HOMECOMING
A JACK CARTER NOVEL

BY
DON NICHOLAS

Homecoming is dedicated to anyone and everyone whose life has been impacted by domestic abuse and to those who help them survive it.

CHAPTER 1

THE LAKE

JULY 7, 2011

1927 EDT

It was a warm summer evening. The sun still hung above the horizon in the west. The lake was calm and quiet here, even though the town beach was only about 500 yards to the north. In the distance he could see cars moving noiselessly over the I-90 bridge.

He walked slowly to the end of the floating dock feeling it rock gently under his weight. He held about four feet of line in his right hand ... line he had found at the base of the dock. His movements were graceful as he lowered himself to a sitting position at the end of the dock with his feet in the cool lake water.

He slowly tied the two ends of the line into a square knot and cinched it tight, testing the strength and correctness of his knot. Then he loosened and released his knot and began again. He tied and untied the knot seven times in all before stopping. It was the seventh of July.

She paused to watch him at the base of the dock. He seemed unaware of her arrival. As she began toward him, walking lightly down the center of the dock, it began to sway ever so slightly. Still, he did not seem to notice.

When she came to him, she stood unmoving for moments and then slowly lowered herself to sit on his left, dangling her feet in the water. They sat without speech or motion for some time. She looked at him after awhile, but he did not return her gaze.

She began to move her hands, gesturing vaguely as she spoke. He appeared to do the same, still not looking in her direction. He seemed focused on something beneath the water about two feet directly in front of him. She glanced to the same spot several times as if trying to discern what so completely captivated his attention.

As the conversation continued, she became more and more animated. He picked up the line, which was on his right, and began testing the seventh square knot.

After a time, she placed her hands on the dock beside her, straightened her arms, pulled her feet from the water and stood in one clean motion. As she began to turn toward him, he replicated her motion with the effortless movement of muscle memory done a thousand times before.

They were now facing each other at the end of the dock, standing just 18 inches apart. The distance was significant ... close but not too close. These two knew each other well, but things had changed.

The conversation continued until he stopped, fixated by the object that hung on the 16-inch silver necklace she wore around her neck.

In one fluid motion, his left arm came up to grasp her right shoulder, holding her arm and body in place with his powerful grasp. His right hand flew up to grasp the object on the necklace and rip it from her throat. It was over in a flash, and his hands were back at his sides.

She was stunned. Their eyes met and locked with anger, contorting her normally angelic features. She slapped him hard across the face with her right hand.

He shook it off and their eyes locked again. Then with his whole body, he twisted to the left and uncoiled a thunderous backhand fist to her right jaw. The force of his blow lifted her from the dock, her legs moving wildly to regain their footing, but it wasn't enough. She landed in the water about six feet from the end of the dock. After some brief movement, she began to float face-down. Then she was completely still.

He turned toward her as part of the motion in which he had struck her. His arms returned to his sides with his right hand still clutching the object he had so violently removed from her neck. He stood there for what seemed a very long time watching her body drift south away from the dock, away from him, away from everything they had been and would now never be.

He turned and walked slowly away. Once again the dock moved gently under his weight. When he reached the end, he paused and turned back to look at her once more. He could barely see her now, as she had moved even farther south and the sun had dropped behind the tree cover on the west side of the lake.

He stepped off the dock and disappeared into the woods.

Darkness was falling.

CHAPTER 2

THE POND

JULY 7, 2011

2035 EDT

He stood with three silver-haired women in the parking lot behind the Wayside Town Building. The mercury streetlights came on as night began to fall. He shuffled his feet slowly, changing position to avoid the glare of one of the lights. The women spoke animatedly, and one tapped on his chest with her right index finger. He nodded slowly and grimaced, trying to avoid eye contact with each of them while also avoiding the mercury lights. His face flushed and his shoulders slumped while he continued to shuffle his feet.

After what seemed like a very long time, they dispersed, leaving him standing alone in the now near-empty parking lot. He walked slowly to his SUV and carefully climbed into the driver's seat.

As he pulled out of the parking lot, his anger and embarrassment continued to build as evidenced by his increasing heart rate and reddening face.

If he hurried, he could still catch her.

***

Her walk home from the Wayside Town Building was a short one, perhaps 20 minutes. Had she known she would be walking home, she wouldn't have worn open sandals that allowed the gravel and small rocks access to her well-pedicured feet. She was carefully walking along the small gravel shoulder that separated the right side of the country road from Farm Pond. The pond was running high from all the spring and summer rains. The surface was smooth and black, as the daylight was now long gone. The evening was beginning to cool rapidly, and she was in no hurry to reach her empty home.

She saw the road light up from the headlights of a car approaching from behind. She edged farther onto the shoulder to let them safely pass. It was not really necessary, as the road was empty and she wore white. As she turned to look at the passing vehicle, she realized too late that it was going to hit her. Pain shot through her hip, left leg and back as she felt herself become airborne.

She seemed suspended in air forever, then her world went cold and black. She gasped for air and felt a burning in her throat and lungs. She could no longer feel or control her legs. She was underwater and sinking. She began to move her arms, pulling herself toward the surface. There was no light even though her eyes were open wide. She knew she was underwater, but the urge to breathe was overwhelming.

She gasped one last time for the cool night air, feeling the burning again in her throat and lungs. The dizziness took over as she stopped swimming and began to sink again. She felt the blackness surround her as she lost consciousness.

***

As he hit her, there was a loud, dull thump and the sound of gravel hitting his undercarriage. He jerked the wheel back to the left and felt the right rear tire leave the road, tipping the entire vehicle to the right. It seemed for a moment that the SUV would roll down the incline and into the pond. He jerked the wheel back to the right, and the left rear tire pushed him forward until the right rear tire again found gravel. The SUV fishtailed forward, accelerating, as his right foot still had the gas pedal pinned to the floor. The knuckles of both his hands were pure white and he had not taken a breath since the moment he had stomped down on the accelerator. The SUV was now going more than 50 miles per hour. He released the accelerator and stomped on the brakes. The vehicle slid to a stop and he began to breathe again.

After a few moments, he looked to the right, to the left, then behind him to see if anyone had witnessed what he had just done. The road was empty. He lightly put his right foot on the accelerator and pointed himself home. Then he began to cry and shake. He inched along slowly, trying to stay on the road and put distance between himself and the scene of his hideous crime.

CHAPTER 3

JACK CARTER

JULY 7, 2011

1700 EDT

My name is Jack Carter, and until seven days ago, I was the United States Naval Special Warfare Commanding Officer stationed in Coronado, California.

Today, I am the Chief of Police for Wayside, Massachusetts, a sleepy little town of 15,000 just west of Boston. I grew up in Wayside and left in 1974 to attend the United States Naval Academy in Annapolis, Maryland.

After 37 years of living out of a sea bag, I am going home, and I still have no clue if returning to Wayside is a good idea or a bad idea. Let me explain how I got to this turning point in my otherwise rational life.

My father served in the Navy from 1948 to 1954, and I grew up listening to his sea stories. When I was accepted to Annapolis, I was mentally committed to serve 20 years and retire from Naval service in 1994 at the ripe old age of 38. This, I surmised, would give me plenty of time to have a second career in civilian life. Running a sailing charter business was the plan I remember best ... and it still sounds pretty good today.

In 1993, I was offered the opportunity to command SEAL Team 7, and my 20-year retirement plan was rounded up to 30 years.

In 2001, the Twin Towers came down, and in 2002, I was offered command of the Naval Special Warfare Group, which included SEAL Teams 1, 3, 5, and 7.

In 2008, I became the commanding officer for all the 6,500 men and women serving as SEALs and SEAL support personnel on a worldwide basis.

In May 2011, we killed Osama bin Laden. While the war on terror was far from over, killing bin Laden had been at the top of my professional to-do list for nearly a decade. Getting it doneAchieving that on my watch felt pretty damn good, and in some way made it okay for me to retire from the service.

My tour of duty as NSW Commander was due to end on June 30th of this year, and my next duty assignment would be at the Pentagon, which was not appealing to me.

The job of Wayside Chief of Police had opened up unexpectedly in April when the current chief suffered a heart attack and died unexpectedly. My friend Chris Bridger is the senior elected official in Wayside and offered me the job in late April. In early June, I accepted the position.

So here I sit, in seat 3A, headed for Wayside.

"Why Wayside?" I asked myself.

There were many good reasons. It was a job I could do well. My experience and training should make running a 28-person rural police department a piece of cake. And I missed running something small. Running SEAL Team 7 — about 300 troops and support personnel — had been my last hands-on job where I actually spent time in the field. The Wayside Police Department wasn't much bigger than a single SEAL Team Platoon.

My family was in the Boston area, and so was Chris Bridger, my best friend since we were 6. Although I could not always tell Chris where I was or what I was doing, he and I spoke and emailed several times a month and saw each other at least twice a year. Chris was my lifeline to Wayside and the civilian world. His friendship and our relationship were reason enough to go home to Wayside.

There was at least one potentially bad reason to go home and her name was Jenny Hale. Jenny and I had been what she called "dance away lovers" since high school. We had been together for a day, a night, a week, a month, and one time for almost a year … and then we would not see each other for months — sometimes years. Every time I thought Jenny and I were really done, she would dance back into my life again. As I look back, Jenny has been a repeated source of both joy and pain. At the moment and for some time, we have just been friends ... not friends with benefits, but just friends.

Truth be told, Jenny had a lot to do with me leaving Wayside in the first place and staying away for most of the last 37 years.

As I thought about Jenny and Wayside, I nodded off to sleep. Over the years I had learned to sleep anywhere, and this evening would be a long one.

CHAPTER 4

THE GAME

NOVEMBER 16, 1973

1925 EST

From where I stood on the 20-yard line, I could see Jenny Hale and Richard Bates take their seats two rows back near the 50-yard line. I wanted to pull him out of the stands onto the field and stomp his head to pulp with my cleats. As I imagined doing this, I could feel my heart race and my face grow hot.

But Richard was not my real problem. Jenny had chosen the weekend before homecoming to break up with me.

"I'm staying in Boston ... I'm going to Harvard. We'll never be apart," I could still hear myself stammering.

"You don't really want to go to Harvard. You want to go to Annapolis and be a Naval officer," she had said emphatically.

"I don't need to be a Naval officer. I do need to be with you. I love you and want to marry you. That was the plan, and I like the plan," I had said defiantly.

A Jack Carter Novel

"Jack, we need some space ... some time to think about our lives and what we both really want."

"That is your father talking. And we both know he doesn't think I'm good enough for his little Jenny," I blurted out. Jenny began to cry. I just stood there. After a few moments, she hugged me, kissed me on the cheek, and walked away. Contrary to what I had just said, I had no idea if this was Jenny talking or her father. It was true that Jeremy Hale did not think I was right for his daughter, but Jenny had the strongest sense of self I had ever known. I knew she loved me; yet I also knew we weren't going to be together, at least for now.

Still standing on the 20-yard line, I was torn from my thoughts by the sound of the referee's whistle. The ball was in the air and I stepped up to meet it at the 25-yard line. I visually and mentally locked onto the ball coming end over end, cupped my hands in front of my face to receive it, and began scanning routes to move down the field.

As I caught the ball, my right thumb hyperextended and I felt a bolt of pain shoot up my right shoulder. I regained my focus, put the pain aside, and tucked the ball between my right arm and body, trying to also protect my throbbing right thumb as best I could.

I faked a few steps to the left then cut hard to the right where I could see daylight and three of my teammates setting a sideline block starting just past the 50-yard line. I shook one defender near the 42 with a stutter step and then locked eyes with Jenny for just a moment as I prepared to pivot at the sideline and head downfield. Her eyes were sad, and she seemed near tears again.

Then I saw her lips move, saying, "Go Jack, go."

I hit my pivot point just past the 50 and turned on all the speed I could muster. At the 40, a teammate took his man out of bounds and I slid to their inside. A second teammate put himself between me and a defender and they both tumbled to the ground, forcing me closer to the sideline. A third defender was closing fast, angling in from up field to intercept. Patrick Kennedy was moving back to protect me. I screamed past Pat near the 10 just as the defender was on us both. Pat shuffle-stepped to his right, keeping the Weston tackle at bay.

I ran past the goal line, through the end zone, and slammed into the chain link fence at the end of the field at near top speed. My hand throbbed, by head throbbed, and my heart throbbed. Jenny was gone to me, and there was nothing to keep me in New England.

CHAPTER 5

LANDING AT LOGAN

JULY 7, 2011

1900 EDT

"Admiral, we're landing in 10 minutes. Is there anything I can get for you?"

The brown-haired United flight attendant had her right hand on my left shoulder and was shaking me gently. She had a beautiful smile, large deep brown eyes, and a perfect California tan. After six hours in the air, she still smelled of lavender. She stepped back and waited patiently for me to respond.

"Water would be great ... what time is it?"

"Just after 7, sir. We're a little early. Is someone picking you up, or do you need a ride?"

"I have a ride. A colleague is picking me up and taking me out to Wayside," I responded.

"Too bad," she grinned at me. "I live in Weston and could have given you a lift."

"Maybe next time."

"Sure ... or maybe we can hook up at the Red Coach Grill some evening. It's on 20 near the town line. Do you know it?" she inquired.

"I do. I grew up in Wayside."

"Home for a little summer visit with the family?" she asked.

"Nope ... moving back to the old hometown," I said, feeling a knot form in my stomach. This could still prove to be a very bad idea. After 37 years on my own, how would it feel to be home? But that is the point after all; it was home. My parents, my sister, and my best friend were all here in Wayside. And I was tired of big cities, politics, and committees ... committees most of all.

The first-class cabin was full, yet the attendant — Wendy, according to her name badge — seemed to only have eyes for me.

"Will you be working out of the Navy Yard?" she continued.

"I wouldn't call it work. My sailboat will be there. I'm retiring from the service at the end of August and taking a job as chief of police for Wayside."

"Not sure my Weston friends would approve of me hanging out with a cop from Wayside," she joked.

"Chief cop," I corrected, smiling wryly. "Perhaps we should meet up at the Red Coach this Friday and see how they feel about it."

"Perhaps we should," she grinned. "Let's say 7 at the bar ... and just so you recognize me, I'll be out of uniform."

"Something to look forward to," I replied, flashing her my best million-dollar smile. To be honest, I had often wondered exactly what my smile was worth. I used it a lot, and often, like now, I meant it.

She handed me my dress uniform coat, tucked her card into the breast pocket, and said, "Looking forward to it, Admiral. Now this girl needs to get back to business."

She stepped out of view, and I heard her begin the landing announcement over the PA system.

CHAPTER 6

OFFICER CORDERO

JULY 7, 2011

1930 EDT

I was happy to be first in line to disembark. When the all-clear was given, I gave Wendy a wink and a smile, then headed up the Terminal B jetway. I was traveling light with just my Briggs & Reilly backpack, as I had shipped clothes and personal items to the family home in Wayside. This was my fifth trip to Wayside in 60 days. Although I had officially become the Wayside Chief of Police on July 1st, I had spent the first week of July wrapping up my life in San Diego.

The formal Naval Special Warfare (NSW) Change of Command Ceremony had occurred June 30th, and I was now a member of the United States Navy Reserves ... hell, it was better than being US Navy Retired. If the going-home thing turned into the bad idea I thought it might be, I could still request an active duty station and probably get it with a minimum amount of begging and pleading.

I left the terminal to find a Wayside Police cruiser sitting to the right with its motor idling. Officer Kim Cordero was

A Jack Carter Novel

leaning against the back of the cruiser chatting with a state trooper who had his back to me as I approached. Cordero wore a khaki Wayside Police uniform with black shoes and a black gun belt, including a Glock 19 in the holster. Cordero was five foot six, 120 pounds, and drop-dead gorgeous.

"Evening, Admiral," she said brightly as she stepped to the side of the trooper, came to attention, and rendered a snappy salute with her right hand.

"Evening, Cordero," I said, returning her salute.

The trooper spun around and appeared a little flustered.

"Evening, sir," he said, coming to attention and saluting.

"Good evening, Trooper Bachman," I replied, reading the name above his left shirt pocket and returning the salute. "How are things at Logan Terminal B this evening?"

"Just fine, sir. Thursday evenings are usually pretty uneventful."

I handed my backpack to Cordero, who put it in the trunk of the cruiser. The trooper opened the right rear door, and I slid into the backseat.

"Welcome home, sir," he said, bending to maintain eye contact.

"Happy to be here," I replied with mixed emotions as he closed the door.

The front door closed, Cordero buckled in, and we pulled away from the curb.

"Did he have to salute you?" inquired Cordero.

"No ... and neither do you," I said with a grin.

"I know, but I'm trying to ease your transition to civilian life. And besides, it's the first time I've seen you up close and personal in your full dress duds."

"Duds? Who says 'duds' anymore?" I inquired with a chuckle.

"Once again, sir, I'm just trying to speak in a way that will make someone of your years feel at home."

"You are a becoming as big a smartass as your dad," I chided.

"Becoming, sir? Yes, sir," she said and was quiet for a few moments navigating traffic as we merged into the Ted Williams Tunnel.

CHAPTER 7

CAVE MEN

JULY 7, 2011

1940 EDT

I had timed my return to Wayside to attend a special Board of Selectmen meeting scheduled after a Massachusetts Department of Environmental Protection Hearing. Apparently, a small group of Wayside residents known as the CAVE Men had been doing everything possible to hold up construction of a new multimillion dollar town center on the north side of town. My friend Chris Bridger was chairman of the selectmen and the driving force behind me being hired as the new Wayside Chief of Police. Chris was also the reason I was in my dress blues, as he wanted to remind the other selectmen of my esteemed military career.

"Do the town center opponents call themselves the CAVE Men and does it mean something?" I asked Cordero.

She laughed and replied, "It mean 'Citizens Against Virtually Everything,' and they hate the label."

"How many of them are there in Wayside?"

"Maybe 300 to 400 who actively show up at town meetings, but there are really only about half a dozen leaders and organizers: Mason Teller, Peggy Dolan, Annie Close, Maureen Jackson, Bessey Clark, and Jim Watson," Cordero explained without any hint of emotion.

"Are they troublemakers?" I asked, always alert to anything that might threaten the tranquility that I was now sworn to protect.

"Depends on how you define 'troublemakers.' They don't break the law. Just the opposite; they manipulate the law to make it much harder for the majority to get things done that need doing. Cell towers, the new high school, the new town center, and pretty much any form of commercial development gets held up with legal filings and requests by this small group. They almost always lose in the end, but they slow things down, waste everyone's time, and cost the town a lot of money," concluded Cordero.

"Anything else?"

Well, since you ask ... as a police officer, I worry that someone is going to murder one of them someday. They've pissed off a lot of important and very powerful people in Wayside and beyond. There hasn't been a murder in Wayside for 36 years, and I'd like to keep it that way on my watch. Sir," she added.

We pulled into the parking lot behind Town Building and Cordero circled to let me out at the curb nearest to the building. The car came to a stop.

"See the man and three women off to our left standing by the crosswalk?" she paused and continued when I nodded acknowledgement. "That's Mason, Peggy, Maureen, and Bessey ... CAVE Men, one and all. And from the looks of it, I'd say the DEP hearing did not go their way."

She and I exited the car, she retrieved my backpack and handed it to me.

"Officer Cordero, it has been a pleasure."

"No problem, Chief. Do you need me to hang around to give you a ride home?"

"No thanks ... I'm sure I can hitch a ride home from here. Will I see you in the AM?"

"You bet. My duty shift starts at 8 ... that's 0800," she said and grinned.

I chuckled and headed for the building.

CHAPTER 8

PATRICK KENNEDY

JULY 7, 2011

2013 EDT

As I approached the building entrance, I saw Patrick Kennedy standing in the walkway speaking with three other men who I did not know. They walked by me on their way to the parking lot, each nodding recognition as they passed, which I returned with a low-wattage smile. No sense wasting the million-dollar smile until I at least knew whether they lived in Wayside.

Pat was waiting for me by the door to the building, grinning from ear to ear. He was a year younger than me and had also grown up in Wayside. We had not been friends until high school, where we had played football together. Pat, Chris Bridger, Kim Cordero's dad Doug, and I had all been on the Wayside High School football team that won the Massachusetts State Championship back in 1973. They had all stayed in the Boston area.

Pat was now CEO of Wayside Holdings, which, according to *The Boston Globe*, was the largest real estate development company in Middlesex County. He was well

A Jack Carter Novel

over six feet tall with broad shoulders, a ruddy complexion, and thinning strawberry blond hair.

As I approached Pat, he extended his hand, which I met and grasped. He pulled me closer, hugged me tightly, and quickly let go as we bounced off each other.

"So Jack, you old sea dog, how's it feel to have your feet back on dry land?" he said, still grinning with just a hint of an Irish accent that he could turn on and off as he pleased.

"I'm a SEAL Commander, Pat, I spend a lot of time on dry land in boring conference rooms."

I still could not bring myself to say *was* a SEAL Commander.

"Then you should feel right at home here, me boy ... we've plenty of boring conference rooms," he said.

"What, may I ask, are you so happy about?"

"Ah Jack ... we put a stake in their heart tonight. The heads of the Planning Board, the Historical Society, chairman of the selectmen, the town manager and even your own mother ... testified as to their support of the project. This was their last shot at delaying us and after seven long years, they are dead," he proclaimed triumphantly.

Last I knew, my mother had stayed neutral in this fight. My father supported the project, as did most of my mother's friends, and more than 80 percent of Wayside's voting population. Most thought a town center in north Wayside would be a gathering place for the community and that it would more than replace the commercial property tax revenue that had been lost when the old Dow Chemical plant closed 10 years ago. But my mother was dating the leader of the opposition and remained publicly quiet on the topic in deference to him. Apparently her respect for him, his position, or both had waned since we last spoke about the town center project.

"What did my mother say?" I asked cautiously.

"She spoke as both an abutting resident and as one of the owners of the Wayside Shooting Club. The club is the largest abutter and also uses the town sewer system. Her support was the icing on the cake. To be frank, I was a wee bit worried. Since she and your father separated, she's been seeing that weasel Mason Teller, but after tonight that relationship may be over. Mason was so mad when she was testifying that I thought his head would explode. It was a fine thing, Jack, and your lovely mother is much the better for being rid of him," concluded Pat. "Ah, but you should be getting to your meeting. We'll have plenty of time to catch up now that you're home to stay."

He hugged me with both arms this time, and I tried to reciprocate.

I loathed Mason Teller — had since I was a boy. What my mother was doing with him mystified me. And if that relationship was over, perhaps she and my dad could work out their issues.

Pat released me, saying, "Later, Jack." He gave me a final grin and strode off toward the parking lot.

I continued into the old brick building that had begun its life as the Wayside School, grades K-12, and began looking for the meeting room. The corridors were narrow enough to remind me of the passageways on a submarine and lit with fluorescent overheads that distorted everything a little to the green side of the spectrum. The walls were brick and the linoleum was worn, but clean and polished. The Great Recession that started in 2008 had taken a heavy toll on Wayside's state and federal funding. I experienced the budget tightening firsthand at NSW, and the SEALS were a high-priority asset in the US war on terror. I could only imagine how federal funding to states and towns might have been cut. I made a mental note to find out.

I could see Chris in a knot of people and headed in his direction.

CHAPTER 9

SELECTMEN

JULY 7, 2011

2020 EDT

Chris turned to greet me as I approached. He was my age, but his hair was now silver-gray, while I was still salt and pepper brown. Chris and I both wore our hair cropped short. He was a full three inches taller than me at 6'2". And while he was in good shape, he simply was a bigger man with a bigger frame. I weighed in at about 185 and was pretty sure Chris had a good 40 pounds on me. His complexion was pale from spending too much time indoors. Chris was clean-shaven and classically handsome with a square jaw and a cleft chin. I was very glad to see him, as I always felt somehow calmed by his presence.

"Hello, Admiral," he said, loud enough for others to hear. "How are things in San Diego?"

"Everything's all wrapped up and my successor has taken over my old command. The rest of my personal goods will arrive in about two weeks," I replied in detail for the benefit of the entire group.

There were five men and two women present. Chris had been speaking to Laura Nowicki, the town manager, and Linda Ralston, who was vice chairman and a former Massachusetts state senator. Laura was technically my direct supervisor, as she was for all town government department heads. That said, I suspected every one of the six selectmen thought I reported to the board and would act accordingly. Laura was 47 and formally trained as an accountant. She was about 5'6" and shapely with lots of curly light brown hair. She had been town manager for about three years and had previously been the CFO for several high-tech start-ups. The most recent had been funded by Crimson Matrix Ventures, where Chris was a founder and managing partner. Laura had two kids. Her son would be a senior at Wayside High School in the fall, and her daughter who would be a sophomore at Roger Williams University in Bristol, Rhode Island. Laura and I had gotten to know each other pretty well during the hiring process, and although she was quiet by nature, I got the sense that Chris and the other board members respected her and gave her a lot of latitude to run day-to-day operations for the town. This impression was key to my decision to become chief of police. I did not generally respond well to being micromanaged.

While Laura was dressed casually in white slacks and an orange polo, Linda Ralston was dressed for success: dark blue business suit and a white cotton shirt that look freshly pressed. She wore a "Jackie O" pearl necklace, pearl earrings, dark hose, and recently polished two-inch black pumps. She was perhaps 65, blonde, and in good shape. Her make-up was light and her facial expressions animated.

"How are you, Chief?" Laura inquired with a smile.

"No worse for the wear," I replied as we shook hands.

"It's good to have you here," said Linda. The position has been open too long."

"If everyone will get seated, we can get started," said Chris as he led the way into a small conference room.

Of the other four men, I knew only Joe Dolan personally. Like Chris and me, Joe had grown up in Wayside but was about 10 years younger than us. Joe wore blue jeans and a denim short-sleeve shirt and work boots. Joe was a carpenter by trade and looked as if he had put in a hard day's work outdoors. His curly brown hair was matted with what appeared to be dried sweat and dirt.

The remaining three men were largely a mystery to me. Robert Giovani, 62, drove for a big linen delivery service and lived on the south side of town, as did Linda and Joe. Robert Farmer, 59, worked in biotech, and Thomas Mars, 47, was an attorney in Boston. Farmer wore khaki pants and a blue Oxford shirt with the sleeves rolled up. Mars was in a simple light blue suit and white shirt with a red tie worn loosely as if it had been a long day. Giovani donned a dark blue uniform of sorts with a red and white patch on his shirt that simply read "Bob."

CHAPTER 10

AN ARMED CAMP

JULY 7, 2011

2030 EDT

There were exactly eight chairs in the room. Chris sat at the head of the table with Laura and Linda in the chairs nearest him. I ended up at the other end with the two Bobs on my flanks. Tom and Joe took the middle seats on each side. There was a white board on the wall behind Chris and an exterior window on my right, where we could see the near-empty parking lot brightly illuminated. The furniture was standard-issue Herman Miller with a gun metal gray table and black Aeron chairs. I liked the Aeron and recalled being happy to see one in my new office at the Public Safety Building. I'd injured my back a long time ago, and an old-fashioned wooden chair was hell on it.

Chris called the meeting to order, and Laura began taking notes on an Apple laptop.

"We're very happy to have you here, Jack," began Chris. "Lieutenant McPherson has done a great job of holding down the fort, but as we all know, his specialty is public affairs, not command. We have concerns about his ability to cope with the town center once construction begins."

Everyone was looking at Chris and nodding.

Joe leaned forward and began to speak. "There's gossip going around that the CAVE Men may step it up a notch or two if they lose this appeal and construction actually begins."

"Step it up, how?" I asked Joe.

"Hard to say," Joe replied. "This is stuff I heard the other night at The Haven and on one of my job sites. It's hard to know what's fact and what's rumor."

The Haven was an old bar and grill on the north side of Wayside Lake that dated back before I was born. It was a guy hangout for townies and 20-somethings. It was also a source of noise, occasional fights, and more disturbing-the-peace complaints than any other single address in Wayside. As a youth, I wanted to get into The Haven more than anything. Now, as the chief of police, I was wishing it were in someone else's town.

Chris picked up the ball. "The other issue is that Patrick Kennedy has heard the rumors, too," he said. I spoke with him briefly after the hearing tonight, and he assured me that I need not worry, as his security team could handle anything the CAVE Men could muster."

"Tell me about his security team," I requested.

Now Laura spoke up, referencing information from her laptop screen. "Wayside Holdings had 2010 revenue of $412 million. Its revenues come from leasing mostly commercial properties in New England and upstate New York. Near as I can estimate, it employs several hundred security people. The Wayside Holdings Security Division includes everything from greeters to patrolmen plus management. Most of the management are former Army Rangers and Marines. I couldn't do background checks on the rank and file as I don't have access to their personal data at this time."

"You pulled background checks on their management?" I asked, trying to hide my surprise. I still thought of Wayside as the sleepy little town I had grown up in. Apparently someone had given them computers and taught them how to use them.

"I pulled background checks on the entire Wayside Holdings Management Team as part of the due diligence we've done and redone around the Town Center Project." Laura smiled at me and gave Chris, who was grinning just a little in my direction, a side glance.

"That's good," I said, nodding. "And if their security management team are ex-Rangers and Marines, you can bet their troops are, too."

"There's nothing *good* about this," said Linda. "It looks to me as if the Wayside Town Center Project is becoming an armed camp, and someone could get hurt."

I agreed with Linda on this point, but felt the need to assure her that everything could be handled.

"We'll meet with Patrick's security people and get agreement on the rules of engagement, their role, and the role of the Wayside Police Department, and I'll have a chat with Mason Teller to enlist his cooperation," I said with the total confidence of a trained security professional.

What the hell had I gotten myself into? I asked myself, while continuing to project total confidence to the group. At least I hoped that was what I was projecting.

The meeting devolved from there into a discussion of all the bad things that could happen, with occasional questions to me about how a trained SEAL Commander would deal with each contingency they could dream up. Linda was particularly imaginative, and Bob Giovani never said a word.

When Linda wanted to know how I would respond to a hostage crisis involving the CAVE Men, Chris decided to step in and end the meeting. "Linda, Jack has run security for US embassies in hostile countries and trained government security forces for the Philippines, Singapore, and New Zealand. I think he can handle the CAVE Men versus Wayside Holdings," he said, patting her on the arm and smiling.

"I know, I know." She gave him a worried smile with a furrowed brow and relented.

The meeting, soon thereafter, adjourned.

Thank the Lord.

CHAPTER 11

JEEP COMMANDER AMG

JULY 7, 2011

2135 EDT

Everyone cleared out pretty quickly, leaving Chris and me to turn off the lights.

As we walked to the parking lot, I asked Chris, "Are we still on for dinner and perhaps a little background on what you think is really going on here?"

"Sure," said Chris, putting his arm around my shoulders as we walked through the crosswalk and into the parking lot. "But first, I have a little surprise for you," he said and shook me a little, causing the hair on the back of my neck to stand up.

Chris was grinning like a little kid on Christmas. I surveyed the lot to see that everyone else had gone and noted that the only remaining vehicle was a jet black Jeep Commander.

"You got a new ride, I see."

"Nope ... *you* got a new ride," Chris said, barely able to contain his emotion.

"Wow," I said, caught just a little off guard. I had not owned a car in years. My last ride had been a somewhat nondescript gray Ford Taurus that belonged to the Navy. This SUV appeared identical to the Jeep Commander I had been assigned when I was stationed in Berlin working for the NATO Joint Terrorism Task Force.

"This looks like the Jeep I had in Germany," I said, wondering if Chris had somehow managed to acquire it and have it shipped to Wayside. That would be a very *Chris* thing to do.

"Looks can be deceiving," said Chris lifting his eyebrows twice and grinning at me. Then he produced a set of keys from his pants pocket, tossed them to me, and gestured to the car, doing his best Vanna White, which was not that good. "This, Jack, is the Jeep Commander AMG. It was introduced at the 2006 North American International Auto Show as a limited edition 2007 model. It features a 6.2 liter M156 V8 engine producing 550 horsepower that was handcrafted in Germany. The engine is added to an AMG Speedshift 7G-Tronic seven-speed automatic transmission. It can accelerate from 0 to 60 in 4.8 seconds. This makes the Jeep Commander AMG the most powerful naturally-aspirated V8 SUV in the world."

"Wow," I said again. "Impressive that you memorized all that, given that you have trouble remembering your own

Social Security number," I replied. smiling and shaking my head. "How did you get your hands on one, and what is it going to cost me?"

"Answering your second question first, it is going to cost you dinner tonight. The town of Wayside actually owns it, but it's yours to use as long as you remain chief."

"Kind of an expensive bribe to retain me, wouldn't you say?" I asked, frowning at him in mock seriousness.

"Wrong again, dog breath," said Chris, laughing out loud. "It costs the town far less than what we spend to buy new Crown Vic patrol cars for your officers. And it has a few added features that should make you feel warm and fuzzy cruising the streets of Wayside."

Chris was really enjoying the moment.

"Like what?" I inquired, encouraging him to continue. He had been planning this for a while, I suspected, and I was going to let him make the most of it.

"I'm glad you asked," he said, now sounding a little too much like a used car salesman. He patted the Jeep on the hood and said, "In addition to the mother of all SUV engines, this baby has been upgraded with bullet-proof glass all around, Kevlar in the door panels and roof, plus a padded weapons locker in the boot that is fully stocked."

"Bought this from a German arms dealer, did we?"

"Close," said Chris. "We bought it from the German government. It was most recently one of three in service to the German ambassador. They're upgrading to the new 2011 M Class, so we picked up this one for you. I remember you saying how much you liked the one you had in Berlin. This baby makes the one you had in Germany look like a milk truck," he concluded.

"Thanks, Chris. This is a great surprise."

"Seriously, Jack … I want you to be happy here, and I'll do anything in my power to make that happen. You're my best friend, and I want you to stay in Wayside for purely personal reasons. We're not getting younger, and I miss you. I have never had another friend that comes even close to the relationship we've had over the years. This means either I suck at making friends, or you're a very special guy. Perhaps a little of both," he said, looking me straight in the eye and nodding.

"If you don't stop now, you are going to make one or both of us cry," I said, meaning it.

"Okay, okay ... let's go get something to eat," he said, walking around to the passenger side door.

I climbed into my "new" Jeep, started the engine, and stopped for just a moment to listen to her purr. A 550-horsepower engine has a very reassuring purr. I put her in drive and off we went.

"By the way, Cordero has already nicknamed her "The Beast," said Chris, chuckling in the dark.

"Great," I said moaning a little. "That's going to stick."

We turned right onto Route 20 and headed east for The Prime Grill.

CHAPTER 12

THE PRIME GRILL

JULY 7, 2011

2155 EDT

Chris and I walked into The Prime Grill just before 10 p.m.
and sat at the corner of the U-shaped bar farthest from the
front door. We could have sat almost anywhere, as the
place was practically empty.

The Prime Grill was less than a year old. It had replaced an
Italian restaurant, which had taken the place of Callahan's
— a burger and beer joint that was here when I was
growing up. Wayside was upscaling. The Prime Grill
sported a huge U-shaped granite bar with flat-screen
monitors on the wall at the top of each side of the U. I'd
never seen them turned to anything but sports. The
windows had been blacked out and covered with dark
wood. The lighting was dim, and the lights were large
round canvas affairs that looked very Pottery Barn. As I
thought about it, the whole place looked pretty Pottery
Barn. I liked it and wondered if that meant my taste in
decor was trendy. I decided it did not, as I would probably
still like the look when it went out of fashion.

"Good evening, Chris. Welcome back, Chief," said Mike, one of the two bartenders on duty. "Kitchen closes at 10, so if you're here to eat, I'll need to get your orders placed in the next few minutes."

"Do you know what you want?" asked Chris.

"Sure," I said, turning to Mike. "I'll have a Blue Moon and the shrimp cocktail to start. Then, let me have the rib-eye with a sweet potato and broccoli on the side."

"I'll have a Grey Goose martini with three olives, shaken not stirred," said Chris. "Then I'll do the seared ahi tuna as an appetizer. And I'll have the seven-ounce filet, medium rare, with broccoli and a baked potato."

"How do you want your steak, Chief?" asked Mike.

"Medium rare is good for me, too," I said.

Mike had my beer in front of me almost immediately and proceeded to work on Chris's martini. Chris and I both watched Mike do his thing shaking Chris's drink vigorously. Mike poured the martini and garnished it with three olives.

Chris lifted his drink and said to me, "It's good to have you here."

"It's good to be here," I replied. For the first time today, I felt really happy to be home. "Now, tell me what you think I can really expect from Patrick and his people."

We both drank. Chris retrieved the garnish from his glass and carefully removed one olive with his teeth, chewing it thoughtfully. He finished chewing, took another drink of his martini, and began, "Our friend, Patrick Kennedy, is a very powerful guy. He has money, resources, and connections that go all the way up to the governor. At the same time, he is the same Pat you and I grew up with, and he's also a ruthless businessman who's used to getting what he wants. At some level, I've been amazed at his patience with this whole Town Center Project. Seven years is a very long time to get something like this approved, and he's had the town, county, and state officials on his side from the get-go."

"Are you saying you're surprised he hasn't used violence against the CAVE Men?" I asked.

"I am," Chris said nodding.

We both sat and stared at our drinks for a while. The shrimp and tuna materialized from over our shoulders. I turned toward the corner of the bar to discover the source and came face-to-face with a brown-haired young woman whose nametag said "Pam."

"Thanks, Pam," I said and smiled.

"You're welcome, Chief," she said smiling back. "Mike has told me a lot about you. I hope to see you here often."

"I suspect you will, Pam," I replied.

Pam departed, and I noticed Chris staring at me and grinning. "Do you flirt with every pretty woman you see?"

"That was not flirting. I was simply being friendly."

"Sure it was. And I'm an Algerian midget," said Chris, shaking his head and taking a bite of his tuna.

"Let's get back to Patrick and the CAVE Men," I said, changing the subject.

"I don't know what else to tell you," said Chris, continuing to shake his head. "There are plenty of rumors about bad things happening to individuals who have gotten in the way of a Wayside Holdings development project. At the same time, Patrick and his people have never been charged or convicted of anything."

I let out a long sigh and tried to decide what I thought about my old friend Patrick Kennedy. Nothing came to me. It was still just after 7 p.m. in San Diego, where my day had started. I shouldn't be brain-dead, but I was. Often, if I slept on a problem, my subconscious would work on it and I would wake with a much clearer picture in the morning. I decided to go with that thought and changed the subject again.

"So, how's the family?"

"Mandy and the kids are all fine," Chris said. The girls will be starting at Skidmore in the fall. So I'll be sending two teenage girls and two horses to college," said Chris, chuckling a little. "Jeb is working for me this summer and is looking forward to his senior year at Dartmouth. Charlie just left McKinsey to become CFO for a start-up with funding. The company makes solar-powered trashcans designed for public places like beaches, parks and street corners. The things need to be emptied about one tenth as often and notify a central computer when they're full. The computer then sets the routes for the drivers who empty the cans. The cans cost about $4,000 each, but the cities say that they get that back in manpower in less than 12 months. Not to mention the fact that the cans are never left to overflow creating a mess and slowing the drivers down. It's really pretty cool."

By now, we had finished our appetizers and our steaks had arrived. I drank the last of my first beer and nodded to Mike for a second. I cut into my rib-eye and savored the first bite.

"How is Susan feeling about your move back to Wayside these days?" asked Chris, digging into his steak.

"Well, she's happy to have me living on the same coast. At the same time, I no longer have any reason to visit

Washington, DC, on business. My job at NSW meant going to DC at least once a month."

"All true old buddy, but the shuttle to DC should mean you two can see each other more than once a month. That is, assuming you want to see each other more than once a month," said Chris, glancing at me while he continued to work on his steak and potato. I noted that his broccoli was not getting much attention.

I had been seeing Susan Oliver on and off since 1994. Susan was a Navy doctor stationed at Bethesda Naval Hospital. Her specialty was orthopedic surgery, which is how we met. I arrived at Bethesda back in '94 pretty busted up from an operation in Latin America. After I had recovered, I asked Susan out, she accepted, and we began seeing each other on a pretty regular basis. Susan still saw other people, as did I. Yet somehow, Susan had become an important and predictable part of my life.

"Susan and I have a complicated relationship. To be honest, I'm not sure how being closer to each other geographically is going to impact things. She's flying up on Saturday to see me and help me figure out where I'm going to live in Wayside."

"I guess it doesn't look good for the chief of police to be living with his dad," said Chris, grinning. "Where *are* you going to live in Wayside?"

"Dad wants me to take one of the houses on old Sudbury Road near him. But as much as I'd like to be near Dad, I'm not wild about having to take care of a 60-year-old house by myself."

"You know," said Chris, "there are 32 brand new townhouses being built near the new town center. You'd be near your dad, near the public safety building, and the association would take care of all the exterior maintenance. For a happy-go-lucky bachelor such as yourself, that might be just the ticket."

"I'll consider it. But right now I need to get home to see Dad and Bandit and get some sleep. I plan to get into the office early tomorrow so I can start researching and get a handle on exactly what you've gotten me into here," I said, slapping Chris on the back with my left hand.

"Works for me. It's time you started showing us why we hired you. Hell, you've been on the job almost three hours, and you haven't even arrested anyone yet," said Chris, yucking it up and slapping the bar. "Mike, give Jack the check."

I paid the check and left a large tip.

CHAPTER 13

CAPTAIN GLEASON HOUSE

JULY 7, 2011

2315 EDT

I turned left onto Route 20 and drove toward Wayside Center. I hung a right on 27 and headed north. Just before my dad's house, I turned right on Gleason Lane. Chris, Mandy, and the kids live in the oldest colonial on the street. Mandy had managed the restoration, which took three years. The house was originally built in 1775 and was stately once more. I pulled the Jeep Commander into the circular driveway and stopped in front of the portico to drop Chris off.

"Saturday night — you, me, Mandy, and Susan. Let's say dinner at 8 at The Haven?" asked Chris.

"Sure," I said, smiling broadly.

Chris exited the Jeep and leaned back in to shake my hand. Maybe Wayside really was where I belong I thought as we shook.

Chris closed the door and waved as I drove away.

CHAPTER 14

DAD, BANDIT, AND JAMESON

JULY 7, 2011

2335 EDT

I retraced my path back west on Gleason Lane and turned north on Route 27. I turned left into Dad's driveway and parked. This was the home I grew up in. We had moved here from South Wayside in 1962, a couple of months before my seventh birthday. Pretty much all my childhood memories took place in or around this house.

Today, only my dad lives here. My parents split up back in 1994. They had never divorced but were legally separated. I never understood it and still don't today.

My mother lives in the house my parents built back in 1994 on a lot off Farm Road that was part of the old Hale family farm. My father has never lived there and made it clear to all the family that he never will.

His house — my house — was on the southern edge of what had been the Carter family farm. The Carters, Bridgers and Hales were all Wayside founding families who settled the place back in 1639. My dad has a copy of the map that shows how the eight founding families had divided up most of Wayside. Pretty much everything else that exists today was originally part of one of those eight original family farms. My ancestors have been living in Wayside for a very long time.

The house was a 2,200-square-foot Cape with three bedrooms upstairs, a kitchen, dining room, living room, and study on the first floor, and a walkout basement that Dad and I had built out as a TV room. There was an enclosed farmer's porch between the one-car garage and kitchen door. No one who knew us ever used the front door. Everyone came in through the kitchen. Although the lights were on, I wasn't sure if Dad would still be awake. I quietly opened the screen door on the front porch and closed it behind me without making a sound. I repeated the exercise, silently entering the kitchen. Both doors had been unlocked, but Dad would have left them unlocked for me, as he always had when I was out late. Most people in Wayside only locked their doors when they went to bed or left their house.

No one was in the kitchen, study, dining room or living room. I could hear muffled sounds coming from the basement and quietly proceeded to investigate. I made it halfway down the basement stairs before all hell broke loose. Bandit and Buster both began barking as they ran to greet me. Buster, a 10-year-old font-colored pug, reached me first as I took a seat on the bottom step. Bandit, a 16-month-old pug with similar coloring, was right behind Buster. They flanked me, Buster on the right and Bandit on the left, and greeted me by licking my chin, face, and ears. After a couple of minutes, I rose and walked over to the sofa where Dad was sitting watching Jay Leno.

Dad turned down the volume and asked, "So, how was your first day as Wayside's new police chief?"

"The selectmen's meeting was a trip. Linda Ralston, in particular, has a very vivid imagination. There does seem to be some genuine concern about conflict between Wayside Holdings and the CAVE Men. Did you know that Mom spoke out in favor of Wayside and Patrick?"

"I was there," said Dad. "Nothing your mother does surprises me anymore," he said with something of a sour expression.

"I gather from Patrick that Mason was hopping mad about Mom taking sides," I added.

"He was," said Dad. "For me, that was the most enjoyable part of the evening. And it does seem like the CAVE Men have run out of steam. Looks to me like the Town Center Project could get started in the next couple of months. To be honest, I felt pretty guilty about the delays given the fact that I sold Patrick the land seven years ago."

"I understand, Dad, but Patrick's a big boy and he knew what he was getting himself into from what I've recently learned about the CAVE Men."

Dad and I were sitting on opposite sides of a large brown and white sectional sofa. There was a 63-inch flat screen on the wall surrounded by bookcases. The cases themselves sat atop a built-in cabinet that ran the entire length of the room. While most people would assume the set-up was primarily a home theater, I knew Dad spent much more time using it to listen to music. There was a Yamaha AV receiver powering the flat screen and a 7.1 surround sound Boston Acoustics speaker system that I had helped him install.

Buster had his head in Dad's lap and was now snoring loudly. Bandit, who was a gift to me from Susan, sat between Dad and me looking back and forth as if he was following the conversation.

"How has my boy Bandit been behaving?" I asked.

Upon hearing his name, he looked at me, cocked his head and pulled back his ears. Then he got up, came to me, and put his paws on my chest and stretched. I scratched his belly and flipped him onto his back next to me. I continued to scratch, and he pretended to try to get away.

"Bandit has been doing fine. I take him and Buster on walks three to four times a day over at the shooting club. In the 10 days you've been gone, there have been no accidents."

"I think Buster must be a good influence on him," I said. "Normally, there's an accident about once a week."

"He's still a puppy, Jack," my dad said and smiled. "And I think being around Buster is good for him. This week he's also taken to lifting his leg when he pees. He watches Buster lift his leg and pee on a tree or a post and then he comes to the same place and does the same thing," my dad said, now chuckling. "Every little dog has to have a big dog to learn from."

I sat staring at my dad, grinning and absorbing the full meaning of his comment.

I adored my father, he adored me, and we both knew it. I had joined the Navy to be like my dad. Now, I had become the Wayside Chief of Police, a post my dad held from 1980 to 1995. I had skipped working for the Massachusetts State police, which he did from 1960 to 1980. But at some level, we both knew my career in the SEALs was just another kind of police work.

Dad rose and both dogs jumped to their feet. "Time for me to go to bed," he said. "It's good to have you home, son."

I stood up and we hugged. Dad was in pretty good shape for an 81-year-old. He was a couple of inches shorter than me and weighed a good deal less. His weight loss worried me a little, but otherwise, he seemed to be in good shape. We patted each other on the back one final time, and Dad headed upstairs with Buster close behind.

I was still pretty wound up and on San Diego time. I walked over to Dad's wet bar, selected a large tumbler, and poured myself about four ounces of Jameson, adding a splash of water. I took a pull and felt the Irish whiskey trickle through my body. It felt good.

The day had ended much better than it had begun.

CHAPTER 15

FIVE-MILE RUN

JULY 8, 2011

0600 EDT

The alarm on my iPhone went off at 0600. During the night, Bandit had burrowed to the bottom of the bed. He heard the alarm, too, and burrowed his way back to the top. His little black face popped out next to mine. He sneezed, shook, and began licking my face. I gave him a hug and rolled out of bed.

The house had just one full bathroom at the top of the stairs. My dad's bedroom door was closed, yet I could still hear Buster snoring. Bandit watched as I washed my face and brushed my teeth. We went back to my bedroom where I pulled on navy blue running shorts and an ash-colored t-shirt. As I was putting on my running socks, Bandit grabbed one, ran to the other side of the bed, and began shaking it like a rodent he was trying to kill. When I went to retrieve my sock, Bandit sprinted to the other side of the bed, looked up at me, and cocked his head, tail wagging.

"Release," I said firmly.

Bandit dropped the sock and waited for me to pick it up. I finished putting on my socks and took my black New Balance cross trainers from under the bed and put them on.

In the kitchen, I made myself a strawberry banana smoothie. While it was blending, I gave Bandit a half-cup of dry food, which he inhaled. I drank my smoothie, washed it down with some spring water, and headed outside.

My chosen outfit gave me no place to carry a gun or cell phone. Carrying a weapon when I was off duty was not a Navy requirement. As I stood in the driveway, I wondered if it might be for a Wayside police officer. At that moment, I wondered what Chris had meant by "a fully stocked boot."

I went back into the house and retrieved the key to the Jeep. When I opened the boot, I was confronted with a raised floor panel and a fixed, six-position combination lock. Chris had not mentioned the combination lock, although I thought it a good idea. I dialed the lock to 551207 and lifted the top panel. Chris and I had both agreed long ago that dates should be displayed in a year/month/day format. While I was happy Chris had used a combination I could easily guess, it occurred to me that using my birthday for the combination might not be the right long-term decision.

The arms locker included a Smith & Wesson 38 with a two-inch barrel, a Glock 17, a Remington pump-action shotgun, and a Remington hunting rifle with scope. All the weapons appeared to be brand-new, and there were three to five boxes of ammunition for each plus a spare magazine for the Glock. There was also a Kevlar vest, high-powered binoculars, smoke canisters, and tear gas canisters. What was Chris anticipating, World War III?

I closed the arms locker and spun the combination lock. I locked the Jeep and put the key back in the house. While I had been investigating my new toy box, Bandit had been relieving himself in the side yard. When he finished, he ran to me wagging his tail.

"Good boy, Bandit. It's good to have your tanks empty before you start to run," I said, squatting down and patting him on the head and back.

After stretching out, I hooked his leash to his harness and we started south down 27 and turned east on Gleason Lane. As we passed the Bridger house, I noted that all was quiet. We continued east and crossed 126 at Red Hill Road. We both moved easily up the hill toward Red Hill Elementary School. Bandit had been running with me since he was about 8 months old.

When we arrived at the point where Red Hill Road intersected Farm Road, we headed west on Farm Road. When we came to the corner of Farm Road and Farmview Road, we slowed to a walk in front of Patrick Kennedy's house. Patrick lived at 2 Farmview Road; Mom lived at 4 Farmview Road; and Dave and Shelley McLaughlin lived at 5 Farmview Road. Dave was COO and general manager for The Carter Company (TCC), which ran all the things my family owned in Wayside and a few surrounding towns. When my grandfather died in 1995, my dad resigned as Wayside Chief of Police to run TCC. After about six months, he hired Dave to be his general manager. While Dad had no experience running a small business, Dave had been chief marketing officer for a start-up called The Coffee Experience. Dave had been a Wayside Shooting Club member for some time. When Starbucks bought The Coffee Experience and its 19 locations, Dad hired him. I liked Dave personally and thought he was an honest and hard-working entrepreneur. Under his leadership, TCC had done well. While Dad still went to work every day at the Wayside Shooting Club, Dave ran the larger business that included Carter Farms and a bunch of commercial and residential real estate.

I was now standing in Mom's driveway. The place was absolutely quiet at 0630.

There was no way my mom was awake at this hour. My mother had always been something of a night owl, often staying up until 2 or 3 in the morning, and then sleeping until noon. While there were many things I did not understand about why my parents did not get along, I did understand this one. My dad was normally up by 6 a.m. and only recently began sleeping in until 7. As a child, I can remember listening to my mother yelling at my father until well after midnight on many occasions. Now and then, I would quietly sneak to the top of the stairs and peer down into the living room. My dad would be seated on the sofa, apparently listening intently to all his shortcomings and those of his ancestors. There were times when I watched from the dark for more than an hour before returning to bed and crying myself to sleep. Even today, it makes me feel very sad to remember him sitting there, being belittled. A Navy shrink once told me I would never marry because I had no positive role model for what a good marriage could be. At age 55, I was beginning to think he was right.

As I emerged from Mom's driveway onto the street, I saw Dave McLaughlin bending to retrieve his newspaper in his driveway.

"Hey, Dave," I hailed. "It's good to see I'm not the only person awake in Wayside at this hour."

Dave retrieved his paper and began speaking as he moved to greet me. "Hey, Jack, it's great to see you. I may be awake, but look at you up and exercising at the crack of dawn. I guess you can take the boy out of the SEALs but it's pretty hard to take the SEAL out of the boy," he said, grinning and putting his hand out to shake mine.

"Old habits die hard," I said. "This may seem like an odd question, coming from me, but do you have any idea why my mom chose last night to take sides on the Town Center Project?"

"Well," said Dave, "I do. It seems that a few of her friends told her 'enough is enough' and that she needed to do the right thing for Wayside. To be honest, Jack, Shelley was one of them. If DEP had ruled against the project, it could have killed it. The density of the town center, as planned, means it must be connected to the town sewer system. Individual septic systems just aren't a viable option. Your mom has always been in favor of the new town center. She's just been unwilling to support it publicly because of her relationship with Mason. Frankly, I was a little surprised she blindsided Mason the way she did last night. She and Mason drove to the meeting together. Hard to believe she thought they'd be leaving together, given what she planned to do."

"Wow, I wish I had been there to see Mom put it to him," I said, nodding my head.

"It did surprise a lot of people, not the least of whom was your father. Your mom hadn't even told Shelley what she planned to do last night before she did it."

"I'll have to stop back by later to give her a hug and congratulate her on finding her backbone," I said.

Bandit had been sitting quietly in the grass, resting. I nodded to Dave, gave him a wave with my right hand as I turned to resume my run, and said, "Give Shelley my best, and tell her thanks for getting Mom to do the right thing."

"I will," said Dave. "Have a great first day on the job, Jack!"

A Jack Carter Novel

I almost turned right onto Farmcrest Road, but decided to check in with Mason later in the day. Mason Teller was probably not an early riser, either. Bandit and I continued to the circle at the end of Farmview and picked up the rail trail heading toward Wayside Center. We jogged along the dirt path adjacent to the abandoned commuter railroad track. When we hit Wayside center, we turned north on 27 and headed home.

CHAPTER 16

MISSING PERSON

JULY 8, 2011

0710 EDT

When Bandit and I arrived home, Dad and Buster were in the kitchen. The smell of bacon filled the air.

"Good morning. How did you sleep?" Dad asked.

"Just fine. How about yourself?"

"I sleep pretty well these days," said my dad. "Have a seat, and I'll pour you some coffee and orange juice. Bacon, eggs and toast will be ready shortly."

The eggs would almost surely be from our farm. The bacon would be applewood smoked. The bread was whole wheat from the Carter Farms Bakery. It was good to be home, I thought. Breakfast was my favorite meal. It occurred to me that this was so because, at least in part, of the time I had spent as a child eating breakfast with my dad. On both weekends and weekdays, Dad was up with me in the morning for as long as I can remember. My mother was always still sound asleep.

My dad was a quiet man. Most of our time together in the mornings was spent just being quiet, or with Dad listening to me. I would tell him about school, my teachers, my friends, and girls. In high school, he came to every football game, and I would often see him watching from the sidelines during practice. Many of my high school mornings were spent talking to my dad about football. While this was 40 years later, it still seemed like yesterday to me. When times have been tough over the years, I often thought about sitting here in this kitchen talking to my dad about football and eating scrambled eggs, bacon, and whole wheat toast.

"I ran into Dave this morning," I said. "He tells me Shelley and some other friends of Mom's put some real pressure on her to back the Town Center Project."

"That would explain a lot," said my Dad. "Your Mom cares a great deal about what her friends think. Still, I am surprised she was willing to cross Mason in such a public forum."

"Whatever her reason," I said, "I am sure glad she had a change of heart. I like Patrick, and I think the project is good for Wayside. Speaking of which, Chris suggested I take a look at Wayside Commons. As much as I appreciate the offer to live in one of the family homes, I think I need a fresh start. And I like the idea of a place where I can walk to work, to dinner, and to see you."

My dad paused and nodded. "Son, if that's what makes you happy, then it certainly works for me. I'm just glad you're back in Wayside. Having you down the street is an added bonus."

"Thanks ... for breakfast, and for understanding." I said.

I rinsed my dishes, put them in the dishwasher, and headed upstairs to shower and get ready for work.

"Jimmy dropped by yesterday morning and delivered a dozen clean uniforms for you, plus two hats, a gun belt, and two pairs of spit-shined black work boots," Dad called to me as I bounded up the stairs.

"Thanks," I yelled back.

It's good to be chief, I thought.

***

It took me about 10 minutes to shower and shave and another five to dress. The uniform — khaki pants and a khaki short-sleeve shirt — was pretty much identical to the one I wore for the past 37 years, minus the ribbons. There was a black and orange Wayside Police Department patch on the left shoulder of my uniform and an American flag on the right. There was a silver and black name badge over my left shirt pocket that simply read "Carter." I liked the simplicity.

When I checked my iPhone before putting it in my pocket, I noted a missed call and a message from Rose Callahan. I had already programmed the work, home and cell numbers for all department personnel into my phone.

I hit the "play" button on the message from Rose and listened. "Hello, Chief. This is Rose. We have a situation developing around a missing 18-year-old Wayside girl. Her name is Kelly White. She's been missing since last night. Her parents only discovered she was missing this morning. We just found her car at the lake. Call me when you get this. Thanks."

Rose was one of three Wayside detectives. She was also our Youth Liaison Officer and worked closely with the faculty and administrators for all the Wayside public schools. Rose was in her early 60s and had been formally trained as a social worker, not a police officer.

My mind ran through her message. A missing girl. Gone for less than 12 hours. Her car by the lake. If her parents had noticed she was missing this morning, that probably meant she still lived at home.

I hit redial on my iPhone.

The phone rang three times, and Rose picked up. "Hello, Chief. Sorry to bother you so early, but I've got a bad feeling about this one."

"No problem," I said. "Tell me what you think."

"It's more of a feeling, Chief. I know Kelly. I know her family, and I've already spoken with a number of her friends. I'm convinced she went missing around 8 p.m. last night, which is reinforced by finding her car here at the lake. The vehicle was unlocked, the keys are in the ignition, and her purse and cell phone are in the front seat. She's missing, Jack."

"I'll be there in 10 minutes, Rose."

"I've got three officers following up leads. I should know much more by the time you get here," she said.

"Anything you need from me, Rose?"

"Not yet, Jack, but the day's young."

I was already in the driveway and climbing into my Jeep.

"See you in 10, Rose."

CHAPTER 17

CRIME SCENE

JULY 8, 2007

0815 EDT

I headed south on 27, turned west on Front Street, and then left on Lake Street. About half of Wayside Lake and the surrounding park were actually in Wayside. The other half of the lake and park were south of I-90 in Natick. While there was a public beach on the Natick side, Wayside Town Beach was for Wayside residents only. The Wayside Beach complex included about 400 yards of sandy beach, boat docks, a large wooded picnic area, and a clubhouse with a snack bar. The most recent addition was a boathouse for the Wayside/Weston Crew Team.

Lake Street terminated into the town beach parking lot, which would have normally been empty before 0900 on a Friday morning. Not today. There were four Wayside police cruisers scattered around the southwest corner of the parking lot. Two of the cruisers still had their blue emergency lights flashing. There was also a black Crown Vic sedan that was one of ours. I also noted several civilian vehicles, including an older Ford F150 pickup. Beyond the parking lot, I could see the picnic grounds, beach, and lake.

The day was clear and warm. The sun had not yet begun to warm the lake, its early morning rays still blocked by the high tree line. This made the lake look almost black. There was little wind, and the surface of the lake was almost perfectly still.

I parked against the south tree line and exited the Jeep. While doing so, it occurred to me that I had no weapon in my holster. I wondered momentarily whether I should retrieve the Glock from the boot and decided against it for the time being.

Rose approached me with a man and a woman I didn't recognize. The man looked to be a bit older than me with longish silver-gray hair. He was clean-shaven and about my height. He was wearing light gray slacks, a white polo shirt, and light brown boat shoes with no socks. The woman was somewhat younger, medium height, and had bright blonde hair that was cut short. She was thin to the point of being shapeless, and wore a light brown sleeveless top, light gray shorts, and sandals. Both the man and woman appeared visibly upset. Rose was on the right with the woman in the middle. As they approached, Rose put her arm around the woman's shoulder as if she were trying to calm or reassure her.

"Hello, Chief. This is Judy White and her husband Nathan. Kelly White is their daughter."

"Morning, folks. Sorry to be meeting you for the first time under these circumstances. Rose tells me that Kelly didn't come home last night."

"That's correct, Chief Carter," said the man, nodding gravely. "I noticed her car was missing from the driveway this morning. I checked her room and was pretty sure her bed had not been slept in. These days, Kelly seldom gets up before 10 in the morning. Even though it was early, around 7 a.m., I was worried so I called her boyfriend, William Campbell. Will told me Kelly had failed to meet him here at the beach last night. He said they had planned to watch the sunset together. When she was late, he texted and then called her and got no response. By 9, he was becoming worried and called three of her girlfriends. None of them had heard from Kelly in several hours. He says he finally gave up, went home, and hoped that she would call."

Judy White was nodding slowly and fighting back tears. She pulled a tissue from her right pocket, blew her nose and dabbed at her eyes. With what seemed to be a great deal of effort, she began to speak. "Our Kelly would not do that. She's responsible and caring, and when she says she'll be someplace, she is either on time or she calls when she's late. I just do not understand what could have happened to her." She began to sob quietly.

Rose took Judy into her arms and patted her tenderly on the back. Nathan and I stood quietly watching the two women. After what seemed like a very long time, Rose stepped back from Judy slightly, turning her gently toward Nathan.

"If you two can excuse us for a moment, I need to report to the chief," said Rose to the Whites.

Rose began walking slowly toward my Jeep Commander. I followed. The Whites started to drift back toward what I was now thinking of as a crime scene.

CHAPTER 18

DETECTIVE CALLAHAN

JULY 8, 2011

0829 EDT

Detective Callahan was petite and thin. Her movements were contained and graceful. Her skin was milky white, with more than a hint of freckles showing through her makeup. The freckles also appeared on the backs of her hands, and I suspected many other places. Her hair was medium in length and blondish red. As I walked beside her, it occurred to me that I had never seen a woman who looked more classically Irish. As we turned toward each other to stop and speak, I noted that her eyes were bright green.

"I thought it best to let you hear from the parents directly," said Rose. "I've known both Judy and Nathan for a while, and I believe them. Their characterization of Kelly is also pretty much on the mark."

We were standing with my Jeep between us and the crime scene. Rose continued to glance to her left toward the crowd, beach, and the lake. In the woods behind Rose, I could see a man with a large dog moving away from us.

"Are the man and the dog part of the search?"

"Yes," said Rose. "That's John Trumbull and his dog, Gabriel. John's a trainer, and Gabby is his best tracker. I called John as soon as we found Kelly's car unlocked with her keys, purse, and cell phone left inside. It's possible she left with a friend, but I don't think so. An 18-year-old woman does not leave her cell phone behind, much less her purse and car keys. Kelly didn't plan to be gone from her car for very long. My hunch is that she's somewhere nearby. I have officers knocking on doors to wake her friends and ask about her. Unless they're working, none of these kids get up too early. So far, none of her friends have heard from her since yesterday afternoon. As for her workplace, I have no way to contact anyone there until the store opens at 10 a.m."

Rose looked at me steadily, while she delivered her assessment of the situation.

"I've had a chance to review her texts and voicemails from yesterday afternoon," she continued. Kelly was quite busy, even though she was working at Nordstrom's from 11 in the morning until 7 in the evening. There are more than 60 text messages, 12 phone calls, and seven voicemails, all but one of which had been played by someone."

"Someone?" I asked.

"The last three voicemails were from William Campbell. The first was at 8:16 p.m. and the second at 9:14 p.m. The third was left at 7:09 this morning and just said, "Please, call me." Both earlier messages have been played. In the first, Will left a short message indicating he was on Town Beach. In the second, he left a somewhat longer message indicating he was worried about her and that he was tired of waiting. He was going home."

I nodded at Rose, processing the alternatives. Either Kelly had listened to William's messages, not returned them, and then left her cell phone in her car sometime after 9:14 p.m. last night, or she had left the cell phone in her car earlier and never heard the messages. This second alternative meant someone else had played back her messages.

"I've also called in an MSP forensics team to work the crime scene. We just don't have those resources here in Wayside. And for the record, I did use crime scene gloves when investigating her vehicle purse and cell phone. Still, I hope I didn't damage any fingerprint evidence on the cell phone when I played back the messages. At the time, I was focused on finding her."

"Rose, don't beat yourself up. It is what it is. Just make sure you let the state patrol know what you did, so they can take that into account when examining the phone."

"Right, right," said Rose. "As soon as the staties arrive, you and I should take a ride to Mr. Campbell's house.

Something just doesn't add up here, and at the moment, I can't figure out what."

As if on command, a Massachusetts State Police van rolled slowly into the parking lot toward the crime scene.

"While you meet up with our colleagues and explain what we know, I'm going to follow the man and the dog," I said to Rose.

Rose nodded at me and headed toward the van.

I went to the back of the Jeep, opened the boot, and retrieved the Glock 17. I examined the weapon to make sure the magazine was full, the chamber was empty, and the safety was on. I placed it in my holster and secured the cover. There were occasional reports of bears in the park, and I was not prepared to meet a bear, unarmed, today.

I climbed the embankment out of the parking lot and into the woods, heading in the general direction where I had seen the man and the dog earlier. After about five minutes of tromping through pine needles and underbrush, I could see John Trumbull and Gabby standing at the end of a long dock that extended into Wayside Lake. It was a floating dock next to the boat launch ramp. When I reached the base of the dock, I proceeded, walking down the middle. The dock swayed under my weight, and Gabby, and then Trumbull, turned to look at me.

When I got close enough, Trumbull commanded Gabby, "Sit," and stepped toward me with his hand extended.

"You must be the new sheriff," said Trumbull, shaking my hand and smiling broadly.

"Something like that," I replied, still shaking his hand.

Trumbull was not from around here. My keen since of language told me he was most likely a Texan. It's also possible that the cowboy boots, rodeo buckle, and Stetson hat had something to do with my opinion of his origins.

"This where the trail leads?" I asked.

"Yep," he replied, nodding over his right shoulder at the dog. "Old Gabby had no trouble following the scent. Led us right here to the end of the dock and stopped."

"What does that tell you?" I inquired.

"I suspect it means our missing girl took a swim and came out of the water somewhere else — I hope."

"Me, too," I said nodding and hoping it was so but fearing it was not.

I shook Trumbull's hand again, gave Gabby a rub on the head, turned, and headed back toward the shore. Trumbull and his dog followed me down the dock. While I headed back toward the woods, Trumbull and Gabby went south along the lakeshore looking for Kelly's exit from the water. I wondered why he chose south instead of north, given that I was pretty sure he was just making an educated guess. I made a mental note to ask him later about his choice.

As I hiked through the woods back to the parking lot, I noticed that the number of vehicles had greatly expanded. In addition to two more police vehicles, I could clearly see a Channel 7 news van.

I adjusted my trajectory to make sure I emerged from the woods inside the crime scene area, which now measured about 100 feet square. Only Kelly's Lexus SUV remained inside the area, which was bordered by orange pylons and yellow and black crime scene tape. I could see several uniformed Wayside police officers searching the woods and the beach. As I neared the edge of the woods, I noted that Rose was speaking with an older, blonde-haired man who was wearing khaki pants and a long-sleeved white shirt, with the sleeves rolled up. Clipped to his belt, on his left hip, was a Smith & Wesson 38 Chief's Special. He was a cop, and he was not a Wayside cop.

CHAPTER 19

HOMICIDE COMMANDER

JULY 8, 2011

0927 EDT

As I approached Rose and the unknown cop, the pair stopped talking and turned to meet me.

"Chief, this is John Rizzo. John is the State Police homicide commander for Middlesex County. He lives here in Wayside," explained Rose.

Rizzo extended his hand to shake, while tilting his body to the right and giving me a once over.

"Pleased to meet you, Chief Carter. I've followed your naval career with interest for some time. Wayside is damn lucky to have someone of your caliber as its chief of police," he said as we shook. I examined him.

Rizzo looked to be about 60 and in very good shape. He was about 5'8" and had the build of a long-distance runner. I could now see that his blonde hair was partially gray and medium in length. Neither his pants nor his shirt were crisp, giving him a somewhat rumpled look. His Cordovan loafers, while expensive, were definitely in need of some tender loving care.

"Are you here in your official capacity?" I asked, looking first at Rizzo, then at Callahan, and back to Rizzo.

"No, no, nothing like that. The forensics guys gave me a heads-up on the call, and I decided to stop by on my way to work. That said, if there's anything I can do to help with your investigation, please let me know," said Rizzo.

"Well, since you've already offered, we're going to need divers, I fear. So far, Kelly's trail leads to the end of the boat dock and stops. Our tracker is searching for an alternate exit from the water, but we should plan for the worst."

If it was possible, it appeared that Rose's milky white skin was becoming even whiter. I understood how she felt. I had seen a lot of people die over the past 37 years, some of them not much older than Kelly. Still, this was somehow very different as evidenced by the knot in my stomach. I had never grown comfortable with death and had somehow believed that coming home to Wayside would remove it from my life, at least for a while.

Rizzo nodded. "I'll put a call in to the sergeant who leads the Underwater Recovery Team based in our Framingham HQ. We can have them in the water in under an hour."

A Jack Carter Novel

"Thanks, Captain. I hope we don't need them, but it's best to be fully prepared," I said.

"I hate to be a pain in the ass at a time like this, but have you been briefed on your jurisdictional authority in the event this becomes a homicide?" asked Rizzo.

"I have," I said nodding. "It's my understanding that the State Police have absolute jurisdiction over any homicide that occurs in Wayside, or anywhere else in Middlesex County, for that matter."

"That is the letter of the law, Chief. But at the same time, I would prefer to pursue any investigation as a joint operation between your office and mine. And for the record, I have the sole authority to make that call. Now just to be clear, I'm doing this because I think you, Rose, and the rest of your department can make a valuable contribution to any crime that occurs in your town. But at the end of the day, I'll call the shots on any homicide investigation that happens in my county," said Rizzo.

"I can live with that. In my past life, 'joint operation,' was my middle name," I said, trying to lighten things up a bit.

Rizzo paused to look me up and down again and said, "Tall, handsome, a military hero, and funny. Who knew you could get all that in one package?"

Even Rose was smiling now.

"Well, it's good to see you boys are getting along. I was a bit concerned you two might have taken an immediate disliking to each other. Happy to be wrong," said Rose, now grinning widely.

"Rose and I are going to take a little ride and interview William Campbell, Kelly White's boyfriend. Care to tag along in the spirit of our newfound cooperation?" I asked Rizzo.

"No need," said Rizzo. "I think my time can be best utilized by making sure our URT guys engage as quickly as possible. But before you two run off, any thoughts about what you want to tell the media about what's happening here?"

"I suppose they can serve a purpose. It's possible someone who actually watches television might see the report and provide us with some useful information. Hell, it's possible she's sound asleep on one of her girlfriend's sofas. That would be a lovely outcome," I opined.

"My guess," asserted Rizzo, "is that you've had some pretty thorough media training and are just the right guy to manipulate the media into helping us find Kelly."

Rizzo was certainly correct about the amount of media training I had endured while I was the NSW commander. I was actually pretty good at dealing with the media, and ironically, still hated doing it.

"My competency aside, I'm pretty sure it's my job," I said.

"Mind if I tag along?" asked Rose.

"Happy for all the help I can get," I said and sighed deeply.

Rizzo pointed his forefinger at me and dropped his thumb to his forefinger like dropping the hammer on a revolver and said, "Good luck."

Rose and I turned and headed toward the news van.

CHAPTER 20

MARIA LOPEZ

JULY 8, 2011

0942 EDT

I recognized Maria Lopez in the crowd of people standing around the Channel 7 van. Maria was tall, perhaps 5'10", with a mass of black curly hair. Unsurprisingly, she was gorgeous with dark skin and dark brown eyes. She wore gray slacks, a plain white shirt that was newly pressed, and a fashionably cut blue blazer. As Rose and I approached, Maria took note, broke off her conversation with the man wearing a t-shirt, blue jeans, and white running shoes.

As she neared, she extended her right hand, smiled, and said, "You must be Chief Carter."

"I am, and this is Detective Callahan," I said, shaking Maria's hand and nodding to Rose.

Maria's hand was cool to the touch, and her grasp was firm. She was 40ish and shapely and radiated an intense energy. She nodded her head toward Rose to acknowledge her presence then returned her attention to me.

"Detective," she said to Rose, and then to me, "What can you tell me about the missing girl?"

Maria was not fooling around; she was moving quickly.

"Kelly White has been missing for about 14 hours. The Wayside PD found her vehicle here just before 8 a.m. There is no sign of foul play. Our officers are canvassing her friends as we speak," I said evenly.

Maria was smiling, but seemed impatient.

"Can you tell us, Chief, who was the last person to see her, and when did that happen?"

I paused, thinking carefully how to best enlist Maria's help in locating Kelly alive. I decided to sidestep her question, realizing that we didn't know for certain who saw her last or when.

"We have very little information about her disappearance at the moment. We have investigators following up on a number of leads to nail down the timeline on when she went missing."

"Are you treating this as an abduction?" she pressed.

"Not at this time. At the moment, we know three things. First, it appears very likely she did not return home last night. Second, it appears she failed to meet a friend here at the beach last evening, as was previously arranged. Third, her car appears to have been abandoned here, along with her purse and cell phone. We believe Kelly is in trouble and needs to be found quickly," I said evenly. "If we get you a current photo of Kelly, how soon can you get this on the air?"

"We already have a current photo from her Facebook page. I can be ready to go live with you in five minutes," said Maria. She gazed at me steadily, waiting for me to agree to the live broadcast.

"Ready when you are," I said, as my stomach turned upside down, backwards, and spun back into place.

"Okay," she said. "Just one more thing on a separate topic."

I nodded, wondering what was coming next.

"I know now is not the time, but will you commit to an interview about the death of Osama bin Laden with me, at a later date?"

"Maria, you help me find Kelly White, and the interview is yours, exclusively."

"Admiral, you have a deal," she said, beaming.

The standup with Maria took less than five minutes and hurt much less than I thought it would. After the interview ended, Maria asked why I was not asking for an Amber Alert. While I suspected she knew the situation did not meet the Amber Alert guidelines on several levels, I explained that Kelly White was too old at 18 and that we did not have a confirmed abduction. Personally, I felt the situation should have allowed an Amber Alert, and at the same time, I understood how the whole Amber Alert System could be undermined if every missing teenager began showing up in the system.

We said our goodbyes to Maria and her team and began walking to my Jeep.

"Nicely done," said Rose when we were out of earshot of the news team. "Do you really think there was any chance she wasn't going to air this as a missing person story?"

"I'm never sure what the media will and won't do with a breaking story. On the one hand, they want to be first. On the other hand, they don't want to look foolish if the person turns out to be asleep on someone's sofa. We're still less than 15 hours into this assuming we can confirm she left the store last night at 7. You think she's missing. Her parents think she's missing. And there's something about the timing of the rendezvous with William Campbell that's not making sense for me."

"Let's see if William can help us out with that," said Rose as she opened the passenger door to my Jeep.

CHAPTER 21

WILLIAM CAMPBELL

JULY 8, 2011

1005 EDT

The Campbell home was on Red Hill Road, about two blocks north of Route 20. As we pulled into the long gravel driveway, Rose finished a call with officer Kim Cordero. The house was big and old. The detached garage looked as if it might have been a stable in a prior life. In early July, the gardens were lush and in full bloom. There were two vehicles parked outside the garage: a gray Honda minivan and a dark blue Honda Civic. I rolled around the circular driveway and parked in front of the garage, blocking both vehicles.

"Cordero confirms that Kelly left the store last night a few minutes after 7. Kelly's manager, Cheryl Marshall, told Cordero that Kelly was in a hurry to leave. She indicated that Kelly had been distracted on and off during the day by what Kelly had described to her as 'boy trouble.' Ms. Marshall further allowed that Kelly had had boy trouble in the past."

We were now sitting in the Campbell driveway, with the motor idling and the windows closed.

"Do we know if the boy trouble was with William?"

"No, we don't," said Rose, "and that is one of several things bothering me. While all the calls that Kelly took yesterday were either from William or a girlfriend, there are text messages from two boys. One is William Campbell. The other is Douglas McIntyre. Douglas was dating Kelly up until about three months ago, when they broke up. About a month later, according to friends and family, she started dating William exclusively. And there's one more thing, Jack, that's bothering me. Kelly's Facebook page says she's 'single,' not 'in a relationship.' Makes no sense, if she's dating William exclusively."

While I barely knew how to use Facebook, I understood how prevalent it was among teens. And it made perfect sense that Rose would know all about Facebook, given her beat.

"Maybe she just hadn't gotten around to updating her Facebook page to reflect her relationship with William?" I asked.

Rose turned in her seat to look at me more fully. She was shaking her head slightly from side to side and chewing on her left lower lip.

"Jack, these kids post to their Facebook page to tell their friends what they had for lunch. There is no way Kelly would not update her status to show she was in an exclusive relationship, if she were in one."

I nodded at Rose and pondered my lack of knowledge about teenagers. The fact that I had been one several decades ago seemed to have little relevance to my understanding of how today's teens communicated with each other. In my day, we talked on the phone or in person. That was pretty much it. Today, teenagers seemed to broadcast their lives over the Internet. I wondered whether or not this was a good thing.

"What do I need to know about the Campbells?" I asked.

"William Campbell just graduated from Wayside High School and will be attending Harvard in the fall. He was class valedictorian and captain of the soccer team. He is generally well liked by his peers and their parents. In my personal experience with William, he can be a bit of a smartass. His father, Benjamin, runs fundraising for the Museum of Fine Arts in Boston and is active at the Unitarian church and in Wayside politics. William's mother, JoAnn, is a real estate agent with Coldwell Banker and works out of the Weston office. JoAnn and I are close friends, and we all socialize with the White family."

As I nodded, it occurred to me that everyone in Wayside seemed connected to everyone else they knew primarily via their children. Apparently, some things had not changed.

"If it's all right with you, Jack," said Rose, "I'd like to take the lead here. While some might feel I'm too close to these people to be objective, I feel my understanding will help us get to the truth faster."

I thought about Rose's request for a moment. I could see both sides of the argument, but it seemed to me that more knowledge of the situation was better than less.

"Rose, I have no problem with you taking lead whatsoever. I'll hang back in the conversation, unless you pull me in."

"Great," said Rose. "I'm glad we're on the same page."

We exited the Jeep and walked back down the gravel driveway to what appeared to be a side porch. Before we reached the door, it opened and a tall, nearly bald man wearing running shorts and a green shirt emerged.

"Hello, Rose," he said. "Have they found Kelly yet?"

"No, I'm afraid not. We did find her car in the town beach parking lot, and there are more than 20 officers searching the park and canvassing her friends. Is William here?"

Benjamin Campbell looked startled. His gaze shifted from Rose to me and back again.

He regained his composure and said, "Of course, how stupid of me. You're not here to update us; you're here to question William."

"*Question* might be a little strong," said Rose, "but we would like to speak with William to get clarity about his planned meeting with Kelly last evening."

"Of course," said Campbell. "And you must be Jack Carter. Rose has told us so much about you, I feel I already know you. Please, won't you both come in, and I'll get William."

The porch opened into a farmer's kitchen. There was a family room on the left and a large round table in the kitchen. Benjamin offered us coffee, and we both accepted. Rose took hers black, and I added some milk to mine. I could hear a shower running upstairs. Other than Benjamin Campbell, there appeared to be no one on the first floor of their home. Campbell excused himself after getting our coffee and went in search of William. Rose and I sat quietly waiting for them to return.

A woman with dark hair emerged from the stairs that I presumed led to the second floor. The woman was not much taller than Rose and appeared to be in her early 50s. She had no shoes and wore a sleeveless top and shorts that were both a similar shade of light gray.

We both stood. Rose approached the woman, and they embraced. It seemed to me that both women were attempting to comfort the other. I could hear muffled voices from the second floor, and the shower turned off. The women parted and both walked toward me and the large kitchen table.

"JoAnn, this is Jack Carter, our new chief of police."

JoAnn extended her right hand, and we shook as she said, "It's a pleasure to meet you, Jack. Is it okay if I call you Jack? Rose hasn't stopped talking about you since you accepted the position a few months ago."

"Jack is fine," I said. "Sorry to be meeting you for the first time under these circumstances. Given your relationship with Kelly and her family, this must be very hard for you. I understand William and Kelly are very close."

JoAnn seemed fully composed and undaunted by the situation. She was an attractive woman and wore no makeup. Her Mediterranean complexion and lack of shoes caused me to think of the TV show "*The Barefoot Contessa*. I wondered if JoAnn was a good cook.

"I am worried about Kelly. I'm also terribly concerned about Will. I don't think he slept much last night," said JoAnn.

The three of us sat at the kitchen table. JoAnn now seem a bit less composed.

"When did you know something was wrong?" Rose asked JoAnn.

"When Will got home last night around 9:30, he was pretty upset. He had waited for Kelly at the beach for more than an hour. I don't recall her ever standing him up like this, and they've been good friends since elementary school. He was calling and texting their friends until well after midnight. I really don't know when he went to bed," JoAnn said, sighing.

The women were quiet. Benjamin appeared in the hallway to the right of the kitchen, walked into the kitchen, poured himself a cup of coffee, and joined us at the table. Everyone, including me, turned to look at him.

"Will was in the shower and will be joining us shortly. I let him know Kelly is still missing, which, while it didn't seem to surprise him, certainly darkened his mood," said Benjamin.

The women engaged in small talk that mostly revolved around other people's kids. Benjamin sat quietly, occasionally checking his wristwatch. He struck me as a very proper individual. I hypothesized that having a police officer waiting for his son made him somewhat anxious. After another five minutes, I heard someone coming down the stairs, at what sounded like two steps at a time. William Campbell appeared in the hallway to the right of the kitchen at the base of the stairs. He walked quickly into the kitchen and stopped by the table filled with adults. Will was well over 6', lanky, and very blonde. He wore black athletic shorts and a white shirt. The shirt had an image of a soccer ball in the center with the words "Wayside Soccer" split above and below the ball.

"Have a seat," said Rose, apparently comfortable giving William orders in the Campbell household.

"Dad says that Kelly is still missing," said William, as he pulled out a chair and sat down.

"That's correct," said Rose. "We're trying to understand the timeline from yesterday. Can you walk us through your communications with Kelly step by step?"

"Sure, if you think it will help," said William.

"Will, right now, I don't know what's important and what's not important. The more information I have, the better the odds that we can find Kelly, sooner rather than later," said Rose.

William seemed to consider this for a moment and began talking. "Kelly sent me a text around 3 yesterday afternoon asking me to meet her at the beach after she got off work. I said okay and told her it should be a great sunset. Around 6 p.m., I got another text from Kelly saying she couldn't meet me until about 8. I said, 'No problem, we should still be able to catch the sunset and then go eat.' That was the last message I sent her, until a little after 8. When she was a little late, I sent a text telling her where I was sitting. She never replied," said William, shaking his head and looking like he was on the verge of crying.

"Did you see her Lexus at the beach parking lot?" Rose inquired gently.

"I did," said William nodding. "I tried to call her when she didn't respond to my text. Then I went looking for her. Her car was parked on the south side of the lot near the trees. So I kind of hung out there for a while to see if maybe she was talking to somebody else, you know, and had maybe lost track of time. Then I went back to the beach, thinking maybe I'd missed her. Then I started asking around if anybody had seen her. Nobody had. Then I called her phone again and told her I was worried and looking for her and that she should call me back right away. So then I went back to her car again and discovered that it wasn't locked. The keys were in it and her purse was on the front seat. So I looked at her purse to see if her cell phone was there, and it was. So, now I knew why she wasn't answering, but I still had no idea where she was," said William, becoming agitated and upset.

"Did you do anything else with her cell phone?" asked Rose.

"Well, yeah, I checked her messages and played the two that I had left her. I just wanted to make sure her phone was working, but then I realized it didn't matter because she didn't have her phone."

"Then what happened?" asked Rose.

"I waited around a little more, then went home. Heck, by midnight, I called everybody I could think of, and nobody had seen her all day. I must've fallen asleep around 2 or 3 a.m. and didn't wake up until just after 7 when her dad called. The first thing I did after talking to her dad was call Kelly. She didn't answer."

William seemed exhausted. His shoulders slumped, and he seemed to have trouble holding his head upright. Both parents remained stoic. I can only assume they did not want to interfere with what they imagined to be a formal interrogation of their son.

I did my best to remain perfectly still.

Rose leaned forward across the table toward William. She put her hands together on the tabletop and clasped them together.

"Will, there's just one more thing I need to understand."

William raised his head with some effort and looked directly at Rose, tipping his head slightly to the right. His expression was both pained and quizzical.

"When did you and Kelly break up?" said Rose evenly.

"What?" said William, leaning back in his chair with a look of stunned surprise. "We ... we didn't," he stammered.

"Will, Kelly's Facebook page says she's single," said Rose, almost as if it were a question.

William rose from the table suddenly and went into the family room where he picked up an iPad. As he slowly walked back to the kitchen table, I could see he was entering commands. He stopped about five feet from the table and began shaking his head violently from side to side, as he dropped the iPad and his right hand to one side. The adults were frozen in place and staring at William.

"This … this is wrong. It wasn't like this yesterday. Somebody else must've changed it. Kelly wouldn't change her Facebook page without telling me."

Now William began to cry in earnest. First, a single teardrop rolled down his right cheek. Then, he simply sat down on the kitchen floor and began to sob. His mother could no longer contain herself. She pushed her chair back, went to her son, knelt, and put her arms around him.

I looked at Rose for some direction.

"Sit tight," she whispered. "Let's see where this leads."

William was no longer sobbing openly. JoAnn released him, and he began entering commands into the iPad again.

"This makes no sense. She changed her status from 'in a relationship,' to 'single' yesterday at 3:42 p.m. Why would she do that without telling me first?" William asked without really expecting an answer from anyone in this room.

"Now we can go," Rose whispered to me.

JoAnn was still kneeling beside her son. When Rose stood, Benjamin followed suit, as did I.

Rose spoke quietly to Benjamin. "We're probably going to need to speak with Will later. For the moment, it seems best to let him calm down."

"Thanks, Rose," said Benjamin. "JoAnn, Will, and I will be here all day and all weekend. Please let us know if there's anything we can do to help you find Kelly."

JoAnn stood to hug Rose, and William got to his feet, too. We were all standing near the door at this point.

Rose, who was about 12 inches shorter than William, stepped directly in front of him and took his left hand with both of hers.

"We are doing everything possible to find her. If she contacts you, call me immediately," said Rose to William. She took a business card from an inside blazer pocket and handed it to him. "Use my cell phone number, and call me any time, day or night."

William nodded vigorously and said, "Thank you. Please find her."

CHAPTER 22

DOUGLAS MCINTYRE

JULY 8, 2011

1050 EDT

Rose and I did not speak as we walked to my Jeep.

Once inside, Rose said, "Please put 75 High Ridge Road into the GPS. The McIntyre home is a bit hard to find."

I complied, and we were off.

"Can you explain what we just learned?" I asked.

"Of course. It appears Kelly and William were in a committed relationship. For reasons I don't yet fully understand, it appears Kelly decided to unilaterally, and very publicly, end their relationship yesterday. From the timeline, it looks like Kelly made a date to meet Will at the lake about 45 minutes before she updated her Facebook page. And then for reasons unknown, she sent William a text message at 6 p.m. moving their rendezvous back about 30 minutes."

So far, I was following the story. But I suspected that Rose had more puzzle pieces to share.

"Do you have a theory as to why she moved back their meeting time?"

"I do," said Rose. "There were three text messages from Douglas McIntyre between 4:30 and 5:20 yesterday afternoon. The messages from Douglas said, 'Call me; please, call me,' and 'I need to see you,' in that order. Then, at 5:31, Kelly called Douglas. Then at 5:58, she sent William a text message moving their meeting time back to 8:00. My bet is that Kelly agreed to meet Doug at the lake after work and before seeing William."

I absorbed the implication.

"So that would make Douglas, not William, the last person to see Kelly before she disappeared?" I asked.

"Possibly," said Rose. "But we can also place William at the lake until well after 9 p.m. Either boy could have been the last person to see her before she disappeared."

"So does that mean you think William is lying about not having seen her at the beach last night?

Rose paused for a moment then said, "Actually, my gut tells me that William is being truthful. But so far, we have nothing but his word. I'm hoping Douglas McIntyre can help us fill in some missing pieces."

We drove in silence, except for the turn-by-turn directions provided by the Jeep's GPS.

***

"You have arrived," said the GPS, as we entered the long gravel driveway at 75 High Ridge Road.

From the front of the drive, I could see only trees. When the driveway curved to the right, the house — or perhaps I should say castle — came into view. The residence was at least 100 feet across the front and three stories tall. The building was made of stone, and there was a large turret on its left corner. There was a large arched entryway in the center. The driveway opened into a large circle in front of the house. In the center of the circle was a fountain with three tiers. Water spurted intermittently from the top tier of the fountain. Water from the top tier fell to the second and then continued to the bottom tier, which was perhaps 20 feet in diameter. The edge of the bottom tier was surrounded with English boxwoods and ground cover. The landscaping was precise and well maintained. I had seen gardens in England and Germany that I imagined were the models. On the far side of the fountain there was parking for six vehicles. As all six spaces were empty, I guessed that this was guest parking and that the family vehicles were garaged elsewhere. The gravel drive continued between the house and the parking area along the front of the house and turned to disappear behind it.

Rose and I emerged from the Jeep and walked back into the driveway. We both stood and stared at the magnificent home. There were some elaborate estates in Wayside, but I had never seen anything like this.

"Okay if I take the lead here, too?" said Rose.

"Sure," I replied, "Are you close to the McIntyres too?"

Rose began walking toward the archway and marble steps that led to the front door, and I followed.

"Not really," said Rose. "I know the family. They have three children in the schools. Doug is the oldest. They also have a younger son, James, and a daughter, Catherine. Joe, the father, is probably the wealthiest man in Wayside and one of the most powerful in the state of Massachusetts. He's the founder of Genesis Capital, which spun out of Genesis Consulting about 20 years ago. Joe is in the business of buying, fixing, and selling billion-dollar companies. As you can see, business is good. The mother, Ellen, does not work outside the home and is involved in more charities and philanthropies than I expect even she can keep track of."

I was nodding and considering the implications. In my experience, the truly wealthy did not respond to rules and regulations like the rest of us. I was remembering, in particular, a former US ambassador to the Philippines. When the SEALs had been tasked with upgrading embassy security in Manila, the ambassador had fought us every step of the way. He and his family routinely ignored security protocols. In the end, his 16-year-old son slipped his protection detail and was kidnapped, tortured, and murdered by terrorists. The failure occurred on my watch, and yet I still believe that there was nothing my team could have done to prevent it. The basic truth of personal protection is that it's impossible to protect someone who does not wish to be protected.

The door opened, and we were greeted by a cheerful Asian man of about 30 who wore blue jeans and a pink Black Dog polo shirt.

"Good morning," said the man in perfect English. "How can I help you?"

"I'm Detective Callahan, and this is Chief Carter. We need to speak with Douglas McIntyre," said Rose in an even and cool tone.

Judging by his appearance and accent, the Asian man appeared to be Filipino. I was guessing this individual was a member of the household staff. While Filipino staff was common in both San Diego and DC, it was out of the ordinary in Wayside.

"I'll need to check as to whether Douglas is available. In the interim, would it be convenient for you to speak with one of his parents?" the man inquired, looking first at me, then at Rose, and then back to me.

A Jack Carter Novel

"It would," I replied in Tagalog. "Your kindness is much appreciated."

"Ah, I see you speak my language," he replied, grinning widely and also speaking in Tagalog. "Please, come in and I will attempt to find one or both of Douglas's parents."

We entered a large foyer that was cool and dark. I glanced up to see that the foyer was a full three stories. There was a curved marble stairway and balconies on both the second and third floors. At the top of the foyer was a dome that appeared to be finished in gold. The floor was white marble with black inlays in every third tile. There were two doors to the right, two doors to the left, and a three-story glass wall at the back with oversized double doors that opened onto a rear patio where I could see another huge fountain.

"My name is Xavier," said the man, now switching back to English. "Please, make yourself comfortable, and I will return shortly."

Xavier walked the length of the foyer and disappeared to the left. I watched him go and turned my attention to Rose, who was staring at me and nodding.

"How many languages do you speak?" asked Rose.

"Ten or so, depending on how you count. It helps to speak the language of both your enemy and your ally," I replied.

"You are just full of surprises, Jack Carter. May I assume that Spanish is one of the 10?" asked Rose.

"Sí, yo hablo español bastante bien. He dedicado mucho tiempo al sur de la frontera," I responded.

Truth be told, I probably could speak closer to 20 languages well enough to communicate and carry on a basic conversation. I have always had a good ear for languages and accents. At the same time, my ability to read and write in other languages is far more limited. Over the past decade, I had spent thousands of hours cross-training with special forces, regular troops, and police from dozens of countries. There's nothing like combat and simulated combat to accelerate your understanding of another language.

"I have some thoughts about putting your language skills to work at the high school," said Rose, smiling. "But we'll talk about that later."

Xavier popped into view at the other end of the foyer and motioned with his right arm to join him saying, "Please, come with me. Joe and Ellen are waiting to receive you in the study."

We proceeded through the foyer and down a hallway to the left. We then turned to the right and entered a large office with windows on three sides. To our right was the large rear patio and fountain we had seen from the foyer. To the left and rear were gardens and lawns that seemed to

continue into eternity. In the middle of the room, facing the patio, was a massive maple desk with a leather top.
Between the desk and the patio were four maple and leather captain's chairs. Against the rear windows was a 12-foot leather sofa. There were two Turkish carpets used to define the two seating areas. The larger was predominantly dark blue and extended from behind the four captain's chairs to the far side of the massive desk. A somewhat smaller carpet, with red as its principle color, sat under the sofa and burled wood coffee table. As we walked farther into the room, I noted a fireplace and flat-screen monitor on the interior wall and large built-in display cases. The four captain's chairs had been rearranged to face each other, instead of the desk. Ellen and Joe rose from two of the chairs to greet us.

"Joe, Ellen, this is Jack Carter, our new police chief. Thank you for agreeing to see us. It's fortunate that you are both at home," said Rose.

We shook hands, and Ellen said, "Please, sit. Xavier, would you be so kind as to bring iced tea for everyone?" she asked.

While Ellen had made her request sound like a question, it clearly sounded like a command to me. I thought it interesting that a choice of beverage was not being offered and that Ellen was deciding what the group would drink.

"Very good," said Xavier as he turned and left the room with nary a sound. As he departed, I noted his black cross trainers. Apparently peace and quiet were important at the McIntyre home.

"How can we help — has Douglas done something wrong?" inquired Ellen.

Being both calm and careful, Rose began, "Kelly White is missing and hasn't been seen since last evening. It appears that Douglas may have been the last person to see her."

The McIntyres appeared genuinely surprised. They looked at each other and then back at Rose.

"Oh, my! You don't think something's happened to her, do you?" Ellen said looking at each of us. As her gaze made the rounds, she shifted in her chair. She had short curly brown hair and was dressed casually. She was in good shape, average height, and perhaps in her early 50s. Joe was tall and thin. He wore running shorts, a T-shirt with a Harvard emblem emblazoned on the front, white socks, and white Nike cross trainers. Joe was balding and what hair he had left was trimmed short on the sides. While Ellen seemed upset, Joe seemed utterly calm.

"We don't know whether Kelly is in trouble or has simply forgotten to check in with her parents. We're hoping Douglas can help us with that," said Rose.

With that, Joe rose from his seat and said, "Excuse me, I'll get Douglas right now."

After Joe left the room, Xavier returned with the iced tea, which he efficiently distributed. I wondered if Xavier had made any attempt to locate Douglas, or if he had simply gone to Joe and Ellen first. I would bet on the latter.

Rose gave Ellen a brief overview of the events surrounding Kelly's disappearance. I noted that she carefully omitted any mention of William Campbell, text messages, voicemails, or Facebook.

After about 10 minutes, Joe returned with his oldest son. Doug appeared to still be half-asleep. His feet were bare, and he wore blue jeans and a black shirt. Both boy and clothing appeared rumpled. I wondered if Doug had slept in these clothes. Joe steered Doug into the chair he had been using. Doug was well over six feet and muscular. His light brown hair was cut short.

"Doug, you know Detective Callahan. This gentleman is our new chief of police, Jack Carter," said Joe.

Doug was sitting directly across from me. Without getting up, I leaned forward and extended my hand to him. His gaze lifted from the floor and met mine. Slowly, he extended his right hand and met my grasp. I shook his hand slowly, giving me more time to hold him and checked his pulse and pupils, while saying, "It's good to meet you, Doug. Detective Callahan has told me a great deal about you. We're hoping you can help us find Kelly White."

As I spoke to Douglas, his hand began to sweat, his pulse was racing, and his pupils opened wider. The mention of Kelly White caused him to flinch, such that I could almost feel an electric current moving through his body. After mentioning her name, I held his hand a bit more firmly, and, as I anticipated, he tried to release my hand and pull away. Every sense in my body, my soul, and my mind told me that this boy had killed Kelly White.

When I released Douglas's hand, he sat back in the chair. He looked away from me to his mother and then turned to stare up at his father. Douglas McIntyre was behaving like a trapped animal looking for a means of escape.

Rose began softly. "Doug, when did you see Kelly last evening?"

Doug appeared startled by Rose's question. He looked to his mother again, who nodded almost imperceptibly, and then back to Rose.

"We met at the boat dock around 7:30. We just talked for a while and then she went off to meet William. I haven't seen her since then," he said, shaking his head and shifting his eyes.

"What did you talk about?" inquired Rose.

"We talked about getting back together, after she finished breaking up with Will. Kelly and I were together for a long time, and the thing with Will just wasn't working out. She was ready to come back to me. Has anyone checked with Will?" he asked, looking at Rose.

"When did she tell you she was meeting William?" asked Rose, carefully avoiding his question.

"When she left the dock she was going to meet him then. If Kelly is missing, you need to talk to Will," he said, becoming more agitated.

"When did you learn that Kelly and William were breaking up?"

"She and I had been talking about it for a while. When I saw that she'd done it, I texted her to call me. I wanted to see her, to make sure she was okay."

"Were you and Kelly planning to meet after she saw William and broke it off with him?"

Perspiration began to form on Doug's forehead. He broke eye contact with Rose as his pupils began to dart from side to side.

"No, no. We were going to see each other tonight, after work. I had other things to do last night, and I don't know if she knew how long she would be with Will. She was also going to see her girlfriends later."

"Doug, I know this is hard, but can you tell me any more about what you and Kelly talked about?"

His head popped up, and he stared directly into Rose's eyes and said, "William, it was all about William. If Kelly is missing, you've got to talk to Will."

Doug was staring at the floor again. Rose took a business card from an inside pocket and handed it to Doug. His eyes came up to meet her once more, and he took the card.

"If Kelly contacts you, you call me on my cell day or night," said Rose, calmly and clearly.

"I will," said Doug, nodding.

We all stood, and Rose addressed the parents. Handing a business card to each of them, she said, "Same goes for the two of you. If you learn anything that can help us find Kelly, call me day or night."

"We will," Ellen almost blurted out.

She and Joe were both nodding.

As if on cue, Xavier appeared on my left and said, "With your permission, I will show the two of you back to the front of the house."

The silence in the room was solid enough to cut. Xavier turned and began walking toward the entrance to the study. Without hesitation, Rose and I followed Xavier out of the study, down the hall, through the foyer, and into the front driveway.

Once in the driveway, we stopped. Rose reached into her blazer and retrieved a business card. She faced Xavier and carefully held her card by the top two corners with her thumbs and forefingers, bowing slightly to Xavier. Xavier squared himself to face Rose and took the card from her by grasping both of the bottom corners with his thumbs and forefingers. I had seen this done hundreds of times in dozens of Asian countries and wondered where Rose had been exposed to the protocol.

As the card was exchanged, Rose said to Xavier, "If you know or learn anything that can help us find Kelly, please call me day or night. This could be a matter of life and death."

"I understand, Detective Callahan. I very much like Kelly White and will do anything I can to help you find her. I will pray for her safe return," said Xavier.

"Chief Carter, it was a pleasure to meet you," said Xavier in Tagalog.

We shook hands and departed.

CHAPTER 23

LUNCH WITH DAD

JULY 8, 2011

1137 EDT

Rose and I sat quietly as I drove us back to the lake. I was processing my encounter with Douglas. While we had no proof that Doug killed Kelly, yet I felt certain it was so. At the minimum, I reasoned with myself, Doug knew something about Kelly's disappearance that literally made him sweat. I rolled through the alternatives in my mind. Perhaps Doug witnessed her death. Or maybe he had kidnapped her and had locked her away somewhere for us to find. Whatever it was, it was bad, and Douglas McIntyre was guilty of something.

As we neared the lake, I noted that Rose had been equally quiet.

"Penny for your thoughts," I said.

Rose continued to be quiet. Out of the corner of my eye, I could see she was, once again, chewing on her lower left lip. I imagined Rose was processing, too. And she had much more data than I.

"Was his pulse racing back there?" she asked.

"It was," I replied.

"Jack, I spend a lot of time with these kids. Either Douglas McIntyre killed Kelly, or he's kidnapped her, or some other variation. What amazes me the most is that this kid was sound asleep after doing whatever he did. Douglas McIntyre is not a stupid kid. Whatever he did, he thinks he got away with it. He was shocked to see us there."

"That doesn't bode well for Kelly," I said.

"No, it does not," said Rose, shaking her head as we pulled into the parking lot at the town beach.

"Jack, let me work on this for a few hours and see what I can put together from all the sources. What I need is a witness to Doug and Kelly's meeting. Let me see if I can find one."

Rose was right, and it appeared she felt she could do her job more quickly without the chief of police in tow. I decided on the spot to give her some room.

"Okay," I said stopping near her vehicle. "If you need anything, or if I can help in any way, call me."

Rose opened the door to exit the Jeep, got out, and turned to look me in the eye.

"I'll find her, Jack. One way or the other, I will find her," said Rose, and closed the door.

I sat for a moment, thinking about what I should be doing next. I could go to the station. Or, I could go to lunch and get some advice. I decided on the latter.

***

Fifteen minutes later, I was sitting at the lunch counter inside the Wayside Shooting Club talking with my dad. There were eight empty stools at the counter. I sat on number nine all the way on the right. Sally Richmond, who ran the lunch counter, had already taken my order for a turkey BLT on whole wheat and a large unsweetened iced tea. I felt safe here, as safe as I felt anywhere on this planet. The club was as much home to me as the house across the street. I had played here, worked here, and grew up here. From cashier to cook to range master, I had done every job at the Wayside Shooting Club. And while it's been decades since I worked here, in some strange way, it feels like yesterday.

After Sally took my order, I gave Dad all the details of my morning, including my dismissal by Rose.

Dad listened intently, nodding, grimacing, and stroking his chin while not saying a word.

"So, what's bothering you more: the missing girl, or the fact that you're not leading the investigation?" said my dad, cutting to the heart of the matter.

I thought deeply about the question. For just a moment, I considered giving my dad the politically correct answer and then thought better of it.

"Dad, should I be leading the investigation?"

"Jack, should you have led the mission to kill bin Laden?"

"No," I said. I thought about objecting. I thought about telling him that in my old job, I was responsible for 6,500 people, and that in my new job, I was responsible for 28. And as I thought about saying it, I knew it was wrong. In both cases, I was an executive with many specialists reporting to me. Rose Callahan was an experienced detective with a much greater knowledge of everything about this case. My job was to make her job easier, support her in every way I could. And if that meant getting out of her way, then that was the right thing to do.

"Then what should I be doing right now?" I asked.

Sally arrived with my BLT, smiled, and said, "Hope you enjoy it. I doubled up on the applewood bacon, just the way you like it."

Two more customers had wandered in and seated themselves at the other end of the lunch counter. Sally gave me a wink and went to greet them. Sally was in her late 60s and had worked for the Wayside Shooting Club since I was a teenager. She was about 5'6", in great shape, and sassy as ever. Her hair was still jet black and curly, pulled back in a ponytail. She had always treated me like a little brother. Over most of the years, I had treated her like a big sister. I remembered fondly the crush I had on her when I was 15 and she was 27. Years later, she had explained to me, as a big sister would do, that there had been two reasons why she had never given me a chance. While she had considered it, she had decided the 12-year age difference was just too much. And if it were not enough, the fact that I was the boss's underage son convinced her that I was much better suited to the role of little brother than Romeo.

Once Sally was busy with her customers, Dad looked me in the eye, smiled, and said, "Right now, you should be giving your full attention to the BLT platter that Sally has so lovingly prepared for you. Once that's taken care of, you might drop by the station and see what your other 27 employees are doing. All kidding aside, Wayside can be a busy little place."

I felt myself nodding my head slowly and smiling broadly at my dad.

"Sounds like a plan I can handle," I said, picking up my BLT.

CHAPTER 24

SUSAN OLIVER

JULY 8, 2011

1245 EDT

For the next two hours, I immersed myself in being a bureaucrat. Lieutenant Kyle McPherson gave me a quick overview of all the open cases including seven burglaries, five cases of domestic violence, and 12 cases of property damage that McPherson assured me were perpetrated by Wayside teenagers. He briefed me on traffic issues including road construction and speed traps.

When I asked about Patrick Kennedy and the CAVE Men, McPherson assured me that all was under control. Patrols for the construction site had been doubled, and he recommended we continue the practice for the foreseeable future. He had met with the head of Wayside Holdings' security department and gotten agreement that they would limit their protection detail to inside the chain-link fence that surrounded the property and construction site. They had been happy to hear about the increased patrols and a dedicated hotline for them to use to reach the WPD dispatcher on duty. All in all, it sounded as if McPherson was on top of the situation. Nonetheless, I asked that he set up a meeting with their security chief and me, if for no other reason than that I had promised the selectmen I would do so.

McPherson also indicated that he had personally spoken with Mason Teller and other leading members of the CAVE Men and received assurances that any further opposition on their part would be peaceful. I still wanted to meet with Mason and take my own measure of his commitment to peaceful protest.

I met with our other two detectives for about half an hour each to review their current cases. Once again, everything seemed to be under control. I also got to spend some time with Julie Kellog, the senior dispatcher and self-described "keeper of the chief's calendar." Apparently Julie's job description included screening my calls, managing my calendar, and making sure that all 28 members of the Wayside Police Department were on the job, per the schedule she maintained. She informed me that she had scheduled a meeting for me with Laura Nowicki for 3 p.m. to review our annual budget. Toward the end of our meeting, Julie asked if there were any family and friends who merited, as she called it, "priority handling," in terms of scheduling and phone calls.

While I had a hard time imagining that anyone on the list I gave her would go through the station switchboard, I nonetheless complied with her request. On the list, I included my dad, Chris Bridger, Jenny Hale, Susan Oliver, and much to my surprise, Wendy Baker, the United flight attendant I would be meeting for drinks at 7 this very evening. I had thought briefly about canceling my date with Wendy and my dinner date with Jenny Hale at 8 this evening. But I needed to see Jenny, as she had made something of a production of seeing me as soon as I was back in Wayside. While she would give no details, her tone and language implied that we had something very important to discuss. Naturally, my imagination ran wild. I conjured up a scene where Jenny declared her undying love for me and her desire to be with me forever, now that I was no longer in harm's way and had returned to Wayside. The scene played out for me over and over again at the Red Coach Grill. I was pretty sure this was my fantasy and nothing else, but the fact that the fantasy was mine caused me to ponder deeply how I really felt about Jenny and what I wanted from her now that I was home. And since I was going to the Red Coach Grill tonight anyway, I felt that keeping my date with Wendy seemed both appropriate and yet so *inappropriate* on many levels.

***

Laura Nowicki arrived precisely at 3 p.m. About 20 minutes into the meeting, Julie knocked on my office door and said, "Chris Bridger's office just called. The selectmen have scheduled an emergency meeting for 5 p.m., and your presence is requested."

"Topic?" I inquired.

"Kelly White," said Julie, with no hint of emotion.

"No surprise there," I said. "Would you track down Rose, let her know about the emergency meeting, and ask her to give me an update on her progress with the case?"

"You got it, Chief," said Julie as she closed the door.

Laura and I were seated at a small round conference table at the end of my office nearest the door. My office was big, about 10-feet wide and about 25-feet long. At one end was a large pedestal desk with a credenza and two guest chairs. One of the long walls and one of the short walls were floor-to-ceiling windows with a lovely view of the public safety building parking lot. Other than furniture, the office was devoid of clutter. The desk and credenza were empty except for the 27-inch iMac sitting on the corner of the desk. There were three oak bookshelves on the inner wall, also empty. The office walls were beige and blank.

"The selectmen are going to freak out about this," said Laura with a calm but concerned tone.

"Any advice?" I inquired.

"Nope," said Laura, shaking her head, "I suspect you've had much more experience than anyone at the table dealing with this kind of thing. So, I guess I do have some advice for you. Do your job and don't let people less experienced than you tell you how to do it."

"Probably some pretty good advice," I said, nodding.

Laura got up, packed away her laptop, and headed for the door. As she left, she turned to me and said, "Not that I think you'll need it, but good luck with the meeting and the case."

Laura departed, closing the door behind her.

I understood, or at least I hoped I understood, the right reasons for meeting with Chris and the selectmen. Any one of them could be contacted by Wayside voters, the media, or other interested parties, and they would need to sound informed on the investigation. At the same time, I needed to make sure they weren't sharing information that could compromise the investigation. The easiest way to make sure they didn't do that was to limit their knowledge of the investigation and be clear with them about what I wanted them to share. Of course, telling your superiors what to do can be a delicate and hazardous discussion.

As I sat contemplating our discussion, my iPhone vibrated. Susan Oliver was calling. My mind flashed for just a moment on Jenny, Susan, and Wendy all sitting at the Red Coach Grill bar, side by side. They were all dressed to the nines, and deep in conversation. I imagined they were discussing me, but I was having trouble imagining exactly what they were talking about. My iPhone vibrated for the fifth time, and I answered it.

"Hello, gorgeous," I said, doing my best Cary Grant imitation.

"I'm looking for the chief of police. I'd like to report a crime," Susan purred into the phone.

"I can help you with that, ma'am" I replied, staying with my Cary Grant persona.

"I seem to have misplaced my libido and was hoping you or one of your detectives might help me find it," she continued.

"I would be happy to help you with the recovery process," I replied.

"I plan to hold you to that, Jack Carter," said Susan. "So, how's your first day going?"

I told her — the good and the bad. Susan listened intently for several minutes while making minor acknowledgments to let me know she was listening and that she cared.

"Is it still okay for me to come up tomorrow?"

"I would be devastated and lost if you did not. It seems as though we haven't seen each other in a very long time, and I miss you."

"It's been a very long time. And I miss you, too."

"Like I said before, case or no case, I came home to Wayside to get some balance back in my life. My dad and my staff all seem to think I should have a life. They all seem to have a life and think having one is normal. I could easily let this case consume me. But I'm pretty sure that's not the right thing to do."

"As your doctor, your lover, and your friend, I can assure you that it is not the right thing to do. Glad to see you're doing your best to hold the new course, sailor," said Susan in a much lighter tone. "I have your dad's address, and will be there around 6. Don't worry if you're not there to greet me. I'm a big girl and can entertain myself."

"I will be there at 6 sharp, if humanly possible. We're meeting Chris and Mandy at The Haven for dinner."

"Dress code?" Susan inquired with a lilt.

"It's a local dive, so bring your boots."

Susan was born and raised in Houston, Texas. Her parents are both professors at Rice University. Susan could ride, rope, and jump a horse as well as any man. And yet she was the most feminine of women and a career Navy doctor. Susan was perhaps the most complex woman I had ever met.

"Shall I bring my hat and my spurs, too?"

"I wouldn't try putting spurs in your carry-on luggage," I said with a chuckle. "I don't think you'll find anyone else at The Haven wearing a cowboy hat, or a cowgirl hat for that matter, but don't let that stop you."

Susan giggled and said, "See you at 6," and hung up.

CHAPTER 26

CASE REVIEW

JULY 8, 2011

1620 EDT

As I sat at my conference table, I thought about Susan wearing nothing but her cowgirl hat and a red bandanna. Her dark black curly hair and her cream-colored Stetson surrounded her beautiful face like a picture frame. She wore a red bandanna around her neck that completed the bottom of the frame. Susan's body was both round and firm. She enjoyed riding horses, sex, and being naked. This combination led to many afternoons of horseback riding that culminated with several hours of lovemaking.

Susan enjoyed being on top, riding me as if she were still in the saddle. She would hold the hair on my chest as if it were the mane of her horse. We would buck, turn, and twist until we were both sweaty and spent. And through it all, she would never lose the hat. I did love that hat.

My musings were interrupted by a knock on my office door. Rose Callahan opened the door a few inches and leaned in far enough to see me.

"Emergency meeting?" she asked.

"Yep. Apparently the selectmen would like to know what we know."

"You plan to tell them everything we know?"

"I plan to tell them what they need to know," I responded.

"Good," said Rose as she entered the room. She closed the door and sat down at the conference table.

"So, what do we know?" I asked.

Rose still looked as fresh and cleanly pressed as she had early this morning. She placed both hands on the conference table and stared at me thoughtfully.

"I've interviewed five of Kelly's friends this afternoon. I told them nothing beyond the fact that Kelly was missing and that we had located her car at the town beach parking lot. Each one of them indicated that I should talk to Douglas McIntyre and find out where he was when Kelly disappeared. Each of the five recounted interactions between Doug and Kelly involving outbursts, threats, and yelling."

"Can you give me an example?" I inquired.

"I can. There was a New Year's party at the Grant family home, which included adults and their families. The Grant home is a split-level. Most of the adults were upstairs along with the younger kids. The older kids, including Kelly and Doug, were in the bottom level. At this point in time, Kelly and Doug were together. Caroline Grant, who is one of Kelly's best friends, was the first to tell me about the fight, and two other girls provided similar accounts. A little after 10 p.m., it appears that Doug saw Kelly dancing with William. Doug grabbed William by the shoulder, spun him around, and slugged him in the gut. When William doubled over, Kelly slapped Doug across the face. He responded by putting his hand on her chest and shoving her back into the crowd, which caught her before she fell.

"Three or four of the boys grabbed Doug and took him outside. Doug didn't return to the party, and no one reported this to the police. I could go on," said Rose, shaking her head slowly.

"So Douglas may have been the last person to see Kelly. They had a history of violence. And Douglas reacted to our interview badly," I concluded.

"All true," said Rose. "But we have no witnesses, and no Kelly."

"Where are we on the search?" I asked, assuming we were nowhere.

"We have many dead ends," said Rose. "Roger and Gabriel have walked nearly two miles of shoreline and found no alternate exit point. If Kelly left the dock, she left exactly the same way she came, which seems impossible unless she followed her own tracks exactly and departed in a vehicle that was parked next to hers."

"Doesn't seem very likely, does it?" I asked.

"It doesn't," agreed Rose. "Beyond that, no one we've interviewed — and that includes more than 50 friends and coworkers — has seen Kelly since 7 last night. As of 10 minutes ago, neither the Whites nor the Campbells have heard from Kelly. The McIntyres are not answering their phone at the moment."

"Do we think Doug is a flight risk?" I inquired.

"Hard to say. Joe certainly has the resources to make Doug disappear if he chooses to do so. That said, we don't have enough to bring Doug in, in my opinion. Beyond that, I've got two officers watching the house to see what we can see."

"You concerned that Joe might complain about having his house, his family, or his son placed under surveillance?" I inquired.

"I am," said Rose. "I'm even more worried that the presence of uniformed officers may stop Doug from leading us to Kelly. So the officers doing the surveillance are doing it from the woods dressed in civilian clothes. Jack, following Doug may be our best shot at finding Kelly, if she's still alive."

"Do we have officers trained in covert surveillance?"

"That's the one advantage I can clearly point to from the war in Iraq and Afghanistan," Rose said. "About one-third of our patrolmen are former military. The two boys watching Doug are both former Marines with strong recon training who did multiple tours of duty in Iraq and Afghanistan. So far, Doug and his parents are at home."

"But still not answering their phones?" I asked.

"No, they're not."

"Should someone drop by for another visit?"

"I would advise against it," said Rose. "My gut tells me that letting Doug and his parents stew for a while is our best shot at getting them to lead us to something of interest. Besides, until we find Kelly or a witness, I don't think we have anything else to question Doug about."

"Anything else?" I asked.

"The URT divers have three men down. They've found nothing relevant so far. I understand they'll be at it until dark and then start up early tomorrow morning as required," concluded Rose.

"Okay, keep at it. I'll let you know if anything comes up at the selectmen's meeting that's relevant to your case. If anything breaks, call me no matter what time it is. I'm meeting a friend for dinner at the Red Coach Grill tonight."

"Anybody I know?" inquired Rose with a smile.

"Perhaps. I'm meeting Jenny Hale for dinner at 8. And I agreed to have drinks with someone I met on the flight back yesterday, who lives in Weston," I said carefully.

"I love Jenny's work," said Rose. "Please give her my best."

As Rose departed, I wondered if she knew any details about my long-standing relationship with Jenny. It occurred to me that my life in Wayside was going to be a very public one. Not in the sense that it had been when I was a SEAL commander and media spokesperson for the Navy. No, this would be very different. There were not more than 10 or 12 restaurants and bars in all of Wayside. My personal life would likely be the subject of intense discussion. Tonight, I would be having drinks with a beautiful flight attendant from Weston and then dinner with a famous Boston artist, who was a knockout in her own right, and the daughter of one of Wayside's most influential families. Something told me that tongues would be wagging about the new chief of police at Sunday church services in Wayside. Oh well, nothing I could do about that.

A Jack Carter Novel

CHAPTER 27

EMERGENCY BOARD OF SELECTMEN MEETING

JULY 8, 2011

1700 EDT

I arrived at the meeting room in the town building just before 5 p.m. I was surprised to find all of the other meeting participants already in their seats. I noted with some amusement that everyone sat in exactly the same seat they had the night before. While some people might write the consistency off as simple habit, I knew there was more to it than that. It was easy to discern that Linda and Laura sat closest to Chris because he was the senior authority figure in the room. Chris was what sociologists call the "apparent leader." I had checked the election records to discover that the two Bobs, who sat closest to me, were the most junior members of the board. Hence, the seating chart played out based on seniority, with me, the newest member, seated farthest from Chris. No doubt someone more expert in group dynamics than me could have added further and deeper explanations of the seating arrangement.

As I took my seat at the end of the table opposite Chris, I could feel the knot in my stomach tightening. I left the Navy in some large part to avoid meetings like this. I was far more comfortable dealing with enemy insurgents than politicians and businessmen. In the Navy, the more senior I became, the more suits I found myself dealing with in briefings and planning meetings. While a meeting of military officers could be contentious, the disagreements were framed by the same, or at least similar, military training. While most of the suits had avoided military service, this didn't stop them from having deeply held convictions about military strategies and operations. I asked myself, is this going to be the same thing?

Chris called the meeting to order promptly at 5.

"I am sure you've all heard that Kelly White seems to be missing. I called this meeting so we can all have the benefit of knowing the current facts," said Chris.

When Chris finished speaking, everyone turned to look at me in unison. While most of them seemed calm and genuinely interested in hearing from me, Linda Ralston seemed anxious. She quickly looked back at Chris with an expression that seemed both puzzled and a little angry. I decided it was best that I jump right in, before Linda could interrupt Chris's plan.

"Chris is correct. It does appear that Kelly White is missing. A tremendous ongoing effort has failed to locate her at this hour. She was last seen leaving work yesterday evening at around 7 p.m. She failed to meet a friend shortly thereafter. Her parents reported her missing early this morning. Shortly after that, we located her vehicle at the town beach. Kelly's purse, car keys, and cell phone were in her vehicle. There was no sign of struggle and no witnesses to her arrival or departure from the town beach area. We have conducted more than 50 interviews, searched the town beach area, and deployed a Massachusetts State Police dive team to search the lake. The investigation is ongoing. Each of you should feel free to share any and all of this information with Wayside residents and the media," I concluded.

By now Linda looked as if she were about to burst. The other six meeting members nodded somberly and some looked back to Chris for direction.

"Thank you, Chief," said Chris, nodding at me. "Does anyone have questions for Jack, or other issues related to this matter that require discussion?"

Linda began. "If Kelly White is dead, this would be the first murder in Wayside since 1975," she said. "The bad publicity could impact everything from home values to our ability to attract restaurants and retailers for the new town center project. We need to begin formulating a PR strategy for mitigating the potential negative impact of a murder in Wayside."

Everyone in the meeting room was quiet. Bob Farmer pushed his chair back from the table and gave me the look of a man about to do something that both of us knew needed to be done, and that he did not want to do. His direction was now clearly focused on Linda and Chris.

"Linda, unless you know more than I do, it appears unclear what has happened to Kelly. She could simply be missing. She could also be the victim of accidental drowning in the lake. And, yes, it's possible that she has been murdered. Thus, while I share your concerns, I feel it would be precipitous for us to proceed on the sole assumption that she's been murdered," concluded Farmer.

I was watching as Chris and Laura exchanged glances, apparently deciding not to intervene at this point in the conversation.

"Chief, can you tell us how likely is it that Kelly White has been murdered?" said Linda.

I wondered who Linda had been talking to. There was nothing in the public reports that made murder the most likely outcome. I recounted the events of the day in my head. There were at least four people who believed, at this point, that Kelly White had been murdered. The list began with me and included Rose, my dad, and the murderer — who I believe to be Douglas McIntyre. As I pondered the situation, I concluded that it was unlikely Douglas had confided his crime to his parents. It was much more possible, in my mind, that he had shared what he had done with a close friend. It was also possible that he had involved a close friend in the murder.

"We have no hard evidence that this is anything more than a missing teenager," I said, choosing my words very carefully. "In fact, statistically this is much more likely to be a runaway than an abduction or murder. This case involves an 18-year-old high school graduate, not a younger child. Hence, while we are putting every resource available into the search for Kelly White, the most likely outcome involves her returning to her parents' home on her own."

I had never been good at poker or any activity that required bluffing. From an early age, my dad told me I was a lousy liar and that telling the truth would make my life, and his, much easier.

While everything I had just said was true, it was not what I believed. But my job was not to involve the Wayside selectmen in the search for Kelly White. Further, I could see no good coming from leading them to conclude that Kelly had been murdered when I had no hard evidence to support my gut instincts. And still, doing what I had just done made me feel like crap. I now sat quietly hoping that Chris would pick up the ball and prevent Linda, or anyone else, from pushing me on the matter further.

I stared at Chris pleading with him in my mind to take over the conversation. Happily, he did.

"Chief, thank you for being so clear in describing the facts of the matter. As you know, no one on this board, other than you, has any experience in managing an investigation like this. While I'm very sorry that this has happened, and happened so shortly after you arrived home, I am incredibly relieved to have you managing this investigation."

Linda seemed unsatisfied and said, "Chris, while I understand there are many possible outcomes for this investigation, I feel we would be remiss in not putting together a response that is appropriate to the worst outcome."

Now Thomas Mars took his turn with Linda. "I agree that we should have a crisis management action plan in place that is appropriate to the worst outcome, as you described it. Don't you also feel we need plans in place for the proper messaging about the other likely outcomes of her disappearance?"

"The other outcomes are all neutral in terms of their impact on our community's reputation," said Linda. "I don't mean to sound cold. But if the divers find her in the lake and it's judged an accidental drowning, there is no fallout for Wayside. Likewise if she never comes home, or comes home on her own, no negative impact."

"What if this turns into an abduction for money?" Thomas inquired.

This surprised even me. I ran through all the information I had about Kelly White's disappearance. There were no witnesses. Her parents were not wealthy. There had been no ransom demand. I realize I had ruled out kidnapping shortly after meeting her parents. Hell, Rose had never even mentioned it as a possibility she was considering.

"Jack, has your team considered the possibility that this could be a kidnapping?" asked Chris.

"No, not really. The general circumstances and the lack of a ransom demand make it highly unlikely that this is a kidnapping for money."

"I'm glad to hear that," said Linda. "At the same time, a kidnapping for money would not be that damaging to the reputation of our community. Wayside is considered one of the safest places to live in eastern Massachusetts. Our nightmare scenario is a random act of violence committed against one of our young people on town property. I don't want to belabor the point, but feel we need to prepare for this worst-case outcome."

Chris jumped back into the conversation. "Linda, your point is taken. Laura is hereby authorized to locate and select a PR firm that specializes in crisis management to prepare an action plan that contemplates the murder of one of our citizens on Wayside public property."

Linda sat back in her chair, triumphant.

"Does anyone else have a question for Jack or an issue related to Kelly's disappearance that requires our attention?" Chris inquired.

The room was blissfully silent. I silently prayed that the meeting be over, and it was.

Chris adjourned the meeting, asking that Laura and I stay behind. When the others were gone, Chris closed the door, and the three of us sat at "my" end of the table.

"Okay Jack, what the hell is really going on here?" Chris said in the same tone he might have used decades before when our parents had just left the room and there was a caper afoot.

I looked at Chris, then to Laura, and waited.

"You can tell Laura anything you would tell me, as long as it's not about me," Chris said and grinned. "Now tell us what's going on. I know you, and you were not even remotely forthcoming in that meeting. That said, I knew you wouldn't be and still needed to have the meeting play out the official version for the other board members. Now, will you please tell me what the hell's going on with Kelly White?"

"I'm thrilled that you thought I'd only recite the official version to the rest of the board." I said.

I took one of my new Wayside business cards from my pocket, pushed it across the table to Chris, and said, "In case you forgot my cell number, it's on my new card. The next time something like this happens, give me a heads-up before the official meeting starts."

Now Laura jumped in. "Whenever the two of you are done having fun, I'd like to know what's going on and what I should be doing about it."

We both looked at Laura, grinned sheepishly and nodded. I began, "What I said in the meeting is true. We have no hard evidence that Kelly has been murdered. That said, Rose and I both believe that Douglas McIntyre has either killed or kidnapped Kelly. Circumstances, timelines, their personal history, and me staring Doug in the eye all tell me that he's done something very bad to Kelly."

"Crap," said Chris, shaking his head and absorbing the implications.

Laura looked at Chris, then at me, and said, "So, Linda had it partly right. You believe that Kelly is either dead or abducted by someone who was very close to her."

"That's correct," I replied.

"But you don't believe this is random violence against a Wayside resident committed on Wayside town property," Laura confirmed.

"I do not."

"So," said Laura, "we do need a crisis management action plan. And we need it to include the possibility that two Wayside families will be devastated by this event. And one of those families is among the wealthiest and most powerful in Massachusetts."

Chris and I both nodded at Laura.

"So, here's my plan. I'll engage a PR firm to create a crisis-management action plan for Wayside in two variations. The first will anticipate that Kelly has been murdered by someone she did not know. The second will anticipate she was murdered by someone close to her. I have no idea if those two variations are material but will make sure the firm we hire does," concluded Laura.

"Sounds like a plan," said Chris.

With that, Laura packed up her MacBook and departed without further conversation.

Chris and I were still seated at the table.

"Jack, are you okay?" Chris asked.

"No, I'm not. I didn't come home to deal with the murder of an 18-year-old girl. Chris, I've seen so much death, and I thought I could escape it by coming home. I still have nightmares about colleagues who've died and people I've killed. It feels like death has followed me home." I paused, and Chris said nothing. "And then this meeting was almost too much to take. I'm focused on finding Kelly or finding the person who killed her. I can do that. I was not prepared for the PR action plan discussion. I get it. But I don't like it."

We continued to sit in silence for what seemed like a few minutes. I could feel myself regaining control of my emotions. This was my job. And apparently it was going to be much more like my old job than I could have ever imagined. This was a very depressing thought.

Chris put his hand on my shoulder and patted me slowly. "Jack, I am genuinely sorry that you're having to deal with this after only a few days on the job. At the same time, I'm damn happy to have you in this foxhole with me. I need you here. I need you to do the good job I know you can do. And I need you to not let it consume you or depress you. At the end of the day, it's just a job that needs to be done."

As always, Chris could take a shit sandwich and make it okay. I felt better. I could do this job. I could be good at this job. And there was no one on the planet that I'd rather be working for than Chris Bridger.

CHAPTER 28

WENDY BAKER

JULY 8, 2011

1900 EDT

After the meeting, I went home and played ball with Bandit and Buster in the backyard for a while. Dad watched from the porch with mild amusement. Bandit was faster in getting to the ball, but Buster often took it away from him before Bandit could return it to me. It was a warm day, and I actually worked up a bit of a sweat playing with the dogs.

I threw the ball one last time and headed back to the porch where Dad was sitting. The house was built into the side of a hill, such that it was a full three stories in the back. There was a large wooden deck attached to the second floor with a brick patio beneath it. The yard was only about 100-feet wide, but ran back toward the marsh almost 300 feet. It was a great space for playing catch.

As I approached my dad, he inquired, "So, do I understand correctly that you have two dates, with two different women, both meeting you at the same restaurant?"

"Well, that would be technically correct," I said hedging. "I have a dinner date with Jenny at 8. Drinks with Wendy was a bit of an afterthought."

"Known Wendy for a while?" he probed.

"No, not really. I just met her on the plane yesterday."

My dad was grinning at me, a grin that meant he knew something that I did not.

"What's up?" I inquired.

"You said this woman is a United flight attendant, she lives in Weston, and her name is Wendy Baker. Do I have all that right?" asked Dad.

"Yes."

"My guess is that you don't know who Wendy Baker is, or perhaps more to the point, who her father is," said my dad.

"That would be correct," I replied, happy to let Dad play this out. "Perhaps you can enlighten me."

"Wendy Baker is the daughter of John Baker, the CEO of Colonial Foods, the largest commercial bakery in New England. The family has been in Weston almost as long as our family has been in Wayside. The father is about my age and lost his wife in a boating accident about 40 years ago. Wendy is an only child, divorced, and the proud mother of a 21-year-old son who is a senior at Williams, the father's alma mater."

"Impressive," I said. "Would I be correct in guessing that you didn't look this up on Google this afternoon?"

"You would," Dad replied. "When the mother died, I was involved in the investigation. While no one thought John had murdered his wife, the death still had to be investigated. I remember feeling so sorry for both father and daughter and thinking it was good that they would have each other. Wendy is about your age and probably graduated from Weston High School around the same time you were graduating here."

"Damn," I said, thinking how sad it would be to lose your mother at such a young age. "Wendy seems very full of life. She was bright, cheery, and seemed very happy in her own skin."

"Well," said Dad, "Forty years is a long time to adjust to losing a parent."

I nodded, thinking about all the things my parents had gone through and decided I should count myself very lucky that they were both still alive and healthy.

"Don't wait up for me," I said to my dad with a grin.

Dad pointed his forefinger at me, dropped his thumb like the hammer on a revolver, and said, "Have a great time, son. The boys and I will see you in the morning."

***

I parked my Jeep in front of the Red Coach Grill. As I walked to the door, I grinned just a little at my choice of clothes. I had selected an orange Nautica polo shirt, black Lucky jeans, and black Brooks Brothers loafers. Black and orange are the Wayside school colors. It struck me as slightly funny, and a little twisted, to wear Wayside colors to meet someone from Weston. The Red Coach Grill was on the Wayside–Weston line, but clearly in Wayside. I wondered for just a moment about the fact that I often wore black and orange. In most cases, the only person who knew they were Wayside colors was me. Now that I was home, wearing black and orange had meaning for me and anyone else associated with Wayside High School.

I entered the front door and let the hostess know I was meeting someone in the bar.

At 7 p.m. on a Friday night, the bar was packed. Wendy was sitting between two guys at the far end of the bar. I stopped to stare at her for just a moment. Her smile was electric.

As I headed down the length of the bar to meet her, I realized that my interview with Maria Lopez was airing on the big screen behind the bar. When I reached Wendy, she swung around and hopped off the barstool.

"Good to see you, Chief," she chirped. "It seems that you've had a very busy first day," she said, nodding toward the big screen.

"It has been a very long day," I said.

The gray-haired gentleman who was sitting on the barstool to my right looked at me, then back to the big screen, then back to me, back to the big screen, and then turned on his stool and said, "You're the guy on TV, right?" He said, pointing to the big screen.

"I am indeed," I said, extending my hand. "I'm Jack Carter, the new chief of police in Wayside."

"Simon Young," he said, shaking my hand. "Too bad about the missing girl. I hope you find her soon."

"Thanks, we're doing everything humanly possible."

Wendy slid back onto her barstool and angled herself about halfway between Simon and me. I began to grin ever so slightly as I noted that Wendy was wearing white linen slacks and a maroon polo shirt that included a Weston Wildcats logo over her left breast. Maroon and white were the Weston High School colors, and Wendy's sense of humor was apparently as twisted as mine.

Wendy focused her attention on me like a spotlight that made me feel warm and said, "What can I order you from the bar?"

I returned her gaze, staring happily into her deep, dark brown eyes and replied, "A Dark 'n Stormy would seem appropriate."

Wendy turned to the bartender and said, "Jim, how about a Dark 'n Stormy for my friend?"

At this point, Simon concluded I was here to stay and offered me his seat, moving one stool down to the right. I slid onto the stool and gave Wendy my full attention as my drink arrived.

Wendy picked up her drink, held it out, and said, "Welcome home, Jack. Tell me about your day."

We clinked classes, drank, and I told her about my day. I tried to stay pretty close to the level of detail I had given the selectmen. Wendy's demeanor was so open and empathetic, I found myself sharing a bit more information than I had originally intended. Her face was both beautiful and expressive. For what seemed like a long time, she simply listened, nodded, grimaced, and smiled.

"So," I said preparing to change subjects, "do we know each other from high school?"

The question seemed to surprise Wendy just a little bit. The bartender delivered two fresh drinks. Wendy stirred her vodka tonic slowly and stalled a little while she decided how to reply.

It seems hard to believe that I could have spent time around Wendy in high school and not remember her. I had thought about not asking and waiting to see if it came up naturally in the conversation. But I simply wanted to know and decided that asking was the quickest way to find out.

"You and I met once in January 1974 at a party in Wayside at the Bridger home. We chatted for about five minutes, and the next time I saw you, in person, was on the plane yesterday."

I flashed on the party in question and placed her immediately. At the time, Jenny Hale and I had recently broken up. I had sworn off women and focused all my attention on graduating and going to Annapolis. I remember the event so vividly, in part, because Wendy was, and is, stunningly gorgeous. Chris had also given me an amazingly hard time about not dating in general — and not pursuing Wendy in particular. What a blast from the past.

"I remember," I said somewhat slowly.

Wendy stared at me intently, cocked her head to the right, smiled broadly, and said in a deep voice that reminded me of maple syrup, "Really?"

"Really," I said, nodding and smiling somewhat defensively. "I can still see you in my mind's eye. Your hair was much longer … it was parted in the middle, and you had no bangs."

"Okay," she said. "We both remember each other."

We were both quiet for a minute. My head raced about what to say next. I wanted to know everything about her and didn't want to share the knowledge I had gotten from my dad earlier this afternoon. Doing so, I felt, would just be creepy. And perhaps she was quiet for the same reasons. Anyone could pick up a lot about me on the Internet. Still, I suspected Wendy knew things about me she had not discovered online.

"So," she said breaking the silence between us, "what have you been doing for the past 37 years, and why haven't you called?"

The last part of the question caught me off guard. I must've had a look of either surprise or mild shock on my face. At first, Wendy's expression was serious. After about 20 seconds, her face broke into a smile, and she giggled. Both the smile and the giggle were delightful.

I was desperately trying to think of something clever to say. Movie scenes with Clark Gable, Cary Grant, and Humphrey Bogart flickered through my head.

Unfortunately, Steve Martin prevailed, and I said, "I was kidnapped by aliens."

Wendy looked at me with surprise. "I didn't think a guy like you would have such a twisted sense of humor. Between the high school colors and Steve Martin quotes, it appears I may have been wrong," she said, smiling. "Seriously, give me the highlights of your last 37 years. Career, family, and anything truly bizarre that you'd like to share."

For the next 10 minutes or so, I shared with Wendy the non-classified version of my 37-year career in the Navy. I told her about my parents and their odd living arrangements. And I concluded with the fact that I had never married but had lived with Jenny Hale in Boston during the 12 months I commanded the USS Constitution.

"That year with Jenny was a turning point?" Wendy asked.

"It was the happiest I've ever been. And then three months after I deployed to Europe, she married another guy."

"That's tough," said Wendy. "She still married to the same guy?"

"Nope. Stayed married for about five years. They have one kid. And Jenny and I have never been together since."

The topic of Jenny reminded me that I would be meeting her for dinner in about 20 minutes. I decided this was the time to come clean with Wendy about my plans for the rest of the evening.

"Oddly, I'm meeting Jenny here for dinner at 8. When she discovered I was moving back to Wayside, she insisted on seeing me in person as soon as possible."

Wendy took the information without flinching. I was afraid that she might have thought drinks at 7 was going to lead to dinner .

"I look forward to finding out what Jenny has in mind for the two of you," Wendy said cautiously.

Apparently, that was all Wendy had to say on the topic of Jenny — and the rest of the evening. It was still very possible that I had just hurt her feelings, which troubled me deeply. I was struggling to place my feelings for Wendy. On the one hand, she seemed like an old and dear friend. Someone with whom I shared a past. And at the same time, I barely knew her.

I needed to get the conversation moving again, and I wanted to know more about her.

"I've given you my life story. How about yours?

Wendy hesitated at first, but then began to open up with the condensed version of her life. After graduating in 1974, Wendy attended UC Berkeley and majored in Women's Studies. Her mother had died in a boating accident, just as my father had suggested, when she was 15. Her father had wanted her to join the family business, but instead she had become a United flight attendant.

She was animated when she spoke about traveling the world for United. It was both adventurous and safe. When she was 30, she had married a United captain named Brad Clark. The marriage lasted five years and produced a son, named John after her father. Her son, she felt, was the most important thing in her life and the best thing she had ever done.

"My father and John are spending most of the summer at the family home on Nantucket," said Wendy. "I moved back into the family home in Weston when JJ turned five. The house is huge, and the school system is terrific. So these days, I split my time between flying, Weston, Nantucket, and my little apartment in the Back Bay."

At this point Wendy swiveled to meet three women who had appeared behind us.

"Jack, this is Sally, Sharon, and Linda."

I shook hands with each after sliding off the barstool. The three women were all in great shape and wore the same maroon Weston Wildcats polo as Wendy.

Addressing me, Wendy said, "We all went to high school together and were cheerleaders for the Weston football team."

"That would be the same Weston football team that you and the Warriors trounced 42 to 10 back in 1973," said Linda.

Sharon spoke up. "If memory serves me correctly, the Warriors trounced us throughout our four years of high school football."

The direction of the conversation was beginning to make me a bit uncomfortable. Sharon was correct, and I had played in each of the four years of games she was remembering as a freshman, sophomore, junior, and senior.

Sally now decided it was her turn. "When Wendy told us she was meeting you for drinks, we were thrilled. As much as we hated losing to Wayside, I think we all had a crush on you in high school. By the time we were seniors, you, Jack Carter, were the most hated member of the Wayside football team."

It's possible that I was beginning to blush at this point, and I was certainly looking for an exit.

Wendy came to my rescue, saying, "Now girls, let's not embarrass Jack. That was a long time ago, and we're all grownups now. Why don't you go see if our table is ready?"

The women giggled, said their goodbyes to me, and left. I suspect my relief was visible. Wendy and I were now standing face-to-face.

"Jack Carter, I have had a crush on you since high school. I would very much like to get to know you better. If that works for you, call me."

She hugged me, kissed me on the cheek, and was gone.

CHAPTER 29

JENNY HALE

JULY 8, 2011

2000 EDT

I turned and watched Wendy walked the length of the bar and disappear into the restaurant. My mind was reeling. This woman was beautiful, intelligent, caring, unattached, and clearly interested in me. Was she interested in the me I am today? Or was she interested in the high school football player I had been many years ago? I had no idea, but thought it was well worth finding out.

As I stood there dumbly processing the past 60 minutes, Jenny Hale appeared at the entrance to the bar, saw me, smiled, and headed in my direction.

Jenny was both petite and shapely. Her long blonde hair was pushed back over her shoulders, just as it had always been. As I watched her approach, I could feel my heart racing. And at the same time, I was fearful of the pain that an encounter with Jenny could bring.

She wore a light green linen sundress and sandals. There was no makeup on her lightly tanned face with the exception of a hint of pink lip gloss.

When she reached me, she put her arms around me and her head on my chest and held me tightly. I put my right hand on the back of her head and my left in the middle of her back and held her. Perhaps I imagined it, but it sounded as if she were purring softly.

Slowly, she released me, and I her. She pushed back a bit placing her hand on my hips and staring up at me.

"I have missed you so," she said, letting the words hang in the air.

As 100,000 thoughts raced through my mind, I could find nothing to say. I had loved Jenny since we were 12. And yet, it seems we were simply not meant to be together. "Dance away lovers" Jenny had called us. And after all these years, I knew not why.

"How are you?" Jenny said, as I helped her onto the barstool where I had been sitting minutes before. As I slid onto the stool where Wendy had been seated, Jim, the bartender, shot me a grin, shrugged his shoulders, and quickly cleared mine and Wendy's drink glasses.

"I've been busy," I said, replying honestly.

"I saw the news," said Jenny with a pained look on her face. "You poor baby. I can't imagine this is the homecoming you were prepared for."

"It was not," I said shaking my head.

"Is it okay that you're here with me now and not working on the case?" Jenny asked with sincerity.

"It's fine," I said wondering if it was. "We've got half the department working on finding her, plus resources from the state police and crime lab. The detective in charge is managing what needs to be managed. And if she needs me, she knows I'm on call."

Jenny nodded slowly, absorbing the situation.

She began, "If it's okay with you, I reserved one of the private dining rooms for us?"

"Sure," I said wondering why the two of us needed a private dining room that was normally reserved for parties of six to 12.

"Great," said Jenny as she slid off the barstool, patted me on the thigh, and walked toward the private dining rooms.

***

Each of the private dining rooms was named for a Wayside founding family. Unsurprisingly, the restaurant manager had reserved the Hale Room for us. The room was big enough for 12, but had been set for two. With the exception of the glass door, the room had no windows. The table was positioned so that no one outside the room could see us. The decor was early 1800s, and with the exception of the electric lights, it would have been easy to believe that we had stepped 200 years back in time. The surroundings only added to the surreal nature of our meeting. Why was I here? What did Jenny have to share with me that was so important?

Jenny had taken the liberty of ordering a bottle of Prosecco and a bruschetta. The waiter had poured glasses for each of us, explained the specials, and then discreetly departed, closing the door behind him.

Jenny raised her glass to me and said, "To all things past, present, and future."

We toasted, and Jenny placed her left arm on the side of the table, palm up, and beckoned me to hold her hand with her fingers as she had done so many times before. I placed my hand on top of hers, and our fingers locked in a tight embrace. Jenny was staring at me with a look that was both happy and serious.

She seemed to shake off the seriousness, and her face lightened with a beautiful smile.

"Tell me everything," she said. "Where have you been, what have you seen, and," she paused for just a moment, "who have you become?"

For the next hour or so, I told her what I could of my life, she did the same about hers, and we ate our meals. The food was good, the wine better, and the conversation best of all. Nothing either of us shared seemed to surprise the other. We connected as we always had, like two parts that were built to fit together.

***

After the dinner dishes were removed and cordials served, the waiter departed silently, and the seriousness returned to Jenny's face. It had the effect of clouds rolling in on a sunny day, and the room seemed to become perceptibly colder.

She once again placed her left hand on the table with her palm up and beckoned with her fingers to hold her hand. I complied, with some wariness that I hoped she did not sense.

"I have a number of things to share with you, Jack," she began, "and some of them may make you angry. Before I start, I want you to know that I love you today, I have always loved you, and I always will love you."

A single tear rolled down Jenny's left cheek. I reached across the table and caught the tear with the back of my left index finger. As I caught the tear, I caressed her cheek, and she turned her head ever so slightly to kiss the back of my hand.

She tightened and then loosened her grasp on my right hand, and I slowly removed my left hand from her cheek. Once again, we simply stared at each other. How had I spent my life so that this woman was not a part of it? At the corners of my mind, I imagine the answer involved my commitment to my country and to the SEALs, but at the same time I knew that answer was too simple.

Jenny continued, "I also need to tell you that I don't know where our relationship will go now that you're home. I can tell you I am open to every option I can imagine."

I nodded, not saying a word for fear that I would break the magic of the moment. I sat quietly waiting for her to continue.

"When you left for Europe after we had lived together for a year, I was devastated. I never believed you would leave me. And before you interrupt, I understand your commitment to the Navy."

Again, I thought about objecting, about interrupting. I wanted to tell her that I had no choice in the matter and that I had told her I would be unable to communicate with her for months at a time. Still, I sat quietly waiting to see where she was going.

"About four weeks after you left, I discovered I was pregnant. At first I tried to reach you, but as you had told me, you were unreachable. I thought about where you were, what you were doing, and came to believe that you might never come home from this assignment. In hindsight, I have no idea if this was real or imagined on my part. At the time, I felt very alone and wanted to have the baby. I shared my situation with Matt, and he offered to marry me. At the time, it felt like the right thing to do. Now, I don't know."

I was stunned. What had I done 21 years ago? I had been working behind enemy lines for months on end. When I was finally able to surface, it was Chris who had told me that Jenny had married Matt. After a long drunken weekend, I had redeployed and never looked back. Jenny and I had pretended that our year in Boston had never happened. Tonight was the first time we had ever spoken of it. I had seen Jenny no more than a dozen times in the past 20 years. And tonight, she was walking back into my life.

"So, we have a son?" I said.

"We do," replied Jenny, with tears running down both of her cheeks.

I rose from the table and went to her. She rose to meet me, placed her arms around me with her head on my chest, and we held each other for a long time. We were both crying now. Tears of joy, I hoped.

***

After a time, we sat.

"Tell me about Seth. How is he doing? Does he know?" I asked.

"There are several other things you need to know," said Jenny, visibly steeling herself. "First, Matthew is gay and always has been. His offer to marry me was made in part to benefit his career. There were rumors about his sexual preference that were slowing down his career options. In the early '90s, being a gay banker was not cool. And you should know, he has been and continues to be a wonderful father to Seth. And no, Seth has no idea that I lied to him about the identity of his father. Jack, once the lie was told, I could never find a way to untell it even after Matt and I divorced."

I absorbed the fact that I was a father but that no one beyond Jenny and Matt Carrington knew it. I had met Seth on perhaps three occasions and realized I had not seen him in almost 10 years.

Jenny was speaking again. "While I haven't told Seth, I feel I must now that you're home."

Jenny retrieved her phone from her purse and showed me a recent picture of Seth. It was like looking in a 35-year-old mirror. The boy on the screen could have easily passed for me when I was a midshipman at Annapolis.

"Oh my God," I said, looking at Jenny, shaking my head slowly, and smiling.

"He does look just like you," said Jenny, beaming. "Hence my concern that with you home, others may begin to notice the resemblance."

"When and how would you propose we tell him?" I asked.

"Seth is in London for the summer. He'll graduate from Skidmore next spring. When he's home from school, he stays with me in town. He spends very little time in Wayside, as he doesn't get along with my parents at all. Something else the two of you share in common," said Jenny, grimacing. "I just don't have a clue when and how to do this."

"Is Matt okay with the idea of telling Seth that I'm his son's biological father?" I said, choosing my words very carefully.

"Matt loves Seth, and isn't thrilled about the idea. With that said, Matt and I have been divorced for 16 years, and Seth has lived with me solely for that entire period. In his heart, Matt has always known that you're Seth's real father."

"Okay, then. Job one is figuring out when and how to tell Seth that I'm his father."

I had a son. I was almost overwhelmed at the prospect. At age 55, I had let go of the idea that I would ever have children. And now in the blink of an eye, I had a son. Not a baby boy, but a 21-year-old man who barely knew me. This was fantastic and frightening.

Jenny was watching me carefully. "I've had a lot of time to think about this since I learned you were coming home. I think it would be best if you and I knew where our relationship stands, before we tell Seth that you're his father. I hope that makes sense to you."

"Let's say for the moment that it does. Have you thought about what you want from our relationship?" I said, choking up just a little.

"I have thought about it. I want to have the you and me that we had back in '89 when we were living in Boston. I want the you that goes to a job every day where someone is not trying to kill you. And I know that 1989 was more than 20 years ago and that I have a life that I love and don't wish to give up." She paused, watching my reaction.

I couldn't tell if Jenny was asking me to be someone else. The year we had been together was one in which I held a largely ceremonial post as commander of the USS Constitution. I hosted parties, gave VIP tours, and made sure the boat was well maintained. It was perhaps the safest military assignment a sailor could have. My new job seemed equally safe to me, regardless of the day's events.

"Jack, I'm flying to London in the morning to meet Seth and spend time with him for a couple of weeks. I need to absorb who you are in 2011. Being with you, talking with you, holding you tonight has been wonderful. But I saw you on TV today. You still wear a uniform, you still put yourself in harm's way, and I'm afraid you'll put your job in front of our relationship." Jenny was crying again.

Once again, I rose and went to her. She pushed her chair back from the table and fell into my arms. After a while, she lifted her head from my chest and stared into my eyes. I kissed her, and she kissed me back — a long slow tender kiss.

When the kiss was over, she hugged me and broke away. She turned and picked up her purse from the floor. When she turned back to me, she grabbed the front of my shirt and playfully held my face to hers and kissed me hard once more.

"I do love you. I'm not sure if I can be with you. But I do love you."

"I love you too, Jenny. I always have, and I always will. But I'm honestly not sure what it is you want from me."

"Neither am I," said Jenny, "Neither am I."

Jenny pulled me to her once more. When our lips parted, she said, "We'll figure this out, together. I'll call you from London."

Then she was gone.

CHAPTER 30

NIGHTCAP

JULY 8, 2011

2210 EDT

After Jenny left, I returned to the bar in search of a nightcap. The place was now less than half full. As the chief of police, you've got to love a town where the bars empty out early even on a Friday night.

I picked a row of five empty barstools and slid onto the one in the middle. I was in no mood for conversation or company and probably should have just gone home. I asked Jim to bring me another Dark 'n Stormy. This would be six drinks in a little more than three hours. I asked Jim to also give me a glass of ice water. It seemed appropriate to make sure I wasn't impaired before beginning the short drive home. I downed a long drink of ice water and a sip of my Dark 'n Stormy.

I thought about the day. A new job, a missing girl, three women I had feelings for, and the news that I had a son. I needed to find the girl, or her killer, or both. I needed to figure out if Jenny and I were going to have a relationship that was exclusive. I had wanted to marry Jenny Hale since high school. I had wanted to marry Jenny Hale in 1989. Did I want to marry Jenny Hale in 2011? Being with her tonight felt so natural, so good, so right. Being with Jenny was something I had planned and dreamed about for most of my life. On one level, the dream seemed to be materializing into reality. On another level, I was sitting alone at a bar, and Jenny was on her way to London. This time she was the one going to Europe. There seem to be some great irony here, but I was having trouble grasping it. Hell, I was tired. I was mentally exhausted, emotionally spent, and just wanted to go to sleep.

I paid my check, left my unfinished drink, and went home to sleep.

CHAPTER 31

BRAND NEW DAY

JULY 9, 2011

0645 EDT

I awoke to the sounds and smells of breakfast being made in the kitchen. For a few minutes, I laid in bed and listened to the comforting clicks, clacks, bumps, thumps, and the whirring of the kitchen fan. The view from my bedroom was due west out across the marsh and to the Sudbury River. The sky was blue and cloudless. Through the open windows, I listened to the morning birds sing.

I replayed last evening's emotional meeting with Jenny. She said she loves me and that she always had and always would. We had a son ... a son who didn't know that I was his real, or at least his biological, father. Jenny said she was open about where our relationship could go, but she seemed pessimistic that we could actually be together.

What the hell was I supposed to do with that?

What did she want from me?

Was I supposed to follow her to London and sweep her off her feet?

Or was I supposed to give her some space to decide what she wanted for us, for her son, and for herself?

I had no answers for any of these questions.

I decided three things. First, I would talk to Dad about all of this and see what he had to say about it. Second, I would share with Susan all of this because she was my friend before she was my lover, and I needed a woman's perspective on Jenny. Finally, I would get my ass out of bed and go do my job. The last item was the one I was most comfortable doing.

***

Bandit and Buster were both waiting patiently outside my bedroom door. I was a little surprised to see them when there was food being prepared in the kitchen. Apparently both of them had been fed and had heard me dressing and decided to investigate.

I sat down on the bed and said good morning to the boys. After getting a proper licking, I wiped the dog slobber from my face and ears onto the sleeves of my shirt. Then the three of us headed downstairs with the dogs leading the way.

Dad, whose breakfast timing was always impeccable, was retrieving toast from the toaster when I arrived in the kitchen. There were already two white plates on the counter. Each plate had three strips of applewood bacon and scrambled eggs that were still steaming. There was some shredded cheese and salsa atop the eggs.

"Morning, Dad," I said grinning. "This looks great. Waking up to the smell of bacon and coffee is one of life's greatest pleasures."

Dad grinned back at me and replied, "We live to serve. How did your double date go last night?"

We ate breakfast, and I shared the highlights of the evening in chronological order. I had decided that doing otherwise might mean never getting to my encounter with Wendy. And for whatever reason, the time I had spent with Wendy seemed both relevant and meaningful to me. At a minimum, it was pretty straightforward compared to the time I had spent with Jenny.

My dad listened intently, ate his breakfast, and said nothing until I finished the whole story including my confusion about where to go with Jenny and Seth.

"So, any thoughts about what I should be doing?"

Dad stopped eating, pushed his plate back from the edge of the table, folded his arms, leaned them on the counter, looked me squarely in the eye, and said, "I would suggest you do absolutely nothing about Jenny and Seth and await developments."

I stared back at my dad with what must have been a puzzled expression and said, "Do nothing?"

"Yes," he replied. "Do nothing."

"But I have to do something," I retorted.

"Eventually, you do. But, for the moment, it appears that you haven't decided how to proceed. From what you've said, it doesn't appear that Jenny has a clear path in mind, either."

I nodded.

"I suspect a couple of things will happen over the next few weeks. First, you'll have time to think about this, and perhaps decide how you really feel about Jenny now. Second, Jenny may do the same. You two have waited a long time to get to this moment and rushing any decisions probably won't make them better decisions."

I nodded some more.

"It sounds like the two of you said a lot of things to each other last night that needed to be said. Now you should both take a little time to think about what you both really want from each other and if there's a fit. You're both thoughtful people. No need to rush."

CHAPTER 32

CAPITALIST LACKEY PIG

JULY 9, 2011

0830 EDT

After breakfast, I spent about 30 minutes in the basement gym lifting and stretching. Both Bandit and Buster watched my every move as if they would be grading me at the end of my routine. In my mind, I imagined them conferring and then each giving me a "9" on their pug-sized judging paddles. My imagined scenario amused me, making the workout that much easier.

With my blood pumping, I headed upstairs for a quick shower. I shaved, I flossed, I brushed, I combed, and I dressed. The sameness of the routine was comforting. The uniform was comforting. Discovering who killed Kelly White would be extremely comforting.

I reflected on the thought. I was certain she was dead. It was something in Douglas McIntyre's eyes that made me certain. I recognized the cold emptiness I had seen there. I had seen the same emptiness in the terrorists I interrogated over the years. There was no concern, no remorse, no feelings at all except those of anger and hatred. For the terrorists, I understood how their circumstances, their upbringing, and their training had produced such cold hatred for all things Western, and specifically, anything American. But how, I asked myself, had an 18-year-old boy come to have the same feelings about an 18-year-old girl he had known and loved? How had she hurt him so badly that this was the outcome? What was it in his upbringing or his DNA that led him down this dark path? Would knowing the answers to any of these questions help me prove what he had done beyond a shadow of a doubt?

I said goodbye to Dad and the boys and headed off for work.

As I drove south on 27, I could see what appeared to be a group of 30 or 40 protesters outside the east gate to the Town Center Project. There were two Wayside patrol cars on the scene. I decided to check out the situation and made a right turn onto the town center access road.

The protesters appeared to be quite orderly. I counted five armed security personnel at the gate and four Wayside police officers keeping the crowd about 10 feet back from the gate. As I proceeded up the road toward the gate, the Wayside officers stopped the protesters from crossing the road opening a path to the gate. I decided to give the security checkpoint a test.

When I stopped my Jeep just outside the gate, a tall, lanky member of the security team slipped through a 24-inch opening between the gate and the stationary fence. His uniform was black from head to toe including a black beret. He wore an O4 rank insignia on his collar and moved with the bearing of an officer.

I rolled down my window and said, "Morning, Major."

"Good morning, Chief," said the officer in a loud, booming voice. "What brings you to the party this morning?"

"Thought I'd stop by and see how you and your boys were doing," I replied while flashing my friendliest million-dollar smile.

The officer made a circular motion with his hand, and the motorized gate began to open.

"Pull on in and we can chat a while," he directed.

I drove through the gate and parked my Jeep on the right shoulder out of the way. By the time I had done so, my host had walked over to join me and signaled that the gate be closed.

After exiting the Jeep, I turned and extended my hand, saying, "I'm Jack Carter, the new police chief here in Wayside."

"It's an honor to meet you, sir," said the officer while shaking my hand. "James Thomas, at your service."

"What can you tell me about the situation, James?" I inquired.

"Well, the townspeople began gathering here around 6 a.m. and have been perfectly peaceful, if somewhat annoying. You see, we normally keep the gates open for easy access during the day. However, our security protocol requires that we close the gates if there is any perceived threat on the part of the site commander. That would be me."

"Better safe than sorry," I replied. "Seems a little silly compared to what we've all experienced in Iraq and Afghanistan."

"Certainly does. Most of my men have experienced at least two or three tours in hostile countries. In comparison, this seems downright surreal."

"How long did you serve, Major?"

"10 years in all. After West Point and Ranger training, I did two tours in Afghanistan and one in Iraq."

"How long will you be stationed here?"

"I'm here for the duration, sir. The project timeline is currently estimated at three years and seven months. This will be the longest time I've been in one place since leaving the Point. The wife and I are renting a place in Waltham right now and hoping to buy a nice starter home here in Wayside."

"Glad to hear you'll be joining our little community," I said, handing Thomas my business card. "My mobile number is on the card. Don't hesitate to call me for any reason, any time."

Major Thomas came to attention and rendered a snappy Army Ranger salute, which I returned. I got back in the Jeep and circled to face the gate, which was already opening.

"Stop by anytime, Admiral," said Thomas waving as I departed.

After passing back through the crowd, I pulled my Jeep over to the right shoulder and stopped. Kyle McPherson approached as I exited the Jeep to face the crowd.

"Morning, boss," said McPherson with a broad smile. "Happy to see you had a chance to chat with Thomas. He strikes me as a good man, well-trained, who isn't inclined to take this situation too seriously."

"He does seem to have a good perspective on the situation. Is there a lead protester with whom I might converse?"

"That would be Maureen Jackson, chief. And I would be happy to introduce you to her."

Upon hearing her name, Maureen broke from the crowd and approached. She was a tall woman with mousy brown hair. She wore large spectacles. If not the ugliest woman I had ever seen in my life, she was certainly among the Top 10.

Kyle turned toward Maureen as she approached and began to speak. "Maureen, I'd like to introduce you to Jack Carter, our new chief of police."

Maureen brushed by McPherson and began wagging her finger at me as she spoke. "I know this capitalist lackey pig. Jack Carter, son of Charles Carter, another capitalist lackey pig. After 37 years of enforcing this country's imperialist foreign policy, you've now decided to put your police skills to work suppressing citizens here in the homeland. And don't think for a moment I didn't take note of your oh-so-cozy relationship with the head of Wayside Holding's private security police."

Maureen backed up a step, put her hands on her hips, and glared at me, waiting for a reply.

"Maureen, it's a pleasure to meet you, too. I trust you and your cohorts will not be giving my storm troopers any reason to provide you an insider's view of the Wayside town jail?"

"Our intentions are completely peaceful. I wish I could say the same for those Wayside Holdings goons. This is a quiet little residential community, and those men are armed to the teeth. One can only imagine the mayhem they would do if they thought they could get away with it."

"Maureen, it's been lovely chatting with you. By any chance, do you expect Mason Teller to join your little demonstration this morning?"

Maureen glared at me and replied," I have no idea." Then she turned, walked away, and rejoined her band of civilly disobedient citizens.

CHAPTER 33

TELLER HOME

JULY 9, 2011

0920 EDT

I decided it was time to have a chat with Mason Teller. I drove past the Wayside Public Safety Building on Farm Pond Road, merged onto Farm Road and turn right onto Farmcrest Road.

Mason and his wife Suzanne had been our next-door neighbors while I was growing up. There was generally nothing I liked about Mason. As a child, I remember Mason yelling at me when my ball went into his backyard, lecturing me on civic responsibility, flirting with my mother, and being mean to his wife. Suzanne, my parents told me, died of ovarian cancer in 1991. This had always struck me as sadly ironic given that she and Mason had no children. When Mason retired in 1996, he sold his home on Old Sudbury Road and built a new home two blocks from my mother in the same new development. This and many other things caused me to wonder if my mother's relationship with Mason long predated their becoming a public couple in 1997. I have never spoken to my father about this subject, as I feel no good can come of it. When my parents first split in 1994, Dad and I did spend a great deal of time talking about his relationship with Mom. While he clearly loved her, he did not seem to miss living with her. In some twisted way, this made complete sense to me.

I parked in Mason's driveway, which was empty. I got out of the Jeep and reflexively checked my holster. I suppressed the desire to chamber a round, although shooting Mason Teller in the forehead was an enjoyable prospect. The house was a large Cape with an attached two-car garage that gave the entire structure an L shape.

I tried to banish visions of shooting Mason from my head and rang the doorbell once, steeling myself for the encounter. I had, after all, promised the board of selectmen that I would speak directly with Mason to gauge his commitment to avoid confrontations over the Town Center Project. A part of me hoped that he and his merry band of miscreants would break into the project and be shot dead by the Wayside Holdings Security Team. Once again, I made an effort to banish my fantasies and rang the doorbell a second time.

There were no sounds coming from the house. I noted that the two-car garage door had glass panels across the front. I decided to investigate. Mason's 1971 Porsche Carrera 911 was in the garage, but the garage was clearly arranged for a second, currently missing, vehicle. It seemed that Mason was not at home. I made a mental note to look up the make and model of his second vehicle.

Perhaps I had missed Mason, and he had joined the protesters. Or perhaps he was out running Saturday morning errands. Or perhaps he was two blocks away, sleeping with my mother. Fortunately, my cell phone rang before my mind could further develop that third scenario.

I retrieved my phone to discover that Rose was the caller saving me from my own overly vivid imagination.

"Good morning, Rose," I said with genuine good cheer.

"Morning, Jack. The divers are bringing up a body."

"On my way," I said and terminated the call.

CHAPTER 34

KELLY WHITE

JULY 9, 2011

0950 EDT

After 36 hours in the water, a human body is both recognizable and grotesquely deformed. The body lay face up on a black canvas tarp a few feet from the water's edge. She was still fully clothed and her blonde hair was simply wet. Her skin had been eaten away in many places by the uncaring marine life that called Wayside Lake home.

"I've already called her parents and asked John to let them make the ID here," said Rose.

"I got no problem with that," said John Rizzo, shaking his head slowly from side to side. "To lose a child is a horrible thing. Anything we can do now to lessen their pain is okay by me."

I had nothing to add and remained silent. This was now a murder investigation, which gave over jurisdiction to Rizzo and the Massachusetts State Police.

Death. I had seen so many young people die. Early in my career, I imagined I would become immune over time. It never happened. Every death I had ever experienced hit me hard. Those I knew well hit me harder. But the sight of a dead body, any dead body, always made my blood run cold, and I feel as if I were aging days for every minute I stayed with the dead. I felt this way even when the life that had been taken had been taken by me. Some of those I had killed had been even younger than Kelly White. The world had an ugly side to it, a side with which I was overly familiar and desperate to escape.

"Chief, I meant what I said yesterday. I want you, Rose, and your people to keep working this case. I will give you the widest possible latitude with a couple of conditions. First, you share everything with me when you know it. Second, when, and I do mean when, we bring this McIntyre kid in for questioning, I need to be in the room. You got a problem with any of that?" asked Rizzo.

"No problem at all, Commander, no problem at all."

"Any thoughts about what we do next?" asked Rizzo.

"So far, we have no eyewitness to the murder, or even their meeting for that matter. Here's what we do know: Thursday afternoon, Kelly changed the status on her Facebook page from "in a relationship" to "single." She made plans to watch the sunset with William Campbell, her steady relationship, shortly after making that change. It's possible that someone other than Kelly, who has access to her

Facebook account, made the change. Upon seeing the change, Douglas McIntyre immediately began trying to contact Kelly to meet with her face-to-face. Douglas admits meeting with her at around 7:30 Thursday evening, but says they just talked, and that she was fine when he left her on the boat dock. Her scent has been tracked to the dock from where she apparently went into the water. Now we've recovered her body from the lake. William Campbell asserts that he didn't see her Thursday night nor have we been able to locate any other friends or family who did see her or hear from her after her meeting with Douglas. When Rose and I interviewed Douglas, he was nervous and exhibited all the characteristics of someone who is lying about their knowledge of the events in question. I think the son of a bitch did it, but it seems to me we lack the evidence needed to prove it."

Rose was watching me intently deliver my summary and added, "John, I've never been involved in a murder investigation. That said, my instincts tell me Douglas McIntyre is guilty as hell. We've got them under 24-hour surveillance, although now that we found the body I'm not certain about the purpose of that surveillance. As you know, Joe is a very wealthy man and has the resources to make Douglas disappear if he chooses to do so."

"Is that the kind of guy we're dealing with here?" I asked.

Rose thought about it for a minute and said, "Joseph McIntyre is a very powerful, very wealthy individual. He's also the kind of guy who tries to do the right thing. The question will come down to whether he thinks the right thing is holding his kid accountable for what he's done or whether he thinks the right thing is protecting his kid from harm at all costs. I just don't know them well enough to know which way he'll go."

"If you guys have the manpower to keep it up, I would appreciate it if you maintain the surveillance on McIntyre. I consider him a flight risk. At the same time, I want to see the medical examiner's report before we rattle his cage. Perhaps cause of death will tell us something," said Rizzo.

"We've got the resources and will maintain the surveillance. I assume you'll forward copies of the medical examiner's report as soon as they're available?" I asked.

"Be happy to give you the details later, but I can tell you how she died now," said a black man who was kneeling over Kelly's misshapen body. He stood to face us and continued speaking. "Her jaw's broken, but her neck is not. There are no strangulation marks or other signs of bruising that would indicate a struggle. My guess is somebody hit her — hit her real hard — enough to knock her unconscious. She went into the water, floating face down, and drowned."

"Jack, Rose, this is Alan Jackson, the Middlesex County Medical Examiner," Rizzo said.

We shook hands and exchanged pleasantries. The civility of the exchange stood in stark contrast to the brutality that had befallen Kelly White.

I looked up to see Kelly's parents approaching the crime scene.

This was truly going to suck.

CHAPTER 35

WHITE MOURNING

JULY 9, 2011

1045 EDT

Both Judy and Nathan White had been devastated by the sight of their lifeless daughter. Rose thought it best that she drive them home. I had offered to follow and pick her up.

The White home was near the lake on the south side of town. Like most Southside homes, it had been built in the early 1900s when the town became accessible via automobile from Boston. Many of the homes near the lake had begun their life as summer cottages.

The living room was a shrine to Kelly. There were dozens of pictures of Kelly by herself, with family, and with friends. There were several trophies for public speaking and debate. Her recent high school diploma was proudly displayed on the mantle over the fireplace.

There were perhaps a dozen other people in the living room and kitchen, all of whom seemed to have been here for some time. Rose had escorted Judy and Nathan upstairs followed by Brian Huckleberry, their minister. While

Huckleberry had been at the Unitarian church in Wayside for more than 20 years, he was unfamiliar to me. I had grown up in the Unitarian church, but Jacob Coleman, the minister I grew up with, had long since retired.

Huckleberry's wife Evelyn chatted with me while I waited for Rose to return. She was a pleasant woman, in her mid-50s with silver-gray curly hair and a bright smile.

She turned to greet Rose who was coming down the stairway. "How are they doing?" Evelyn inquired.

"As well as can be expected, I suppose. Kelly was the center of their universe, and they're in shock."

"The community will stand by them. We will get them through this. As horrible as this is, we will get them through it," said Evelyn as she began to cry.

Tears began rolling down Rose's cheeks now, too. The two women embraced each other and cried softly, slowly, steadily.

After some moments, they patted each other on the backs, separated, and Evelyn turned to me and said, "Forgive me, Jack. As a minister's wife, you might think I deal with this better. Personally, I don't ever want to get used to death. The loss of every human life is tragic for me. But right now, I need to take care of the living."

Evelyn started up the stairs.

Rose turned to me, dried her cheeks with a handkerchief, and said, "Come on, boss, we've got work to do."

CHAPTER 36

TELLING WILLIAM

JULY 9, 2011

1125 EDT

Rose and I were seated in the Campbell family living room.
The news of Kelly's death had reached them far before we
did. Benjamin, JoAnn, and William were all mournfully
quiet. While I felt we were intruding upon their grief, I also
felt we needed to get to the bottom of Kelly's murder
sooner rather than later.

"There are a couple of things that I just don't understand,
and I'm hoping you all can help me with them."

Rose glanced at me and nodded ever so slightly. On the
way over, we agreed it was my turn to take the lead.

"Please, tell us how we can help," said Benjamin.

"When we were last here, it seemed to me that William was
surprised by the change in relationship status on Kelly's
Facebook page. I'm hoping William can help me
understand how he was caught so unaware," I said
carefully.

William had been staring intently at his own feet, rocking side to side in overstuffed armchair, while his parents looked on from the sofa. It was hard to know if William was listening or not. Once again, I felt horrible about pushing him to talk about his relationship with Kelly less than an hour after he learned she was dead. I genuinely did not believe he had anything to do with her death, but I could be wrong. It could have been him that killed her after the breakup. He had motive, opportunity, and means. He was a large, athletic young man who could have easily broken Kelly's jaw.

"William," said his father, "what can you tell the chief about your relationship with Kelly?"

William seemed to return to us from wherever he had been. Apparently he'd been listening all along.

"The whole thing was a sham," he began. "Kelly and I were never really going together. We made the whole thing up to keep Douglas off her back. Sorry if I misled anyone. But Douglas … the guy's a son of a bitch, and I would have done anything to keep him away from her."

William's parents, who had been leaning forward, both sat back onto the sofa and stared, first at each other, and then at William.

"Why didn't you tell us?" JoAnn said quietly.

"It was our secret," said William. "We agreed to tell no one that we were faking. Hell, sometimes I think we even fooled ourselves. Or at least I fooled myself, maybe."

"What about the Tiffany heart you gave Kelly for her 18th birthday?" said his father.

"Look, Dad," William began while shaking his head back and forth slowly. "I love Kelly. I've loved Kelly all my life. For a few months, I got to pretend that she loved me, too."

Now JoAnn moved to comfort her son. "Kelly did love you, William. I could see it in her eyes, in her face, in the way she talked to you."

"Not enough," said William. "Not enough to want to be in a relationship with me once she got to college. Don't you get it? She changed her Facebook status so she'd be able to meet new guys at Trinity. She told me she was going to do it. But I didn't know she was going to do it this soon. I told her that Douglas would be all over her if she did. She had promised me she wouldn't change her status till she got to school this fall. I tried to stop her."

Once again, William began to sob.

Rose and I stood, and began moving toward the front door. Benjamin went with us, while William and JoAnn stayed behind.

Once on the front porch, Benjamin said to us both, "I'm not sure I understand entirely what's going on here. But as you might expect, I don't think my son killed Kelly. I just don't think William could do such a horrible and violent thing."

Rose and I both nodded. We shook hands with Benjamin and departed.

Once we were both in the Jeep and headed down the long gravel driveway, I turned to Rose and said, "How sure are we that he didn't kill her?"

"It's all gut, Jack; it's all gut. He could've done it. He loved her, and the breakup could have made him so angry that he broke her jaw and left her to drown. But I don't think so. I just don't see how any human being can hurt someone that they love. And that's the problem, Jack, that's the problem. People kill people they love all the time."

CHAPTER 37

ABIGAIL GRANT

JULY 9, 2011

1215 EDT

Rose got a call from Abigail Grant, the principle of
Wayside High School as we were driving back to the White
house. Grant, it seemed, had something to share with us.
Rose told her we'd stop by the high school to meet her
immediately.

Wayside High School was under construction, to put it
mildly. Two new three-story buildings were under
construction on the south side of the campus. As I
understood it, virtually all of the existing buildings on the
north side of the campus would be demolished once the
new construction was available for occupancy in early
2012.

Even though it was a summertime Saturday, the campus
was bustling with a combination of construction workers,
students, and a few members of the faculty. Grant had
asked that we meet her in her office on the old campus.
Rose and Grant worked closely together and knew each
other well. Rose described her as a no-nonsense

administrator who loved the kids and tolerated the parents. Rose had told me Abigail Grant had been the principal in a poor, inner-city high school prior to landing at this wealthy suburban high school. I wondered how she would compare the two.

"Hello, Rose," said Grant as we entered her office. She was up from her desk and around to meet us in a blink. She was tall, athletic, and appeared to me much younger than the 43 years alleged in her Wayside town biography.

"Abby, this is Jack Carter, our new chief of police."

Abby extended her hand and smiled warmly. "Welcome to Wayside, Chief. But then, perhaps I should say welcome back, as I understand you were born and raised here."

Abby had a strong handshake. It also appeared that she had done her homework on me, much as I had done on her.

"Always good to meet another servant of the people," I said, turning up the charm.

"Please, won't you two have a seat? I think I may have some information that's relevant to your investigation. This is such a horrible thing, and I imagine you two are trying to get to the bottom of it as quickly as possible. It's simply hard to imagine that something like this can happen in Wayside."

We sat, and Rose pulled a reporter's notepad from her bag and prepared to take notes. It occurred to me that she must know Abby well, as I had never seen her taking notes during an interview before.

"What can you tell us?" said Rose.

Abigail leaned back in her chair and began, "I saw William Campbell at the lake near Kelly's car on Thursday evening just before 9 p.m. There was no one else around, so I decided to investigate. William was agitated and told me he had been waiting for Kelly since about 7:30. He indicated he had tried to contact her via phone and text to no avail. I told him not to worry, that I was sure she would turn up. That feels pretty stupid now."

"Don't beat yourself up, Abby. There's no way you could have known that something was wrong at that point in time. What happened next?" Rose inquired.

"I left to meet friends for dinner and didn't think about it again until I heard Kelly was missing on Friday."

"Ms. Grant, can you tell me what you were doing at the lake at 9 p.m. on a Friday night?" I inquired.

"Please, call me Abby. We have several beach parties for the teenagers over the course of the summer. We've got one coming up July 16, next Saturday night, and I was there working on the arrangements."

"What do you know about Kelly's relationships with William Campbell and Douglas McIntyre?" Rose inquired.

"Night and day," she began. "Kelly's relationship with Douglas McIntyre was fiery. There were public arguments, and several screaming matches in the Commons. Douglas, whom I've known since he was a freshman, has become somewhat moody and unpredictable over the past year. And he seems to bring out the worst in Kelly. William Campbell, on the other hand, is the closest thing you'll find to a gentleman in our senior class. He is kind, well mannered, and liked generally by everyone, even the freshmen. And conversely, Kelly seems at her best when she's with William. May I assume that both boys are suspects?"

Rose hesitated for a moment, and then began speaking in a tone I imagined she reserved for her closest friends. "Both boys are suspects. Both were at the lake to see Kelly on Thursday evening. Both boys seem to have what could be a motive to fight with her, which could have resulted in her death. And both boys are certainly capable of harming her physically."

"And it's a tragedy either way it comes out," said Abby.

"That's the one thing we do know for certain," concluded Rose.

CHAPTER 38

CHERYL MARSHALL

JULY 9, 2011

1250 EDT

As we left the building, I turned to Rose and said, "Other than Douglas McIntyre, who was the last person to see Kelly White alive?"

"There are a number of possibilities, but the only one we know of for sure is Cheryl Marshall, Kelly's manager at Nordstrom."

"Perhaps we should drop by the Natick Mall and chat with Ms. Marshall," I said, hoping the conversation might lead somewhere.

"What are you expecting to find out?" inquired Rose.

"I have no idea, but it feels like the right thing to do."

Rose checked her notes, dialed a number into her cell phone, and waited. "Hello, Ms. Marshall, this is Detective Rose Callahan with the Wayside Police Department. (Pause.) We'd like to drop by and get some background information on Kelly White. (Pause.) That would be great. We'll meet you there in about 15 minutes."

Rose terminated her call and said, "You and I will be dining with Ms. Marshall at the Nordstrom Café for lunch. That work for you?"

"Sure," I replied, and we headed for the Natick Mall.

***

We parked in the Speen Street parking lot, and entered Nordstrom through the east entrance. After entering, Rose took a left into the menswear department, and I followed. Nordstrom had become a favorite place to buy civilian clothing while I was stationed on the West Coast. The department store chain had only recently made a foray into the east, building three flagship stores in the greater Boston area. This made me happy. As we headed through the department, I noted the presence of Lucky Jeans and Taylor Byrd dress shirts. I made a mental note to come back on my own time for a little shopping. We stopped in front of the sales counter. There were three people behind the counter. Two were dressed casually, and the third, a woman, wore a black blazer.

The woman in the blazer nodded at us and said, "I'll be with you in just a minute." She finished ringing up a transaction for a 30ish male who was thin, casually well dressed, and handsome. With her customer interaction complete, she stepped from behind the counter and extended her hand. "I'm Cheryl Marshall."

Rose extended her hand and replied as they shook, "I'm Detective Callahan with the Wayside Police Department, and this is Jack Carter, our chief of police."

As Sheryl's attention turned to me, I felt as if I was being sized for a new suit of clothes. She looked to be mid-30s, medium height with dark hair and eyes. She had a round face and a broad smile.

"Good to meet you, Chief." And then she said to us both, "How does the search for Kelly go?"

We were now standing about 15 feet from the sales counter, walking slowly back the way Rose and I had come.

Rose stopped and turned to face Cheryl. "I'm afraid we found Kelly's body earlier this morning."

"Her body? I don't understand. Are you saying she ... she's dead?"

"I'm afraid so," said Rose, as kindly as she could.

We continued walking and took the escalator to the second floor. The café was busy and we took our place in line. It seemed to me that Rose had known where we were going. Cheryl now seemed to be following her, visibly shaken by the news.

When we reached the front of the line, Cheryl and Rose both ordered the chicken Caesar salad and iced tea. For some reason, I felt compelled to do the same. Somehow, it felt as if doing otherwise would have complicated the moment. And besides, I like a good Caesar salad. We found a table, sat, and waited for our food to arrive.

Rose broke the silence. "How well did you know Kelly White?"

"We weren't friends, if that's what you mean. But I liked Kelly, and we chatted from time to time about her personal life."

Rose nodded thoughtfully. "What can you tell me about the relationships in her life?"

"I assume you mean boys, her relationship with boys?"

"Yes," said Rose.

"Kelly seemed to be very conflicted about boys," began Cheryl. "On the one hand, she seemed to want to have a steady boyfriend. When she started working here, she was dating Doug McIntyre, but then I guess you know that. Back then she talked about marrying this guy as if it would be the best thing she could do. But for the last six months, she's been pretty excited about college and all the freedom it would offer her. For what it's worth, I told her to play the field. Settling down with the son of one of the richest men in the state is still settling down. And from what I could tell, Doug McIntyre is a real son of a bitch. Personally, I think there were some drug problems there that seem to screw this guy up even more than his upbringing."

"Did Kelly ever mention Doug hurting her or threatening her?" Rose asked.

"It seems they fought constantly from the start of their senior year. I don't know if he ever hit her, but I wouldn't be surprised. I think Kelly was a good kid, and Doug is bad news."

Rose nodded thoughtfully and continued, "What do you know about her relationship with William Campbell?"

"That was even more surprising. A few months ago she announced that she and Will were going steady — my phrase, not hers."

"What was surprising?" inquired Rose.

Both women were picking at their salads as they spoke. Although I was listening intently, I was also hungry. I had finished all of the chicken and was now working on the lettuce. I was pretty sure this meal was going to be inadequate and that I would be looking for further sustenance.

"Near as I could tell, she and Will were just friends. I don't mean friends with benefits, I mean just friends. Kelly talked about him as if he were a family member, a brother, a cousin, or something like that. And you know what, that didn't seem to change after she announced they were together."

I was regretting not getting dessert while we were at the counter. I was eyeing the line and the menu on the wall, but decided better of it given the nature of the conversation.

"Anything else?" asked Rose.

Cheryl thought about Rose's question for a moment and began, "She was really distracted all day Thursday. Text messages, phone calls, and she just seemed to not be here. I feel bad about it now, but I kind of chewed her out at the end of her shift. I told her she really needed to be at work when she came to work. She apologized and promised it wouldn't happen again. Kind of prophetic, huh?"

Both women were quiet for a few moments, but neither touched their salad and just drank some iced tea. Cheryl looked as if the energy had been drained from her body. Her perky demeanor was flat. Her eyes had gone dull. Kelly's death was becoming real for her. She was replaying that last conversation and wishing it had been different.

Rose broke the silence. "We do appreciate your help and are sorry for the loss of your colleague."

Cheryl Marshall took her napkin from her lap, buried her face in it, and sobbed.

CHAPTER 39

SARAH WALKER

JULY 9, 2011

1500 EDT

After dropping Rose at the White house, I decided to revisit the scene of the crime. As I pulled into the Wayside Lake parking area, I noted that it was packed. The lake and the Wayside Beach Club was a safe place for families with small children to spend a summer day.

I drove down the access road to the boat launch area, parked my Jeep, and headed for the floating dock. I noted its gentle sway as I walked to the end. All evidence of the crime scene was now gone. I stood on the end and looked south over the lake. I could both see and hear the traffic going over the highway bridge that separated the north and south sides of the lake.

I needed an eyewitness.

I scanned the numerous poles that stood above the highway bridge. I wondered if there might be a traffic cam pointed in my direction.

I retrieved my Bluetooth headset from my right pocket, placed it in my ear, and powered it up. "Connected, battery life high," it chirped.

"Call Sarah Walker," I commanded.

She picked up on the third ring. "Jack, how the hell are you?"

Hers was a friendly and familiar voice.

"Not enjoying my new gig," I replied sadly. "I've been on the job less than three days, and I'm investigating the murder of an 18-year-old girl. First time we've had a murder here in Wayside in more than 30 years."

Sarah was my CIA liaison when I was SEAL commander. We had managed operations that had gone both good and bad. Sarah was competent and honest, and I trusted her.

"Sorry to hear that, Jack. I had truly hoped that going home would help you find the peace you were looking for. Anything I can do to help?"

"As a matter of fact, there is. I'm standing at the scene of the murder on a floating dock in Wayside Lake. I'm hoping Nexus saw something and has it stored away safely."

"What's the time window?"

"Between 1900 and 2200 hours on July 7."

"Capturing your current location now. Stand by ... done."

My iPhone still had software installed that allowed the CIA and any number of other governmental organizations to track my whereabouts 24/7. This was both comforting and disconcerting at the same time.

"Sarah, I'm staring at a highway bridge that probably has traffic cams. I'm hoping one is pointed in this direction."

"Jack, if it's there, Nexus will have it. The search may take a little while. I'll get back to you one way or the other."

"Thanks, Sarah," I said with as much sincerity as I could muster.

"No problem. And Jack, try to relax. You're civilian now."

Sarah ended the call, and I stood staring at the highway bridge. Me, Jack Carter, a civilian? Really? I did *not* feel like a civilian.

CHAPTER 40

JEREMY HALE

JULY 9, 2011

1545 EDT

I was back in my office at the public safety building. As I leaned back in my chair with my feet on the desk, I contemplated why Douglas McIntyre was capable of killing Kelly White. Most of the killing in my life was motivated by war. Kelly's death was motivated by love, or at least something that passed for love in the mind of McIntyre. The only thing Rose and I had learned exclusively from Cheryl Marshall was her feeling that Doug probably had a drug problem. Rose was working that angle on her own.

Maybe, just maybe, I could catch a break and Sarah would find something buried in Nexus. Project Nexus was a closely guarded secret that pulled together video surveillance data from hundreds of thousands of sources across the globe. Technically, it was an NSA project, but in reality every federal law enforcement agency had access to the data. This gave the CIA, among others, the capability to do wide-reaching domestic surveillance. Before 9/11, this would have been strictly forbidden. But in 2011, the CIA needed to track terrorists both inside and outside the United

States. The amount of video surveillance data stored in the Nexus Cloud was truly staggering, far surpassing the storage requirements for commercial applications such as search engines and social networks. And the Nexus Cloud was impervious to attack, as the data was stored and mirrored across more than 70 locations around the globe. Privacy advocates would have heart failure, both in the US and Europe, if they ever discovered the scope of the project and the surveillance capabilities it made available to those who had access.

My reverie was interrupted by the buzzing and blinking of my desk phone. It was the first time I had heard my desk phone ring. Virtually all the communication I had with anyone these days came through my iPhone. My desk phone buzzed for the third time and I picked it up and said hello.

"Chief, this is Anne-Marie at the front desk. There's a gentleman asking for you whose name is Jeremy Hale. Are you available?"

I asked Anne-Marie to bring him back to my office.

Jeremy Hale was Jenny's dad and one of my least favorite people on the planet. I had known him my entire life, but had not seen him in more than two decades. I couldn't imagine that Jenny had shared any of what we had discussed the night before with her father. Jeremy had been married to his job as a partner in Hale & Curry. While he was a good provider, he did not appear to be close to any of his children. My memories of the Hale household were almost exclusively of Barbara Hale, Jenny's mother. Barbara was a wonderful mother to her own children and their friends. What Jeremy lacked as a parent, Barbara more than made up for.

What in hell was Jeremy Hale doing here looking for me?

There was a knock on my door followed by Anne-Marie and a man I did not recognize. As I rose to meet him our eyes locked and I knew it was Jeremy. The bushy hair and mustache were gone, replaced with a clean-shaven face and a nearly bald head. He was also far thinner and more frail than I remembered. As I did the math in my head, I realized that he must be nearing 80. His broad gait was replaced with a slow shuffle. As we approached, he extended his hand to meet mine, with not even a hint of a smile on his aging face.

"Mr. Hale, what can I do for you today?"

Anne-Marie exited, closing the door behind her.

"You can explain to me why you have the McIntyre house under surveillance," he commanded.

I gestured toward a seat at my conference table. He slowly maneuvered into position and sat. I pulled out a chair, sat down, and placed both hands on the table in front of me, leaning forward.

"Might I inquire about your interest in the matter?"

Jeremy stared at me intently for a few moments and then continued, "I'm Joe's attorney and have been for years. I assumed you knew that."

"Joe didn't mention that when I spoke with him yesterday."

"Jack, you and I have never much liked each other. Let's put that aside right now and do our respective jobs. Why does the Wayside Police Department have the McIntyre family home under surveillance?"

I was mostly relieved that this visit had nothing to do with Jenny. At the same time, it was obvious that Joe McIntyre or someone who worked for him had discovered our surveillance. Now that Kelly was clearly dead and not kidnapped, one of my two reasons for placing the house under continued surveillance was gone. I could sidestep the question by simply saying it was a request from the staties who were now running the investigation. Or I could tell him the real reason and see where it took us.

"Douglas McIntyre was among the last people to see Kelly White alive. This makes him a person of interest in an ongoing homicide investigation. There is also some concern that Doug could be a flight risk if he is involved."

Jeremy leaned back in his chair and smiled thinly. "Well, it's good to see we're not going to pussyfoot around here anymore. It appears to me that you believe Doug may have been responsible for the death of Kelly White. At the same time, I don't imagine you have sufficient evidence to charge him."

He paused, and then continued, "How am I doing?"

"No comment."

"Guess I shouldn't have expected one," he said, still smiling.

I said nothing, and we just stared at each other for a few moments.

"Jack, I understand that you're just doing your job here. I have no intention of trying to tell you how to do it. I would ask, in fact, I would insist, that you do not speak to Douglas, Joe, Ellen, or any member of the McIntyre household without having me or a member of my firm present. Do we have an understanding?"

"Mr. Hale, I believe we do. I have one question for you."

He nodded at me and waited.

"Can you guarantee me that Douglas will not leave Wayside without first checking with you, and you with me?"

"Jack, I can assure you that I will recommend, strongly recommend, that Douglas remain in Wayside until I tell him otherwise."

I nodded. "I guess that's the best you can offer."

Jeremy nodded and rose. It was a slow, considered motion. I stood and walked him to my door, which I opened. He shuffled along slowly. When he was standing in the door jam, he slowly turned, looked me squarely in the eyes, and extended his hand, which I took.

 "Jack, maybe you're not the asshole I've always thought you were," he said with a smile. He then released my hand and departed.

As I watched Jeremy Hale leave, I wondered the same thing about him.

CHAPTER 41

TIME WITH DAD

JULY 9, 2011

1720 EDT

I decided to swing by the shooting club and see Dad before going home to meet Susan. The Wayside Shooting Club was busiest on Saturday afternoons. As I pulled into the gravel lot and parked, I was assaulted by the sounds of gunfire. Rationally, I knew the sounds were coming from the range. I had grown up on the range, but the sounds for me had changed over time. Now, it sounded like every firefight I had experienced over the past three decades. Rationally, I knew the pattern was different. There was no automatic weapons fire. There were no mortar rounds exploding. But the crackle of small-arms fire would never sound the same to me again.

As I entered the clubhouse, Bandit and Buster came to greet me. Buster watched as Bandit spun around in circles and barked. I squatted down to get the licking that would calm them. Both dogs went through the ritual of licking my face and chin and nipping at my ears. It was a tribal ritual reserved for a returning hunter.

I walked over to the counter and retrieved a dog biscuit for both of them.

"Sit," I commanded.

Both dogs immediately sat and gave me their undivided attention. In return, I gave them each a biscuit.

My dad appeared to one side.

"How are you?" he asked.

I realize that I had momentarily forgotten about the murder investigation. Selfishly, I wished I could put it away until Monday morning. At the minimum, I wished I could put it away for the evening. Perhaps to some small degree, that would happen.

"I'm fine. I'm a little frustrated. But, otherwise I'm fine."

I wanted to tell Dad about the Hail Mary pass I had just thrown called Nexus. I kept telling myself it was not my only opportunity to find an eyewitness, but somehow it seemed like the best. In my heart, I knew this thinking was more about making me feel better than the reality of the situation. Now I was beginning to depress myself.

"I hope you mean that. Crime-fighting is a job just like any other job. You'll live longer if you don't take it home with you," said my dad earnestly.

"Good advice, Dad, good advice."

"Have you heard from Susan?" he inquired.

"I'm assuming that no news is good news, and that she's on time. I promised to meet her at the house at 1800 sharp."

"Then, my boy, you'd better get cracking. Please give Susan my best. I'll be tied up here for another hour or so, and I suspect it's likely that the boys and I will be fast asleep by the time you two come home."

I nodded, gave my dad a hug, and headed home.

CHAPTER 42

WHITE STRING BIKINI

JULY 9, 2011

1800 EDT

I found Susan lounging on the back deck watching the sun move slowly toward the horizon. The deck was large, extending 20 feet off the back of the house. It was about 30 feet wide and 12 feet off the ground. While the sides of the deck were surrounded by tall trees, Dad had always kept the view west toward the river unobscured.

When Susan heard the sliding door open behind her, she rose from the chaise lounge. She turned to face me placing her hands on her hips and cocking her head to one side. She was wearing nothing but a white string bikini, which hid almost nothing behind the three triangular white bits of fabric. The sun was almost directly behind her head and made it appear as if she was glowing. Susan was tan, shapely, and muscular. I knew she rode three to five times a week and worked out regularly. The program was working.

"See anything you like?" she said with just the hint of a giggle.

"I think you're entirely overdressed for the occasion," I said realizing that I was both staring and smirking.

"Really?" she said, lowering her hands ever so slightly to her hips. She untied each of the strings slowly, letting her bikini bottom drop to the deck. While she did this, her eyes never left mine. She shifted her head and her hips and continued. "How about now?"

I noted with interest that her bikini wax was perfect, and that her tan was complete under the missing bottoms.

"The view just keeps getting better and better," I said.

Taking this as her cue to continue, Susan's right hand slowly came up across her flat belly and grasped the string that held her bikini top together. As she slowly pulled the string, she kept her eyes locked on mine as her smile broadened, reflecting my own. With the knot almost undone, she brought up her left hand to hold the top together. She was now using both hands to hold the bikini top in place and cover her breasts. Slowly, she pulled the top aside, to the right, and then to the left, finally allowing it to drop to the deck. Susan's breasts were full and firm. Her large nipples were round and hard.

While still facing me and maintaining eye contact, she took two small steps backward, placing her hands and her now naked ass on the railing of the deck. She completed the pose by spreading her legs and leaning back. Susan was simply irresistible, a force of nature totally at home in her own body. And her body was magnificent.

It was still in the 80s, and I noticed that Susan was now covered with a light sheen of sweat. With the sun still behind her, she was now naked, glistening, and glowing. I noticed I was perspiring even more than she, and wondered if it was the heat or the view.

"I believe it's your turn," she said.

I considered ever so briefly the possibility that there might be a birdwatcher between here and the river with a high-powered camera. I decided to risk it and removed my clothing in far less time than Susan had needed to remove her little white bikini.

As I did, Susan walked to the table and poured me what appeared to be a tall glass of sangria, then refreshed her own. She now came to me slowly extending the icy cold tumbler.

I took it from her, we clinked glasses, and both drank deeply.

We stood staring at each other. It had been almost two months since I had been with Susan. While we had been dating for 17 years, we were never officially together. We had made love in dozens of cities around the world. But we had never spent more than a week or so together at any one time. In fact, we had never lived in the same city at the same time. And still I was closer to Susan than to anyone on Earth, including Chris and my father. I felt complete when she was with me and often empty when she was not.

And here we stood at sunset, on the back deck of my family home, alone and together.

Without asking, she reached out and took my now half empty tumbler. She walked to the table, sat them down, and returned to me.

This time she approached completely, pressing her body against mine, placing her arms around me, and pulling me to her. She lifted her face to mine and said, "Kiss me, Jack."

Our lips met, locked, and held until we were both breathless.

She leaned back in my arms, staring up at me and smiling.

"I've missed you very much," she murmured.

"And I, you," I sighed, relieved to have her with me again.

"I want to hear all about Wayside, your investigation, and anything else you want to tell me. But more than that, first I need you to take me inside, up to your bedroom, and make love to me as if this is the last time we will ever see each other."

The "last time" part scared me, but I put it aside.

I turned, pulling her along with my right arm, and opened the sliding glass door into the house. We stopped in the living room and kissed again. I was beginning to lose track of time. She took me by the hand and led me upstairs. Once in my room, she pushed me gently down onto the bed following me closely.

The weight of her body on mind was intoxicating. We lay there just feeling each other. She was hot, sweaty, and smelling ever so slightly of musk. I breathed her in with my eyes closed. I imagined what she looked like from above, lying on me, covering me, protecting me.

She brought her hands to my shoulders and slowly lifted her head up from mine. Our eyes met. Her cheekbones were high, and her face was flushed. Her long, curly brown hair was voluminous and wild. In one smooth motion, she lowered her face to mine and kissed me deeply while pulling her body forward and then lowering herself and engulfing me. At first she moved up and down slowly. As she began to speed up, her eyes closed and her face tightened, focusing on the place where we were joined.

I placed my hands on her hips to help guide and power our movements. After a few moments, she pulled her knees up alongside my hips and began to sit up. Then she began to lean back. To support each other, I grasped her forearms and she grasped mine. As our movements became more extreme, our mutual grasp tightened. I was now able to thrust upward into her while keeping her body tight against mine. She was now leaning back, trusting me to hold her in place. Her vaginal muscles were contracting with each thrust and holding me inside her on the return motion. She was now drenched in sweat. We accelerated the dance-like routine suppressing our physical drive to climax. There was both pleasure and pain as we pushed our bodies past their normal limits.

After what seemed like both moments and hours, I felt her beginning to climax. To maximize her pleasure, I instinctively began to thrust upward as far as I could, while pulling her arms back toward me. In response, she leaned back such that her back was almost parallel to the bed. As the climax began to take her, she moaned and shuddered. I released the pressure for just a moment then thrust again, causing her to moan and shudder. On the third thrust, I began to climax inside her. There was a fourth, a fifth, a six, a seventh, and then we were done.

I pulled her to me and as we released each other's arms, we hugged each other tightly. She raised her head and stared into my eyes.

"I love you, Jack Carter," she said as she contracted her vaginal muscles around me tightly and kissed me. As we held the embrace I lowered my hands to her ass and pressed my pelvis into her clitoris rolling her slowly from side to side. In a few moments, she shuddered, sighed, and went limp in my arms.

By the time I woke, it was a little after 7 p.m.

I shook Susan gently to wake her. She rolled off me slowly and snuggled up against my right side. I hugged her tightly.

"Planning on taking a shower?" I asked.

"Yes, I am," she murmured and continued, "and I'll be quick."

"I'm happy that you're not quick at everything."

She grabbed a handful of my chest hair with her right hand, pulled herself to me, and kissed me hard.

"I'll bet you are!" she said as she hopped out of bed and headed to the bathroom.

CHAPTER 43

THE HAVEN

JULY 9, 2011

1930 EDT

While we were showering and dressing, I told Susan about my first three days in Wayside. While there was a lot going on, reciting the tale left me feeling there was nothing I couldn't handle. Talking with Susan often had that impact on me. Over the years I had shared much more with her about my work than she was cleared to know. I didn't care. Without her support, I would've left the Navy long ago.

When I told her about my dinner with Jenny, and the revelation that Jenny and I had a son, she absorbed it without comment. I was careful in revealing my confusion about Jenny and my feelings for her. I don't think Susan was unclear about the ramifications. Still, everything she said and asked showed only her concern for me and my feelings. It seemed so unfair as I could also sense the pain she felt over my confusion about Jenny. At some point, we would need to tackle the subject head on. But not right now. Not tonight. I needed to get through the murder investigation. I needed to have time to figure out which

Jenny I was in love with. And I needed to do it all while taking care of Susan, her feelings, and our relationship.

Although it seemed impossible to me, Susan's and my lovemaking had seemed more passionate than ever. Was I missing something? Did my move to the East Coast signal some change in the relationship that I was not fathoming? All things I needed to figure out in time.

***

By 7:45, we were ready to go and headed out the front door.

I noted that Dad and the boys were still not home. My guess was that he was taking his time to make sure Susan and I had an uninterrupted reunion. I love my dad.

Susan, who was born and raised on a ranch, was dressed to the nines cowgirl style. From her white Stetson to her Lee Miller boots, she had pulled out all the stops including skintight black jeans with a white silk shirt embroidered with gold and mother of pearl.

Doing my best to keep up, I was wearing a new pair of Lucky blue jeans and a dark blue denim shirt. I had on my Heritage boots and a custom ankle holster made for me by Heritage owner Jerry Ryan. To top it off, I was wearing my black Stetson with a sharkskin band that matched my boots.

My .38 Special was nestled tightly in the holster attached to the inside of my left leg. My boots were extremely comfortable and did a great job of concealing my weapon. I had discovered that I was not required to carry a gun when I was off duty. Still, after 30+ years of military service, I simply felt more comfortable when I was carrying a weapon.

"Are we meeting them at the restaurant?" inquired Susan.

"We are indeed."

We buckled up and departed for The Haven.

✱✱✱

By the time we arrived, Mandy and Chris had already been seated in the upstairs restaurant by the windows on the south-facing side of the building. The view of Dudley Pond was calming and pristine. From our side of the table, Susan and I had an unobstructed view of the water and surrounding trees. While Mandy and Chris could see the pond from their vantage point, they also had a wonderful view of the parking lot. Chris, always a good host, had given us the best seats in the house.

"McPherson tells me you bought the place?" I inquired of Chris.

"He did," said Mandy with a grin. "From the amount of time Chris spends on it, you'd think it was the most valuable thing in his portfolio."

"The place burned to the ground last year," began Chris, "and I didn't want to see it go away or fall into the wrong hands. So I bought it. As you can see, The Haven has been rebuilt from the ground up. All natural wood, granite bars and tabletops, state-of-the-art kitchen, and professional management. I'll probably never get my money back out of it, but the place makes me happy."

"Happiness is everything," said Susan to the table at large.

Chris recommended the baby back ribs, which we all ordered along with the appropriate sides, including dirty rice and beans, coleslaw, and cornbread. Chris and I started with a couple of Blue Moons and the ladies ordered Grey Goose Cosmos.

"I have a request, or perhaps I should call it a suggestion," said Susan, gaining everyone's attention. "I know the murder is weighing heavily on everyone here in Wayside. Would it be appropriate to make the subject off limits for the rest of the evening?"

"I think that would be entirely appropriate," said Mandy looking at me and then Chris with a questioning glance.

Chris and I looked at each other and nodded agreement.

The drinks arrived along with fresh chips and salsa. The conversation meandered from the Bridger children to the books we were reading and recent movies we had seen. Susan was rereading *Pillars of the Earth,* and remarked how the TV serialization had been such a disappointment. Mandy agreed and asked if anyone of us had read the sequel to *Pillars.* Of course, Susan had read it and recommended it highly to the group. Chris and I had both read the two books, and many others by Ken Follett. We all talked about how different these two volumes were from the rest of his work and how difficult it was to translate a novel into a movie or miniseries.

The whole conversation was so incredibly normal that I could barely stand it. While I tried very hard to remain engaged, I could not keep my thoughts from straying to Kelly White and Douglas McIntyre. Still, I concluded that this was probably a better way to relax than having a deep discussion about the true meaning of love and how people who love each other could kill each other.

CHAPTER 44

TINY MORRISON

JULY 9, 2011

2150 EDT

We finished dinner and dessert and moved on to after-dinner drinks. The ladies switched to white wine, and Chris produced a bottle of Ardbeg single-malt scotch from behind the bar, which he and I were now enjoying.

Chris was staring out the window toward the parking lot. He glanced at me and said, "You've got to take a look at this."

I swiveled in my seat to see three men on motorcycles parking in the lot near the building. The bikes were custom, and the boys looked like trouble.

"Do you know them?" I inquired of Chris.

"The big one with the bald head is Tiny Morrison. The tall, thin one goes by the name of Snake. No clue about the last name. The short fat guy is Sam Keller, a dentist who lives here in Wayside. They haven't been around lately since we rebuilt the place. Before that, they were regulars here.

They've been arrested for assault and battery more times than I've got fingers and toes. For the life of me, I can't figure out why somebody hasn't locked them up and thrown away the key."

"Let me see if I can head this off by letting the boys know that there's been a change in management at the saloon, and that there's a new sheriff in town," I said with a smile. "Just in case that doesn't go well for me, call 911 and let the dispatcher know that the Wayside Police Chief is investigating a possible disturbance at The Haven and needs backup. Make sure the dispatcher tells the officers that I'm off duty, in civilian clothes, armed, and looking forward to seeing them. I'm going to meet the boys in the parking lot, and I would appreciate it if you would tell your staff to keep everyone in the building."

I rose and quickly headed downstairs, trusting Chris to make sure I had backup. I managed to exit the front of the restaurant and meet Tiny and his boys at the edge of the parking lot. Fortunately, the four of us were the only ones present.

I pulled my badge from my right rear pocket, opened it so they could see the shield, and held it next to my face. The three men stopped about 10 feet in front of me, standing shoulder to shoulder, and stared. Tiny was about 6'6" and close to 300 pounds. He looked like a Patriots linebacker. "Snake was about 6' and 200 pounds. Sam was 5'6" and maybe 220 pounds. All three wore motorcycle boots with laces, denim jeans, and jackets. It looked a little like a uniform. While they had no weapons visible, that didn't mean they didn't have them.

My best strategy was to stall until backup arrived.

"I'm the Wayside Police Chief and would like to speak to you boys for a moment."

Tiny advanced toward me with his companions following closely behind. When he was about five feet away, he stopped and said, "You aren't the fucking chief, so why don't you take your dime store badge and get the fuck out of my way?"

I could smell the alcohol on Tiny's breath, which explained his belligerent behavior and made me wonder whether my game plan of stalling was going to work. As I contemplated alternate strategies, I could see Tiny twist ever so slightly to the right while raising both arms and clenching his hands into fists. He took a half step forward with his left and then a full step forward with his right while twisting his body to try and deliver a roundhouse punch to the left side of my head. Most amateur fighters aimed for the head.

I dropped my shield and delivered a right cross to his groin while crouching slightly as his roundhouse went over my head. I quickly followed the right cross with three jabs to his left side as he folded like a tent falling to the ground.

Tiny was now lying on the ground between me and his companions. I stepped back and waited to see their reaction.

The two looked at their leader who was lying on the ground moaning, up at me, and then at each other. Sam turned away and walked quickly toward their motorcycles. Snake looked at me and snarled, "You sucker punched him."

"I did."

"Are you really the chief of police?"

"I am."

Snake continued to stare at me. Sam had reached his bike by this time and was mounting up.

Snake was staring at my badge, which was lying, shield up, next to Tiny, who was beginning to recover.

A Wayside police cruiser appeared behind Snake and ground to a halt in the gravel parking lot. Officer Cordero emerged from the passenger side with shotgun in hand. She pumped the action to chamber a shell. The sound of the cruiser arriving and the shotgun being made ready to fire caused Snake to turn toward the cruiser, forgetting all about me for the moment.

"Evening, Chief. Everything okay here?" asked Cordero.

"Just fine, Officer. I think Snake is on his way home, but before he goes you'd like to take a sobriety test. His friend, Tiny, has bigger problems like assaulting an officer, or at least attempting to."

When Snake turned his attention back to me, I could see him quickly glance to my right hand, which now held my Smith & Wesson .38. Snake, who was not new to the judicial system, slowly placed both his hands behind his head, interlocking his fingers.

By now, Officer Sam Marlowe had emerged from the driver's side of the cruiser and was approaching Tiny and Snake.

I motioned to Snake with my .38 to move to his right, away from Tiny and said, "Snake, please step a few paces to the right so we can take care of your colleague."

Snake complied. Marlowe instructed Tiny to stay on the ground while he was cuffed and searched. He complied.

Another cruiser appeared, and two more officers emerged from their vehicle. It was James Dunn and Jack Curry.

"Jim, please take charge of the suspect who is still standing," said Cordero. "Frisk him, cuff him, read him his rights, and give him a sobriety test."

"Thank you, Officer Cordero," I said.

"You're welcome, Chief. If you'd like to return to your dinner, I believe we have everything under control out here. I'll need a little help with the paperwork tomorrow."

I squatted to holster my .38, which remained happily unfired. I picked up my shield, nodded to Cordero, and turned to go back into The Haven. As I did, I noticed that the windows on both the first and second floors of the building were lined with patrons, who appeared to be applauding.

CHAPTER 45

THE RAIL TRAIL

JULY 10, 2011

0815 EDT

Susan and I had slept in late and were now jogging east on the rail trail toward Weston. I was wearing my standard navy blue shorts and gray T-shirt with black running shoes. Susan was dressed completely in white including her shoes. She used a ponytail and a white terry cloth headband to attempt to control her hair. Susan had once told me that women don't perspire. "Girls perspire, real women sweat." With the temperature and humidity in the high 70s, Susan and I were both sweating.

"How's the swelling in your hand?" she inquired.

"My right hand is still a little sore. Soaking my hands in ice water usually does the trick, but I think Tiny may have been wearing a cup."

"Lucky for him, or you could have neutered him for life," said Susan with a giggle.

We were passing directly behind Mason Teller's house. While most of the homes in Wayside did not have a fenced perimeter, the Teller home did. Although I couldn't see over the fence from the rail trail, I knew that Mason had a swimming pool in his backyard. This was the apparent reason for the fence, but the fence was larger and more encompassing than required to keep small children out of the pool. The fence was a full six feet and solid to the top. Mason's home was a two-story Cape, which meant I could see the second story, or at least part of it, from the rail trail. Because the entire area had been a farm until 1994, there were no forest-sized trees. Still, there were a few maples in the backyard that had managed to reach 20 to 30 feet since the development of the land almost 20 years ago.

We exited the rail trail onto Farmview and slowed to a walk.

I found myself staring down Farmview toward Mason's house.

"Mind if we take a little detour?" I inquired. "I promised the selectmen that I would talk to Mason directly about not escalating his opposition to the new town center. Beyond that, I would kind of like to look him in the eye, now that Mom has dumped him."

"No problem. Any chance you might get the opportunity to punch him in the nuts?"

Susan was keenly aware of my dislike for Mason Teller. She knew I had grown up next door to him and his wife and that I suspected him of having an affair with my mother long before their relationship was public, and that all the above had served to make my relationship with my mom worse than it already had been.

We walked along in silence toward the Teller home.

A Jack Carter Novel

CHAPTER 46

LOOKING FOR MASON TELLER

JULY 10, 2011

0835 EDT

There were two newspapers, still wrapped in plastic, lying in Mason's driveway. Further inspection confirmed that these were the Saturday and Sunday editions of *The Boston Globe*. It appeared very much that Mason had not been home since Friday.

Susan was peering through the glass panels in the garage door.

"The garage seems to be arranged to hold two cars, and one is missing. Does that make sense?" Susan asked as I approached.

"It does. The Porsche was here Friday morning when I last visited. His other car is a 2007 Ford Explorer. Looks like Mason isn't home. Just the same, I think I'll ring the bell."

I went to the front porch and rang the bell while Susan waited patiently. After a few moments, I rang again.

No answer.

We left and headed for my Mom's house on Farmview. Here I found the Friday, Saturday, and Sunday editions of the *Globe* in the driveway. My mom's Volvo wagon was in the garage.

"What are you thinking?" said Susan.

"I'm thinking that my Mom and Mason have made up and gone somewhere for the weekend. This, of course, pisses me off. I had hopes she had dumped the son of a bitch, but there seems to be evidence to the contrary."

CHAPTER 47

PHOTOGRAPHIC EVIDENCE

JULY 10, 2011

1000 EDT

Susan and I were sitting in a booth at the Carter Farm Café enjoying a lovely breakfast. Susan ordered an egg white omelet with tomatoes and cheddar cheese. I was having the meat-lover omelet, which included applewood smoked bacon, country ham, and Italian sausage. The sausage was very spicy and created an amazing contrast to the sweet-tasting bacon and ham. We both had coffee, orange juice, and freshly baked whole-wheat toast. It dawned on me that the ingredients for breakfast I love the best were largely available at home and here at the Café.

Dad stopped by to chat.

"Everyone is buzzing about the little martial arts demonstration you put on last night at The Haven," said my dad with a grin.

"It seemed like the right thing to do at the time."

"Three on one the odds you like to take into combat?"

"Come on, Dad. I wasn't showing off. I just didn't want those guys busting up The Haven after all the work Chris has put into it. And I didn't want the showdown to take place when I was surrounded by a bunch of civilians."

"I know. I'm just busting your chops. And besides, I understand you followed procedure, called for backup, and were trying to stall for time. Sometimes things just don't work out the way you plan," said Dad with an even bigger grin.

"I think it's good for his reputation," Susan chimed in. "An ounce of prevention is often worth a pound of cure."

"Missy," said my dad smiling, "I like the way you think. Most people don't understand the proper use of force."

"Chuck, I'm a Naval commander and a Texan. I understand all about the proper use of force," said Susan, peering at my dad over the top of her coffee cup, which she held and sipped.

"So," inquired my dad, "will I be seeing more of you now that Jack is here in Wayside?"

"I certainly hope so," said Susan, turning her gaze to me.

My iPhone vibrated and buzzed. It was Sarah Walker calling. I excused myself and walked outside heading away from the buildings and toward the trees.

"Hello, Sarah. Good news or bad?"

"Hello, Jack. Both. Let me explain. I have a video that clearly shows a man striking a woman and knocking her into the lake. It further documents that he did nothing to pull her out and simply walked away. That's the good news. I have your eyewitness."

"What's the bad news?"

"It's not from a traffic cam. It's keyhole video."

"What the hell is a keyhole satellite surveilling in Wayside?"

"That, Jack, is need-to-know, and you don't need to know. I can tell you that the video surveillance is part of an active investigation being run by the FBI and DEA. The operation is classified and highly confidential. I had to call in favors to get access to the video. I would've never found it without the geo-locator codes."

"So I can't have the video or use it to prosecute this guy?"

"Giving you the video is both difficult and unlikely. But there's something that I think can help you catch the creep."

"I'm listening," I said hopefully.

"Before he hit her, he ripped something from her neck. Whatever it was, it was important to her. When he took it, she slapped him. Then he hit her, knocked her into the lake, and walked away."

"I think I'm following along. If I can find what he took, it might go somewhere."

"It might, Jack. It just might."

"Can you send me a photo of his face? I need to make a positive ID."

"Sending now. Tell me when you've got it."

My phone chirped almost immediately with the file, and I opened it.

While the photo was a little grainy, it was clearly Douglas McIntyre.

"I've got it."

"Are you tracking the right guy?" Sarah inquired.

"I am."

"I hope you get him, Jack. What this guy did is as coldblooded as anything I've ever seen. He needs to be taken out."

I thanked Sarah and began to ponder how to find the object that Douglas McIntyre had ripped from Kelly White's neck.

CHAPTER 48

JUDGE CLARK

JULY 10, 2011

1030 EDT

When I hung up with Sarah, I called John Rizzo and told him exactly what I had, including the fact that I didn't really have it.

"So, you have a trusted source inside a federal agency with video of the crime, but the video is part of an active federal case, and it's unlikely that we will ever get our hands on it," summarized Rizzo.

"That's pretty much it. Is that enough to get a search warrant for the McIntyre home and an arrest warrant for Doug?"

"Hell if I know. On the one hand we don't have the evidence. On the other hand, we've got a decorated war hero using his government contacts to assure the court that Douglas McIntyre killed Kelly White and that there is physical evidence that could connect him to the murder. It's sure as hell worth a try. I'll call you back."

***

Rizzo called me back in less than 10 minutes and told me to meet him at an address in Wayside at 11 a.m. sharp.

I went back into the café and shared the news with Susan and Dad, or at least the parts that I thought prudent to share.

"Don't worry about me," said Susan, smiling warmly. "Your dad has challenged me to a little skeet shooting contest. I understand that solving this has to be your first priority."

I said nothing, kissed her on the cheek, and stood to leave.

"I'll be home for Sunday dinner, if that is at all possible," I said, turning to depart, and added, "You two have fun."

The plan had been to go house-hunting with Susan this afternoon. I couldn't help but wonder if I was hunting for a house for me, or for Susan and me. It continued to seem like I was missing something. Had my move east signaled to Susan that I was ready to settle down with her? As I rolled that thought around in my head, it occurred to me that my return to Wayside had certainly triggered similar thinking for Jenny. I had never settled down with anyone, save the year that Jenny and I lived together in Charlestown. The entire prospect of settling down seemed foreign to me. I was 55 years old, never married, and never lived in the same place for more than 24 months. Most of my career had been spent living out of a seabag.

I was thrilled that Dad and Susan were getting along so well. While they had met on several occasions, they had never spent time together without me. Something about this was a little scary, too. So many decisions to be made that were anything but rational.

As I pulled off Route 27 into the driveway of Judge George Clark, I could see Rizzo had already arrived. I shifted gears in my head, and focused, happily, on the murder.

***

Rizzo and I were now standing in the basement office of Judge Clark. His home office was crammed with electronics, computers, and stacks of books, magazines, and journals. The judge looked to be in his mid-50s and was tall and lanky. Rizzo explained the situation in as much detail as possible, including his own opinion about the murder.

"You're telling me that there's no way we're actually going to get possession of this video?" Clark asked, as if he already knew the answer to the question.

"My source inside the CIA thinks it's extremely unlikely," I said, purposely revealing the agency.

"Can I speak with your source by telephone?"

I paused, wondering how far Sarah would be willing to go to help me catch and convict McIntyre. After pondering the question for a few moments, I decided to stop guessing and simply ask Sarah.

"Let me find out," I said.

I dialed her number on my iPhone, purposefully avoiding the use of the voice interface, so as not to reveal her name until I was clear about her willingness to be involved and speak directly to Judge Clark. She answered on the second ring, and I carefully explained where I was standing and Judge Clark's request to speak to her directly.

"Sure," she said without any hesitation.

I passed the phone to Clark.

"Hello," he said. "May I know your name and position?"

Judge Clark listened for what seemed to be a much longer time than should have been required to answer his question. He was nodding slowly now and beginning to smile.

"I do. (Pause.) Good. I see that you understand my dilemma. Seeing the video is sufficient for me to issue warrants, at this point. I don't need to have it in evidence."

He continued to nod as if listening to a story or perhaps instructions that he seemed to understand. Clark turned away from us and sat down in front of his computer. He launched the Safari browser and began typing a long numeric URL string. When he was done, he repeated it back into the phone.

When Clark hit return, an almost entirely blank webpage loaded with a small video player in the center. I examined the page and URL carefully, noting there were no identifying marks. The video player was now loading a file and when it began to play, we could all clearly see Kelly White and Douglas McIntyre sitting on the dock in Wayside Lake. After a few moments, they stood and faced each other. In rapid succession, he ripped a necklace from her throat, she slapped him in the face, and then he backhanded her with enough force to knock her into the lake. He stood watching her float face-down for several minutes, then turned and walked away. The video ended, and the video player disappeared.

"Thank you very much," Clark said in the phone. "Do you wish to speak with Chief Carter?" He was nodding as he hung up the phone.

Judge Clark stood and faced us, "I'm granting your warrants under what are the most unusual circumstances I've ever seen. I do believe it's going to be difficult to get that video into a court of law, so you better find that necklace. You're going to need physical evidence to convict Doug."

"I understand," said Rizzo. "We'll do our best."

"And just so we're clear, John," Clark was now speaking directly to Rizzo, "Joe McIntyre is a personal friend and a standup guy. Let's not drag the family through anything more or less than is required to convict his son in this unfortunate incident."

I could tell that Rizzo was containing himself. I wondered why of all the judges in the state of Massachusetts, Rizzo had chosen Judge Clark.

"George, I get that this is a crappy thing for everyone involved. But at the end of the day my job is to make sure Douglas McIntyre is held accountable for what we all just watched him do."

We all just stood there for a few moments, absorbing the video, the situation, and the horrific implications. Kelly was dead. Doug was guilty, and yet it was unclear if we'd be able to prove it in a court of law. Two families were going to be destroyed. Other families in our community would be profoundly impacted. And at the moment, I didn't see how anything good would come from any of it.

CHAPTER 49

GATHERING EVIDENCE

JULY 10, 2011

1615 EDT

I was amazed by the speed at which Rizzo had made things happen. By 1 p.m., both search and arrest warrants had been issued. Just after 2 p.m., Douglas McIntyre had been arrested and taken into custody. To my surprise, Rizzo had asked to hold him in the Wayside jail. I wondered if the goal was to minimize the publicity and press involved. By 3 p.m., there were more than a dozen crime scene investigators scouring the McIntyre household, surrounding buildings, and even the woods.

Rose and I stood in Douglas's bedroom. The room was large and well decorated. The furniture was dark wood, the walls were navy blue, and the carpet appeared black with matching black curtains. The walls were covered with posters of rock bands and movies with which I was totally unfamiliar.

The entire room was covered with what appeared to be dirty clothes. There were more than a dozen pairs of black and blue denim jeans. There were T-shirts in gray, white, and black. I counted seven pairs of athletic shoes, all in black. There were swim trunks and workout clothing. The room included a 52-inch flat screen TV fed by a variety of electronics, video, and gaming consoles.

There were two crime scene investigators methodically examining and cataloging everything they touched with their crime scene gloves.

"The commander asked us to be on the lookout for a necklace. Do either of you have any clue what kind of necklace we might be looking for?" asked the investigator who had introduced herself as Britney.

Britney appeared to be late 20s and in very good shape. Her dark red hair was thick and almost waist length. Her face was thin, and she wore large round glasses that appeared too big for her head.

"I don't think we're clear what the necklace looks like," I said awkwardly, trying not to reveal why I knew there was a necklace but didn't know what it looked like.

Rose was watching me cautiously.

"This is just a hunch," said Rose, "but I think there's a good chance it's a Tiffany heart."

I stared at Rose for a moment and nodded as I comprehended her hunch. It was a good hunch. The Tiffany heart that William Campbell had given Kelly would certainly evoke a reaction from Douglas McIntyre.

"Thanks. A necklace can be a lot of things these days. And I understand the item belongs to Kelly White, the victim. Naturally, we'll be on the lookout for anything that even resembles a necklace," said Brittany in a way that made me feel she was reassuring us.

Rose was answering her cell phone.

After a few moments, I heard her say, "We'll be right out."

CHAPTER 50

TIFFANY HEART

JULY 10, 2011

1720 EDT

Trumbull and Rizzo were standing in the woods about 100 yards beyond the east side of the McIntyre house. As Rose and I approached, treading carefully through the dense underbrush, I also spotted Gabby and one of the investigators. The investigator had his back to us and appeared to be taking photographs of a large clump of vines that had wrapped itself around the base of the dead tree. As we got closer, I could see something metallic, glinting occasionally in the broken sunlight.

When we were about 20 feet from the group, I could clearly make out a Tiffany heart dangling from the vines and turning slowly to one side, and then the other, as it slowly twisted in the wind.

"Howdy, Sheriff. I think old Gabby found what y'all were looking for," said Trumbull proudly.

"Looks like you did," I replied as we met and shook hands.

Rizzo was ignoring us in speaking to his investigator. "I want this thing checked for prints within the hour. They just booked Douglas McIntyre, so his prints are going to be new to the system."

The investigator removed the necklace from the vines with some difficulty. The silver chain snagged in several places on the small thorns that lined the stems of the plant. With some effort, he finally freed the necklace.

"You got it, Commander. I'm going to take it to the van and process it for prints right now. If your suspect is in the system, I should have a match for you in less than 20 minutes."

The investigator was holding the necklace chain in his gloved right hand such that the heart was touching nothing. Everyone present knew how easy it would be to destroy all or part of any fingerprints from the surface of the heart. He began slowly and methodically walking out of the woods, and we all watched him go.

I turned to Trumbull and inquired, "Did Gabby come straight to the heart?"

"He did. He picked up the scent as soon as he was on the ground. There's a light wind coming from the east, and both the chain and pendant are covered with body oil and small particles of dead skin from our girl. We are damn lucky it didn't rain since the necklace was deposited in the vines. We're also lucky that it landed where it did. These thorny vines are enough to discourage critters and birds from taking it. And the elevation made it all the easier for the scent to be carried by the wind. Damn lucky all the way around."

We all nodded at Trumbull's explanation.

"Commander," Trumbull said to Rizzo, "Do you want me to keep poking around or is that the only thing you were looking for?"

"With the necklace found, see what else you come up with. I'm not looking for anything in particular, but that doesn't mean you won't find it."

***

Callahan, Rizzo and I stood outside the CSI van waiting not so patiently. I looked toward the woods where the necklace had been found and imagined its trajectory and point of origin.

"I'd say it's about 50 yards from the edge of the driveway to the vines where we found the heart. That's quite a throw, even for an 18-year-old fullback in great shape," I said, still staring into the woods.

The investigator emerged from the back of the CSI van. He was smiling and nodding his head.

"We have a solid match and three partials. The print from his right index finger that we lifted from the heart was almost as good as the one that was just entered into the system."

We all nodded and exchanged brief glances.

"There's an inscription on the back of the heart that reads 'Kelly and William.' I thought our prime suspect's name was Douglas. Who's William?" asked the investigator, with a puzzled look.

"You're right, Stewart. McIntyre is our prime suspect. William Campbell gave Kelly White the heart you've been examining. Near as I can tell, the fact that Kelly was wearing the heart given to her by William may be what got her killed," Rose offered in a voice that was tightly controlled.

"He killed her over a piece of jewelry?" Stewart asked, looking more puzzled than ever.

"He killed her for love," said Rizzo. "Which makes about as much sense here as it ever does."

***

Rizzo and I stood by the edge of the woods watching the continued bevy of activity. He asked Rose to call the station and inquire about Douglas McIntyre, his family, and attorneys. Rizzo was planning something, and I was hoping to be in on it.

"You know that video that doesn't exist ..." he began.

I nodded.

"I'd like you to arrange another one-time showing, using the same protocols that were in place for Judge Clark."

I understood exactly what Rizzo was asking me to do. Perhaps more to the point, what he was asking Sarah Walker to do.

"I'll do what I can do," I replied.

"You do that, while I pick up the DA and get her to go along with what I've got in mind."

I nodded.

CHAPTER 51

THE DEAL

JULY 10, 2011

1845 EDT

I commandeered the training room in the station's basement to set up the presentation and discussion Rizzo had requested. Sarah agreed to sponsor a second, one-time viewing of the video. While she had not hesitated, I could also sense she was going out on a limb. By Monday morning, there were any number of people in her chain of command or at the NSA who could veto any further viewings. While I was not totally clear about Rizzo's plan, I was certain it involved using the video to achieve an outcome that might later become unachievable.

I had the video player cued up on a 55-inch flat screen that was mounted on the forward wall of the training room. I set up one table and four chairs directly in front of the big screen.

Rizzo and a tall blonde entered the room, and I walked over to greet them. She was muscular and tall. Her blonde hair was curly and plentiful. She wore khaki pants, a white button-down shirt, and a blue blazer. She had on two-inch navy pumps and enough makeup that I was having trouble determining her age. She could have been anywhere between 45 and 65, although I guessed she was probably right in the middle. As I approached, she extended her hand and looked me squarely in the eye.

"Nancy McManus, meet Jack Carter, our new police chief," said Rizzo.

"The pleasure is mine, Jack, although I wish we were meeting under different circumstances. Rizzo has filled me in on your background, and I must say it's a bit different from that of any other police chief I've had the pleasure of working with."

"At the moment, ma'am, I'm just trying to keep up with the commander."

"You seem to be doing just fine. And please, call me Nancy."

"So, Nancy, have you two agreed on a course of action?"

"I don't like it," said McManus, "but I suspect it's the best we're going to do under the circumstances. There will be plenty of fallout, even if it does work. Women's groups are going to hate the outcome and accuse me of being soft on McIntyre because of his family. But a girl's gotta do what a girl's gotta do."

"Jack, let's get this show on the road," said Rizzo.

***

Douglas McIntyre, Jeremy Hale and Betsy Hopkins had joined us and were now seated at the table in the front of the room. Hopkins was a criminal attorney from Hale & Curry who was apparently going to be representing Douglas. Doug's parents were in the building but had not been invited to our little premier.

Hopkins wore a navy blue suit with a light charcoal pinstripe. She had dark short hair and appeared to be in her mid-30s. It occurred to me that both women had probably not been dressed for success on a Sunday afternoon. Rizzo, in comparison, was wearing rumpled khaki boat pants, a green polo shirt, and boat shoes with no socks. Douglas was wearing a Wayside Police Department orange jumpsuit. It struck me as odd that Doug was experiencing Wayside colors from an entirely different perspective.

McManus was seated on the far right side of the table from my viewpoint. Jeremy was next, then Doug, then Hopkins. Rizzo stood directly in front of them, while I stood behind the podium on their left. This gave me access to the keyboard that controlled the flat screen.

"Does your client have anything he'd like to share with us about the murder of Kelly White before we begin?" Rizzo inquired formally.

"Our client has been advised by his attorneys to offer no commentary or information on the matter of Kelly White," said Hopkins.

"Chief Carter, would you please cue the video," said Rizzo.

The video began to load.

Hopkins whispered something into Doug's ear, who then began shaking his head slowly. Jeremy's attention was riveted on the screen. McManus was watching Doug and Hopkins, sliding her chair forward to get a better view of client and counsel.

Once again, the video player sprang to life showing Douglas McIntyre and Kelly White sitting on the dock in Wayside Lake. Once again, the two stood and faced each other in the twilight. Then, in rapid succession, he ripped the Tiffany heart from her neck, she slapped him across the face, and he struck her with such force that she left the dock and landed in the water, motionless. Once again, he stood watching her for several minutes, then turned and walked away. The video ended.

Douglas had stopped staring at his hands during the video. His gaze had become fixated on the screen. His cold, dark eyes had grown wider. Still he did not move. He remained motionless, his eyes growing wider and wider, and sweat beading on his forehead. As the video ended, everyone was now staring at Doug. Although I thought it was most likely my imagination, for a moment, I thought the room was so quiet that I could hear the beating of his heart.

At this moment, Rizzo produced a plastic evidence bag and tossed it on the table in front of McIntyre. The bag contained the Tiffany heart.

"I didn't mean to ..." Doug began before his attorney could interrupt him.

"Douglas, shut up. Shut up now. Do not open your mouth. Do you understand me?" Jeremy was shouting.

Doug stopped speaking and looked at Hale. His expression was both angry and confused. At the same time, he seemed near tears. Seemingly unable to speak now, he simply nodded agreement at Hale.

"Goddammit, John." Hale was now on his feet and directing his anger toward Rizzo. "What kind of cheap stunt are you playing here? I have half a mind to end this interview right now."

"Jeremy, I have a simple deal for your client. Plead guilty to voluntary manslaughter in the murder of Kelly White, and this video goes away. Don't, and this video gets released to the media as soon as this meeting is over. Take it or leave it," said Rizzo without emotion.

"You expect me to make that decision without knowing the source of this video or what this piece of jewelry has to do with anything?" Hale demanded.

"Counselor, your client killed Kelly White. He hit her so hard that he broke her jaw and knocked her unconscious. Then he walked away with that necklace clutched in his right hand and let her drown. We located the necklace at his home earlier today with a clear fingerprint match of his right index finger in the center of the heart. If we go to trial, you know he's going down for murder. We're just discussing the charge and whether he's out in a few years or serves life in prison."

Hale turned to McManus and said, "I take it you signed off on this deal? You think railroading my client into admitting murder without a trial is in anyone's best interest?"

"I'd like to try him for murder and put him away for life. But he comes from a prominent family and it will be difficult, but not impossible, to prove intent. So, to make this go away now, I've agreed to the commander's request to plea bargain this out as voluntary manslaughter. But be clear about this: it's a one-time offer. As soon as this video is released to the public, I'll have no choice but to try this as murder one."

I stood quietly in the corner behind the podium watching the exchange. Rizzo and McManus were playing this as if there were a video that they really could release to the media. It was an incredible bluff, and I couldn't tell if Hale was going for it.

Hale glanced at Doug and Hopkins then returned his attention to Rizzo. "May we please have the room?"

Rizzo nodded to Hale and started for the door. McManus was up and following with me close behind.

"Jack," said Hale loudly to get my attention before I left the room.

I stopped, turned around, and said, "Yes?"

"Do I have your word that this room is truly private and that there are no recording devices monitoring our conversation?"

I thought about it for a moment. While I had never been shown anything that had led me to believe that this room could be monitored, I realized that it could be, and I would not know it.

"Mr. Hale, to the best of my knowledge there are no recording devices currently monitoring this room for either audio or video."

"Carefully said, Jack. But I suspect what you said is enough to make any recording that might be in progress inadmissible. Thank you."

I left the room, not sure whether I won that round or not.

***

Once the three of us were out of the room, I closed the door and turned to face Rizzo and McManus. "Nice performance. Think he bought it?"

"We'll know soon enough," said Rizzo.

"Got a Plan B?" I inquired.

"Several, but I don't like any of them," replied Rizzo.

"Let's just hope we can stick with Plan A," concluded McManus.

There was a small window in the door about head high. Through it I could see that Hale was on his cell phone.

***

After less than 30 minutes, we were back in the room.

Hopkins and McIntyre were still seated at the table. I glanced at the screen and noted that the video player was once again gone. The webpage was completely blank. I wondered if any of them had thought to transcribe the URL that was still displayed on screen. I assumed it wouldn't matter. It seems likely that Sarah had set up the server address so that it was completely untraceable.

"Draw up the plea bargain as voluntary manslaughter and we have a deal," said Hale. "And while I don't want it in writing, I would like personal assurances from each of you that this video will never see the light of day."

"Counselor, you have my word and the word of my colleagues," said Rizzo, taking the lead for us. McManus and I both nodded in agreement. I was doing my best to make sure that my astonishment that this actually worked wasn't showing.

"I'd like to further request," said Hale, "that my client remains here in the Wayside Public Safety Building through sentencing."

This time it was McManus's turn. "Done."

And I hoped that it was.

CHAPTER 52

SUNDAY DINNER

JULY 10, 2011

1945 EDT

I had called Dad to let him know I was on the way as I left the station. By the time I got home, it was almost 8 p.m. Dad told me my timing was good, and the family had decided to wait before sitting down to eat. I suspected the evening had begun around 6 p.m., which meant many cocktails had been consumed prior to my arrival.

As I pulled into the driveway, I noted my brother-in-law's black Bentley. My sister Elizabeth had married well. Her husband, Tom, was a serial Internet entrepreneur. While he owned and operated a number of companies, I understood he spent most of his time managing a website called Trip Advisor, which offered unsolicited reviews of travel destinations and hotels. From what I've read, Tom was probably worth a few hundred million dollars. My sister's wellbeing, at least from a financial standpoint, seemed to be in good hands. While they had married later in life, by all accounts they seem quite happy. Ellie, as I called her, was still a practicing attorney and a professor at Harvard

Law School. Five years my senior, she was simply my big sister.

I found the assembled group on the back deck. In addition to the dogs, Susan, Ellie, Tom, and Dad, Sally was also present. I wondered ever so briefly, if once again I was missing something and decided to look into it later.

Ellie met me at the back door with an extra drink in hand.

"Dark 'n Stormy, little brother?" she inquired with a big smile.

I took a drink, kissed her on the cheek, said thanks, and really meant it.

"Thanks for waiting," I said to everyone. The group had turned to face me. Every single person was smiling, as if they were genuinely glad to see me. I felt like Sally Fields at the Oscars.

"Congratulations on closing your first case!" said my dad, raising his glass in a toast.

"Congratulations," they all said in unison.

I raised my glass and said, "Thank you all. It's great to be home."

Susan was waiting for me to finish my first long pull on the Dark 'n Stormy. When I finished, she put her arms around my neck, and kissed me hard on the lips. Between the drink and the kiss, I already had a nice buzz.

"Nice job, sailor. Ready for a little family time?" she asked.

"You bet," I said, with as much enthusiasm as I could muster.

Dad wandered over to join us and said, "Sally tells me that dinner will be ready in about 10 minutes. I hope you're hungry. We roasted three chickens. And by the way, you could've warned me that your girlfriend here was a skeet hustler."

Dad was smiling broadly, and Susan was blushing ever so slightly.

"Tell me more," I said to Dad.

"We all shot high teens in the first round. In fact, I believe Susan was tied for last place at that point. The guys were razzing her about being a Naval officer who couldn't shoot very well. She suggested to them that we double the bet, and she'd try to do better. We shot three more rounds. Most of us continued to shoot in the high teens. Your girlfriend shot two 25s and a 24, giving her a final score of 91. No one else in the group broke 80," said Dad, looking at Susan.

"It took me a little while to get used to the gun. Your dad was nice enough to let me use your mom's Browning 12. I have a Remington at home and keep the choke set a little wider," said Susan.

"I checked your record on the NSSA website. You average in the high 90s, which should be expected of someone who won junior nationals when she was 16," said Dad, still smiling and now beginning to chuckle just a little.

Susan replied with a grin, "Just because skeet shooting was invented here in Massachusetts, doesn't mean it's not taken seriously down in Texas. I grew up with guns in the house and learning to shoot came right after learning to walk."

I would've paid good money to watch Susan hustle my Dad and his friends. Ironically, I suspect my Dad enjoyed it, too. I was not so certain about his friends.

Sally interrupted the conversation, thankfully, by calling us the dinner.

***

The food was both wonderful and simple. We started with sliced beefsteak tomatoes and buffalo mozzarella. In addition to the roast chicken, there were whole-wheat dinner rolls and fresh corn. Ellie and Tom had brought two bottles of a very dry Riesling that went perfectly with the chicken. Instead of a heavy barbecue sauce, the chicken had been prepared with a light, sweet, bourbon marinade.

My dad and I were seated at opposite ends of a rectangular teak table. Sally was on his right, and Ellie was on his left. Tom sat next to Ellie, which put Susan on my right. As I watched the group chat, I wondered about Sally and Dad. In the handful of times I'd been to the house over the last 10 years, Sally had often been present. I knew that some years ago, she had moved into the house next door, which was also owned by TCC. It further dawned on me that Sally had never married. While I had never seen any sign of affection between them, I was beginning to wonder if Dad and Sally were an item. As a trained investigator, I realized that everything I had observed was merely circumstantial, and yet my gut told me something was going on that I had missed until now.

Most of the food was gone, and we were now chatting individually. Dad tapped his water glass to get everyone's attention.

"Ellie has a little announcement to make," said Dad.

Everyone went quiet, and turned to stare at Ellie.

Ellie, who had just turned 60 in June, looked more like 40 to me. Her skin was creamy white and wrinkle-free. Her shoulder length hair was a dark auburn brown. She had large hazel eyes, a family trademark, and an impish smile. She was all of 5' 2", and I suspected barely more than 100 pounds. She was quiet, yet confident. Ellie was also perfectly comfortable speaking to a crowd of 200 or 2,000. While I knew she was both a professor at Harvard Law

School and a partner in a small law firm, I had no idea how she split her time. Perhaps she was preparing to resign one or the other of those two positions. Perhaps she was going to resign them both and travel with Tom. It occurred to me that I needed to spend more time with my sister.

"There have been some rumors I would be running for the Senate in the upcoming election. I wanted you all to know that I will announce my candidacy this Friday. I will be running as a Democrat and hope I can convince each of you to support me in the race," she concluded.

"A toast to the next US Senator from Massachusetts!" said my dad, raising his glass and meeting each of our gazes one by one, as he looked around the table before clinking glasses with Ellie.

"Hear, hear," said Tom, which we all repeated and clinked.

Ellie was a lifelong registered Independent. She had served as attorney general under Mitt Romney, who was a family friend. I couldn't decide if I was more shocked that she was running for the Senate or that she was running as a Democrat.

CHAPTER 53

ASKING ELLIE

JULY 10, 2011

2115 EDT

Ellie and I had volunteered to do the dishes, a time-honored tradition for Sunday dinner in the Carter household. Once all the dishes had been transported into the kitchen, the other family and guests sat on the deck watching the sunset with an after-dinner drink. I was loading the dishwasher, and Ellie was taking care of the larger pots and pans.

"You do have my full support," I said to Ellie.

"How do you get along with President Obama?" Ellie inquired.

"We get along fine. As commander-in-chief, I found him to be a good listener, intelligent, and decisive."

"Did you vote for him?"

"I did not."

You voted for McCain and Palin?"

"I voted for McCain, in spite of Palin," I said with emphasis.

"Any decisions about who you plan to vote for this time?"

"If Mitt gets the nomination, I'll vote for him. If he doesn't, I may actually find myself voting for Obama."

"Jack, you truly are an independent," she said shaking her head slowly

"And you should be pretty happy about that, Sis, since it appears I'm going to be voting for a Democrat for US Senator," I said with a big grin. "In all seriousness, I think you'll make a great senator. We need more independents in Washington. The partisan bullshit has gotten pretty thick. We've got a lot of problems to solve, and so far I think we're doing a pretty poor job of getting things done."

"That's why I'm running, little brother, that's why I'm running."

"On a completely different subject, are Dad and Sally together?"

Ellie stopped washing the large pot that had been used for the corn, and turned to look at me.

"You hadn't figured that out?" Ellie inquired kindly.

"I've wondered, but I guess I never put two and two together. Have you ever seen them being affectionate, holding hands, anything?"

"I have not, but I have seen the way they look at each other, especially when they don't think anyone's looking at them."

"So, why are they hiding it?"

"That, little brother, is complicated."

Ellie loved calling me "little brother" for reasons I didn't fully understand. Personally, I found it amusing as I was about twice her size. Once the little brother, always the little brother.

"Since you seem to understand what's going on here. Perhaps you could share your theories?" I encouraged.

Ellie took in a deep breath, and sighed. "Sure... Dad and Mom come from families who didn't get divorced. Even though he hasn't practiced in years, Dad still thinks of himself as a Catholic. Catholics don't get divorced. You know they're legally separated, but near as I can tell have never even contemplated getting a divorce. The relationship had been bad for years, and when they built the new house, I think that was a convenient way to separate. Mom always wanted Dad to be something that he didn't want to be. She thought marrying into the Carter family meant marrying into a lifestyle of the rich and famous. Dad, of course, didn't want any part of it. So Mom ended up with Mason the banker. And Dad seems to be with Sally, the restaurant manager. Personally, I think Dad made a better trade."

I was trying to absorb the implications of all things Catholic, the years of fighting, and the feelings I had for Mason and Sally. This was going to take a little getting used to.

"So, they're willing to be legally separated, but not divorced. Mom's willing to be open about her relationship with Mason, and Dad and Sally are keeping a low profile. Do I have that about right?"

"Pretty much," said Ellie as she nodded her head slowly. "With Dad and Sally, I think it's don't ask don't tell. I'm pretty sure a lot of people think what I think, and I don't think anybody's asking either of them about it. I could be wrong, but I don't think anybody is going to push Dad on the subject. I could be wrong. It's entirely possible that his buddies know what's going on. At the end of the day, I figure he'll tell us if he wants to talk about it."

"I like Sally, but I must admit that I'll have trouble thinking of her as anything but another big sister." I said.

"I wouldn't think too hard about it. And I don't think Sally would want you to treat her any differently than you've treated her for the last few decades. Although it probably is a good thing you've gotten over that crush you used to have on her," said Ellie with a little chuckle that reminded me how much she reminded me of Dad.

"Anything else I should know, that you think I've missed?"

"Have you been reading the TCC financials?"

"No, I really haven't been paying attention."

"You should probably take a look."

"Why? Is TCC in trouble?"

"Just the opposite. The book value of the company is somewhere north of two billion, depending upon the stock and real estate markets. Dave is a phenomenal operator, and he convinced Dad that we should invest heavily in equities after the 2008 crash. The company's positions in Apple, Amazon, and Google alone have a current market price in excess of $250 million."

"Wow," I said, somewhat surprised. I had always worried that Dad wouldn't do well running TCC. Apparently, my worries were unfounded.

"Dad also recently had me update his will and the family trusts. He's assuming you'll take his place as CEO of TCC when he dies. You also inherit the bulk of the assets, with about $20 million in cash going to me through the trusts. He wants the company to survive as an independent organization. His biggest concern is that neither you nor I have produced an heir to the family throne. TCC or its equivalent has been passed down generation to generation for 400 years. You and I are the first generation who haven't produced any offspring."

I considered what my sister was saying, trying to decide whether I should share what I knew about Jenny and Seth.

"Why aren't you the primary heir and the next CEO? You're the oldest. And probably the most qualified?" I asked.

"Once again, it's complicated. First, I think Dad is more comfortable with a male heir. The family business has always been passed to the oldest male, and there's always been an oldest male. Next, I don't want the job. I have other plans, and as the executor of the estate and the family's attorney, I was in a position to make it easy for Dad to do what I think he was most comfortable doing anyway."

I was nodding. I knew it all made sense, even if it didn't sound quite fair.

"Did Dad update his estate plan because of some health reason?" I asked, remembering the weight loss. I couldn't even contemplate losing him without feeling my eyes beginning to water.

"No, he updated it to include Sally. Assuming he dies first, she gets the house she's living in and a $5 million trust.

Otherwise, the estate plan is the same since they updated it, after he and Mom separated."

"What does Mom get, if she outlives Dad?"

"The house on Farmview and a $20 million trust, which is more than twice what the pre-nup requires."

"Mom and Dad have a pre-nup?"

"It's a pretty common practice among wealthy New England families. You don't maintain a family legacy by letting the assets get divided between a myriad of siblings and spouses. The Carter family fortune has been passed from generation to generation by protecting and focusing the inheritance. You'll be the first manager in 400 years that will need a different plan for the estate."

"Maybe, and maybe not," I said finding myself smiling. I proceeded to tell Ellie about my conversation with Jenny and the revelation that she and I had a son. A son who would potentially be heir to the Carter family fortune.

"Wow and congratulations, I think. Where does that leave you and Susan?" said Ellie, glancing out the window toward Susan, who was talking with Tom.

"As you've been telling me, that's complicated. I have a lot to figure out over the next few weeks before Jenny and Seth return from London."

"Have you told Dad about Seth?"

"I have. He didn't really react one way or the other."

"That's Dad. He's probably thrilled down to his toes, but there's no way he's going to let you know that if it might influence your decision about Jenny or Susan. Either way, baby brother, you've got a son," she said and gave me her best big-sister bear hug.

With my sister and I still hugging, it did occur to me that the stakes had just gotten much higher. If Seth was potentially an heir to the Carter family dynasty, I needed to make damn sure he was really a Carter. This was getting more complicated by the minute.

CHAPTER 54

MOON RIVER

JULY 10, 2011

2355 EDT

Everyone had left, and Susan and I were in my bedroom upstairs.

I was standing at the window looking west. The moon was full and the night sky was clear. I could see Dad, Sally, and the dogs heading toward the Sudbury River. I was still somewhat amazed that I had missed the relationship between Dad and Sally. All the same, I felt nothing but joy and happiness. I love my Dad, and I thought Sally was one of the most wonderful people I had ever known.

Ellie's explanation of Mom and Dad's relationship had made sense to me, too. While I believe my parents truly love each other, I don't think they really ever liked each other. This was why I had never married. I assume that any marriage would turn out the same way my parent's marriage had turned out. Rationally, I know this is wrong. But emotionally, it's hard for me to understand how I could be happy being married to anyone.

This was a sobering thought that I chose not to dwell on.

As I stood in front of the window wearing only my boxer shorts, Susan came up behind me and put her arms around my chest. I could tell she was naked. Her nipples were hard and she pressed them into my back. She was playing with and pulling my chest hair and then began pinching my nipples.

"Take me to bed now, or lose me forever," she said, quoting one of her favorite movies.

I turned to her and kissed her deeply.

Many things about my life seemed incredibly complicated.

Making love to Susan did not.

I decided to go for the simple life.

As we kissed I slowly maneuvered her back to the bed.

This time it was my turn to be on top.

When we reached the bed, I began to push her back.

In one motion, she put her arms around my neck and pulled herself up wrapping her legs around me. We fell back onto the bed together, and the lovemaking began.

CHAPTER 55

NIGHT MOVES

JULY 11, 2011

0030 EDT

He stood looking at the house at 2 Farmview Road. There were no lights in any of the windows, and the place appeared to be quiet. Even without streetlights, the moonlight made it easy to see all the details of the home, the landscaping, and the vehicle parked outside. It occurred to him that the moonlight would also make it easy for anyone to see him. The thought made his heart beat a little faster, and he felt sweat forming on his forehead. He felt the baseball bat weighing heavily in his right hand. He thought about having to explain to anyone he might meet why he was carrying a baseball bat walking around after midnight. He shook his head as if to clear it of these thoughts and proceeded slowly up the driveway.

The black Ford Explorer was still parked next to the driveway. It had been there earlier when he had driven by, and it was still there now. It was the only vehicle parked beside the driveway in a space that seemed built to accommodate as many as three or four cars or trucks. At this moment, it was the only vehicle parked in the gravel space. As he walked up the driveway, he stayed to the right side as far from the house as possible. As he neared the parking area, he went off the driveway and onto the lawn near the hedge and the front of the SUV. He looked to the house and noted that there was only one room that would give someone a view of what he was about to do. He watched the four big windows over the garage to make sure the lights were out and that he could see no movement inside.

When he was confident he was not being watched, he removed the dark blue towel from his shoulder and placed it against the front of the SUV on the side of the headlight. With the towel positioned to muffle the noise, he slammed the bat into the side of the SUV. He was surprised by the loud noise created even with the towel muffling the sound. He began to sweat more profusely. His heart was now racing as he gripped the bat and swung again. He then hit the corner of the SUV a third, a fourth, a fifth, a sixth, and then a seventh time.

He removed the towel and surveyed the damage. While he had not broken the headlamp, he had severely damaged the trim piece around it. He had managed to crack part of the blinker housing on the side of the SUV. He bent down to pick up some of the small pieces of plastic that were now lying on the ground.

As he rose to his feet, he looked back to the windows over the garage to see that they were still dark. As he headed back for the street he now stayed next to the hedge in hopes of not being seen by anyone from the front of the house. For his plan to work, it was important that the damage go undiscovered at least until morning.

When he got to the street, he turned left and proceeded toward his home. He forced himself to walk slowly so that anyone seeing him would just think he was out for a walk. He held the bat so that it was simply an extension of his right arm and hopefully less visible to anyone who might see him. He held the broken plastic car parts in a towel in his left hand.

As he turned the corner from Farmview to Farmcrest, he looked back down the street to see if there was anyone following him. He was in the clear. There was no movement behind him. He had gotten away with it.

CHAPTER 56

EARLY FLIGHT

JULY 11, 2011

0630 EDT

I stopped my Jeep Commander in front of the USAir shuttle terminal at Logan. Susan and I had woken at 5 a.m. and made a quick run to get her to the airport for an 0730 flight.

I jumped out and opened the rear hatch to retrieve Susan's bag. I stayed standing in the street as I put her bag down beside her. The difference in height between the street and the sidewalk actually made Susan a bit taller than me.

She wrapped her arms around my neck and pulled me to her, kissing me deeply. It seemed to me that we stayed that way for several minutes. While I didn't want her to leave, I also wasn't sure where we were or what was in store for us. But when I held her in my arms, all that mattered was her.

We released and stared into each other's eyes. I was mesmerized by her and tried to find something to say. My mind swirled with all the alternatives and my need to make a decision and set a course.

"Can you come back up this weekend?" I blurted without really having thought about the question before asking it.

"I was hoping you'd ask. Jack, we need to make some decisions but I know you had so many things on your mind this past weekend. I love you, and I want to be with you forever. We need to talk about what that means," she said.

"I know we do, and we will."

We kissed again, this time more lightly. I loved her so.

We broke, she picked up her luggage, and was off.
As I saw her turn to go, I could swear I saw tears beginning to form in her eyes. I hoped beyond hope that I had not done anything to hurt her. But I knew the Jenny and Seth revelations must be killing her.

I needed to work it all out before I could truly commit to anyone.

I watch her disappear through the glass doors.

My iPhone chirped. It was Rizzo.

I answered the phone. "Good morning, Commander."

I was relieved for the distraction.

"Can you meet me for breakfast? We need to talk."

I told Rizzo that I was at Logan and could be back in Wayside in less than an hour. We agreed to meet at 0730 at the Commonwealth Café.

CHAPTER 57

BREAKFAST WITH RIZZO

JULY 11, 2011

0730 EDT

Rizzo was already seated when I arrived.

"Morning, Commander," I said, sliding into the Art Deco booth for four across from him.

"Morning, Jack," Rizzo replied. "I hope you're ready for a little dog and pony show today. We're holding a press conference at 11 a.m., and McManus would like you to be present."

As I took in the information, our waitress arrived and asked for our order. Millie had worked at the Commonwealth Café for as long as I could remember. She was a pleasant-looking motherly sort with an abrasive wit and British accent.

"Ready?" she inquired curtly.

Rizzo ordered a grapefruit, whole-wheat toast without butter, and black coffee. I ordered a jelly doughnut and coffee with milk.

"Only one?" Millie asked.

"I'm watching my girlish figure, and this is my second breakfast," I replied impishly.

"Of course you are," grinned Millie. "I'll let the chef know."

Millie departed.

Rizzo was staring at me, gently shaking his head, "Jelly doughnut? Really?"

"I'm trying to get into this cop thing. I understood that doughnuts were part of the deal?" I said, smiling as if looking for confirmation.

"You're doing just fine," said Rizzo still shaking his head. "Any trouble making the press conference?"

"No problem at all," I replied.

Millie arrived with a hot pot of fresh coffee and poured for both of us. She also delivered a plastic cup that was half full of milk for me, which I carefully added to my coffee, filling it to the brim. I wondered if she planned the amount of milk in the plastic cup based on the number of cups of coffee she believed I would drink. It seemed I always had milk left over at the end of my breakfast. This led me to think that the system was the system and was not self-correcting.

When Millie left, Rizzo continued. "McManus will be announcing the plea and trying to close this up as quickly as possible. You and I are supposed to be standing behind her, nodding thoughtfully, when she shares how well we worked together to solve the case. I don't suppose we need to chat about what we will talk about and what we won't talk about with the media, in the event that either of us gets cornered after the formal press conference?"

"No, I don't believe we do."

Millie return with the commander's toast and grapefruit and my jelly doughnut. Rizzo's grapefruit had been cut in half and placed into individual bowls. It appeared that both halves had already been sliced in such a way that it would be easier for Rizzo to eat his grapefruit. The unbuttered toast look positively boring. I took the first bite of my jelly doughnut, followed by a generous gulp of coffee. It was good.

***

I had long finished my jelly doughnut, and Rizzo was still working on his second grapefruit half and toast. Millie refilled our coffees twice, and I was feeling sufficiently caffeinated. At the back of the diner, I saw Mason walk in and take a seat at the counter. *Bingo*, I thought. *Now I can find out if the son of a bitch is really back with Mom.*

"Mason Teller just walked in and sat down. He and I need to chat about a couple of things. Is breakfast on the state?"

"Sure, you had a doughnut and coffee. I'm pretty sure I've got that in my budget."

"Thanks," I replied brightly.

"Just one question before you go: Do you plan to shoot him in here or take him out back and do it?" said Rizzo, deadpan.

"Oh, I'll be sure to take him out back."

"See you a little before 11 at the station."

"Can't wait," I said as I walked toward the back of the restaurant.

The counter stool next to Mason was empty, so I took it.

"You're a hard man to find," I said to Mason.

He looked up suddenly, obviously surprised to see me. His face seemed to go a little ashen, and he began to sweat. "I was away for the weekend," he mumbled.

"I know," I replied. I just stared at him to see what would happen next.

"Why were you looking for me?" Mason said cautiously.

"I wanted to discuss the security around the new town center. I was surprised that I didn't find you at the protest on Saturday morning. I wanted to get your assurance that any further action by your group would be peaceful and law-abiding."

Mason seemed to relax just a little.

"Jack, you have my word that we'll do nothing to break the law," now puffing himself up a bit to deliver the reply.

"That's good to hear, Mason," I said with just a hint of skepticism.

Mason said nothing and took a sip of his coffee.

"Where did you and Mom spend the weekend?"

Mason put his coffee down and paused. Not looking at me, he said, "I haven't seen your mother since the meeting last Thursday night. In case you hadn't heard, she testified on behalf of the opposition. I don't think your mother and I will be seeing each other any longer."

While this was happy news on the surface, my mind raced to find another explanation for her absence on Friday, Saturday, and Sunday.

"So, you have no idea where Mom spent the weekend?" I asked carefully.

"None whatsoever," he replied, finally looking at me.

"Thanks Mason, I'm sure we'll be talking."

I got up, left the restaurant, and headed for Mom's next.

CHAPTER 58

INKY ALONE

JULY 11, 2011

0820 EDT

I noted that Mom's Volvo was still in the garage as I keyed the security code into the pad to raise the door.

As I entered the garage, I could hear Inky, a 10-year old Scottish terrier, barking on the other side of the door. When I entered the mudroom, I found Inky waiting for me. His tail was wagging slowly, and he appeared a little disoriented. He sniffed by hand as I knelt to pet him. After a little examination, he gave my hand a lick.

"Hey buddy, where's Mom?" I asked, not really expecting an answer, but perhaps hoping for one.

The house smelled bad.

"Mom?" I yelled as loud as I could. I listened for a reply and heard none. I started by checking out the first floor including the family room, sitting room, dining room, and kitchen. Nothing, except two piles of poop by the French doors in the sitting room. Something was wrong. Inky

didn't poop in the house. And two poops meant that he
hadn't been let out in days. I stopped in the kitchen before
going upstairs to give him food and water.

I check the upstairs bedrooms and found everything in
order, but no Mom. When I return downstairs, I let Inky
outside, first making sure that his electronic fence collar
was in place. I walked the perimeter of the property, not
sure what I was looking for.

Still not finding Mom, I walked across the street to the
McLaughlins. While Shelly was home, she confirmed that
Mom had not been seen since Thursday night. I shared with
her that Mom had not been with Mason, according to
Mason. Shelley volunteered to call a few of Mom's friends
to see if anyone knew her whereabouts. I thanked Shelly
and called Rose.

When Rose answered, I filled her in on everything I had
learned that morning. While I was talking to her, my mind
was running through all the possible alternatives that would
fit the facts. I didn't like most of them.

"I'm on it, Jack. We'll find your mom."

CHAPTER 59

CALLING OUT THE DOG

JULY 11, 2011

0850 EDT

By the time I got to the Town Building, it was a little before 9 a.m. It had taken me a few minutes to find a suitable piece of dirty laundry for the dog. Rose, John Trumbull, and Gabby were all standing by the parking lot waiting for me.

I emerged from the Jeep carrying a pair of my mom's sweatpants.

"John was available immediately," said Rose. "If we need reinforcements, I'm sure the MSP K9 Unit can also lend a hand."

"Do we think we know where she was headed?" Trumbull asked.

"We think she was going home. But we have no idea if she got there and left again, or if she never got there at all on Thursday night. Her dog had clearly been alone for some time, but I don't really know how long. The neighbors haven't seen her since the meeting on Thursday night," I concluded.

Rose began, "I've already made a few calls and found no one who has seen her since Thursday night. Shelley McLaughlin has also made a number of calls with the same result. It's beginning to appear that she's been missing since then."

"I've gone looking for her several times over the last three days with no results. I had assumed she was with Mason until he told me otherwise this morning," I added.

"That would make the trail a bit cold," said Trumbull. "If I could have your mom's sweatpants, Gabby and I will get on it before it gets any colder."

I handed him the pants. Gabby examined them carefully. Trumbull had Gabby on a retractable leash. It occurred to me that there was an awful lot of asphalt between the Town Building and my mom's house. This was a completely different exercise than tracking a human being through the woods.

After getting the scent, Gabby put his nose to the ground and began circling in the lawn between the parking lot and the back of the Town Building. Trumbull, Rose, and I just stood watching the dog going back and forth.

After several minutes, Gabby began following a trail down the sidewalk that went around the building. The dog was moving slowly, stopping occasionally to circle. But as we expected, the trail seemed to be leading in the direction of my mom's house.

"If it's okay with you folks, Gabby and I will do this on our own and give you a call as soon as we find something."

Rose answered, "That works for us."

"You have a plan here?" I inquired.

"I do. We're going to call Rizzo and get the staties to help us find out where the hell Mason Teller has been for the last three days."

CHAPTER 60

STATE RESOURCES

JULY 11, 2011

0930 EDT

Rizzo agreed to meet us at the Wayside Public Safety Building at 9:30. He had told Rose about the Kelly White press conference that would be taking place at 11 a.m. at the Public Safety Building.

Rose and I were in my office when Rizzo arrived.

Rizzo began, "The media circus is already setting up on your front lawn, Chief."

"I'm sorry," I said. "I had forgotten completely about the press conference."

"You're allowed," said Rizzo. "Your mother's missing."

He continued after a moment, "I've got two state detectives pouring through Mason's financial and phone records as we speak. While this isn't a murder investigation, I'm taking it over now."

"Why the hell are you taking it over now?" I almost yelled.

"Because your mother is missing, and you're the chief of police. Letting you or anybody on your team investigate this on their own is an extreme conflict of interest. I'm not saying I'm going to keep you out of it. I am saying you need to be accompanied by somebody who doesn't work for you on every step of this investigation. Are we clear?"

I found myself nodding, "Clear."

CHAPTER 61

ROAD TRIP

JULY 11, 2011

1145 EDT

The press conference had been reasonably painless. McManus had done all the talking, and Rizzo and I had both nodded at the appropriate times. A piece of me wanted to blurt out, "My mother is missing, and I need to look for her."

Trouble was, I didn't know where to look.

We needed to follow up on Mason and discover where he'd been for the past three days.

I also knew that I was paying my respects to Kelly White, her family, and the entire town of Wayside by being present for the press conference. This was my job.

***

Rizzo was on his cell phone as soon as we walked back into the Public Safety Building. By the time we reached my office, he was hanging up.

"Our boy Mason seems to have spent the weekend in Bristol, Rhode Island. He spent Friday and Saturday night at the Bristol Harbor Inn. There are also miscellaneous restaurant and gas station charges on his credit cards. The real puzzle is $3,400 in cash he withdrew from various ATMs."

"$3,400 in cash?" Rose repeated with a puzzled tone.

"If he were charging everything on his credit cards, why would he need so much cash?" I added.

"Best way to find out is a little road trip to Bristol," said Rizzo.

"May I come with you?" I asked, ready for an argument.

"I was hoping you'd ask," replied Rizzo.

There was a knock on my door, followed by the entry of an extremely tall, thin, blond-haired man in his mid-30s.

"Commander?" said the man.

"Chief, Rose, this is Detective Scott Britta. Detective Britta will be working out of Wayside to coordinate the investigation here," said Rizzo.

Rose and I both shook hands with Detective Britta and exchanged pleasantries.

"Chief, if it works for you, I'd like you to put Rose on temporary assignment to the state police working with Detective Britta," Rizzo said, half inquiring and half commanding.

I nodded agreement.

"We've got the Teller house under surveillance and will stay with him if he leaves. There has been no activity on Martha Carter's credit cards, bank accounts, or cell phone since last Thursday afternoon," Britta reported to the group.

***

The trip to Bristol took about an hour and 45 minutes. We stopped along State Route 24 to get gas and a quick sandwich from one of the highway rest areas.

Bristol was a lovely seaside town just over the Massachusetts border. While it had a proud sailing history, in more recent days it had been overshadowed by Newport. The old town by the harbor was no more than 10 blocks long and 10 blocks deep. The waterfront included a carpet manufacturing facility, a ferry terminal, various restaurants, and condominiums. The little town was trying to redevelop and having some success. After crossing Mount Hope Bridge, we followed the shoreline into the old town area. For a few blocks, the highway dividing line was painted red, white, and blue. I knew this was the parade route for what Bristol billed as "America's oldest continuously held Fourth of July parade."

Rizzo parked in front of the Bristol Harbor Inn. I noted with some amusement that the waterfront restaurant I knew as Goff's was now called the Thames Waterfront Café.

Over the next two hours, we checked the hotel and every restaurant where Mason had visited. Only the desk clerk at the hotel remembered him. The hotel was small, and the desk clerk was certain that Mason had been alone for his entire stay.

"We include a free light breakfast, which Mr. Teller took advantage of on both Saturday and Sunday morning. A lot of guests will opt for a bigger breakfast at one of the nearby restaurants," offered the desk clerk. "But Mr. Teller ate with us both mornings. I also saw him sitting on the benches on the dock reading on both Friday afternoon and Saturday afternoon. He was quite alone."

Mason had eaten dinner, according to his credit card receipts, at two of the restaurants along the waterfront. No one remembered him at either establishment. Since we had no credit card receipts for his luncheons, we had to assume he paid cash. Rizzo and I were both sure Mason had not skipped a meal.

Having established that Mason was alone and nothing else, Rizzo and I prepared to leave Bristol and head back to Wayside.

Rizzo's phone rang, and he picked it up. I watched him for a few minutes as he listened to what must have been an intriguing story. He was nodding to me and saying, "Yes, go on, go on," into the phone.

He hung up and began speaking to me. "This is a little weird, but I think it's relevant. The Wayside dispatcher took an anonymous tip about an hour ago. It appears that a black SUV parked at Patrick Kennedy's house has some significant damage to the front right bumper and lights. The caller further allowed that the vehicle had no damage on Thursday and that it had been damaged on Friday. Makes it sound as if it's a neighbor."

"I'm not seeing the connection," I said, trying to follow.

"There's more. The SUV is parked outside and clearly visible to anybody driving by. We've got two investigators on the scene now. While the damage is recent, it appears that it happened to the SUV sitting in place. There were fragments of the blinker housing on the ground, but not enough to account for all the missing pieces."

"I'm still not getting it," I said to Rizzo.

"OK, let me spell out for you what I'm thinking. Either the car was damaged in an act of vandalism, or somebody's trying to make it appear as if it was involved in a hit and run. I know this is hard to hear, Jack, but I'm guessing Mason may have been so mad after the meeting on

Thursday that he ran your mom down with his SUV. Did I mention that he has an SUV that's identical to the one parked at Patrick Kennedy's?"

"That's seems to me to be a pretty big leap in logic." I said.

"You're right, but my explanation fits the facts. My detectives have already checked out Mason's SUV. No damage, and the entire vehicle has been polished and waxed recently. Then there's the $3,400 in cash that Mason gathered while staying here."

"So, you're telling me that Mason ran my mom down Thursday night, damaged his SUV, and had it fixed here in Bristol over the weekend?"

"That would be my working theory."

***

It had not taken long to discover that there was only one auto body shop in Bristol. The problem was it was closed on Sunday and Monday. Rizzo and I had gotten the home address of the owner from the Rhode Island State Police. It was another temporary dead-end, as no one was home.

***

We agreed that we would stake out the owner's home for a while to see what developed. By 9 p.m., there was still no sign of him.

My cell rang, and I picked it up. "Hello, Rose, what have you got?"

"A couple of things, Jack. First, Gabby found a woman's sandal near Farm Pond. Trumbull says the dog seems confident that the sandal belongs to your mom. Next, we found pieces of the broken blinker from the SUV at Patrick Kennedy's house near the pond. The blinker fragments make no sense on a couple of levels. First, the damage to the SUV appears to have been done at the home, which means somebody transported the fragments to Farm Pond. Kennedy is adamant that the vehicle has not been moved in over a week. While it is a company vehicle, he says he keeps it there for his son Bobby, who's away on a college trip to Europe."

My gut was twisting. The son of a bitch had run her down and was trying to frame Bobby Kennedy. If I could get my hands on Mason, I would choke the life out of him without a second thought.

"What's the second thing?" I asked Rose.

"Jack, I'm sorry to tell you what I've got to tell you next."

"I know you are, Rose."

"Trumbull is confident that the trail ends by Farm Pond. At the same location, it appears that a large vehicle swerved off the road and then back onto the road before breaking hard. Trumbull and Gabby have scoured the woods near the pond. The only thing left to do is to search the pond itself. We'll have a dive team out here at first light to do just that. The only other explanation we've come up with is a kidnapping that occurred at that location."

"Thanks, Rose. I know that was as hard for you to say, as it was for me to hear. It's beginning to look like our stakeout will become an overnight affair. I guess I don't have to tell you that we need to make sure the staties keep an eye on Mason in the event he tries to flee."

"Not to worry on that account, Jack. The MSP have Mason's house under 24-hour surveillance. If he tries to leave before we get the orders to arrest him, we'll arrest him anyway. Hell, I may just shoot him."

"I appreciate the sentiment. But please don't do that."

"I'll call you if anything else happens."

"Good night, Rose."

"Good night, Jack. And please tell the commander I appreciate him being with you."

I filled Rizzo in on the latest details.

Rizzo said, "I'm sorry, Jack."

"Thanks, John. You were right to take me off the case. If I could get my hands on him right now, I'd kill him."

"Then it's a good thing you and I are both down here. If I could get my hands on him right now, I'd kill him myself."

We sat there in silence for more than 10 minutes. The auto body shop owner was still not home, and it was now close to 10 p.m. I began wondering if we were on the right track, if Mason had killed him, too, or if I was just going crazy.

"Let's go get a meal, a good night's sleep, and we'll track this guy down in the morning," said Rizzo.

"I don't have a better plan."

Rizzo started the engine, and we headed back toward the Bristol downtown area. This had the potential to be a very long night.

A Jack Carter Novel

CHAPTER 62

JUSTICE DONE

JULY 12, 2011

0317 EDT

She stood quietly by the six-foot fence that bordered her target's property. She held a phone in her right hand and carefully observed the pattern on the display. When she was satisfied that her target was asleep, she silently pulled herself over the fence and dropped just as silently onto the other side. The entire backyard was landscaped around the perimeter, with a large swimming pool in the center. She made her way through the shrubbery, around the pool, and stopped at the sliding glass door that led into the house.

Once again, she studied the display on her iPhone and concluded that her target continued to sleep soundly. She silently placed a key in the sliding door's lock and turned it to hear the tumblers click into place. She slid the door open and stepped inside. Now she turned her attention to the flashing alarm LED on the keypad next to the sliding glass door. She keyed in the four-digit code she had memorized. The alarm light stopped flashing. She noticed her heart beating faster. She stopped moving for a moment. She centered her thoughts and slowed her heart rate.

Once again she checked her iPhone display to make sure her target was still asleep. Knowing that he was, she proceeded to the foyer and up the stairs to the second floor. His bedroom door would be the one on the left. She paused before opening the door to check her sleep monitor one more time. Confident that her subject was deep in REM sleep, she entered his bedroom.

As she approached his bedside, she retrieved a small plastic bottle from her pocket. The subject lay on his back. From the plastic bottle, she carefully extracted a dropper full of clear liquid. She gently inserted the dropper between his lips and squeezed the liquid into his mouth. He swallowed and coughed ever so slightly. In under a minute, the powerful neurotoxin put her subject into an even deeper, coma-like sleep.

She bent down and placed her hand under the bed to retrieve the sleep monitor she had attached days earlier. Then she stood and removed the audio transmitter she had placed in the lampshade on his bedside table. She left the bedroom, went downstairs, and made a clean sweep of all the audio transmitters she had planted in his home. Finally, she removed the face of the alarm control panel and removed the small transmitter she had attached to the control circuit.

Now she returned upstairs to retrieve her subject. She pulled back his bed covers and removed his pajamas. He was white, flabby, and disgusting on so many levels. She carefully folded his pajamas and placed them at the foot of the bed. She retrieved a pair of swimming trunks from his dresser. She slid them onto him. Now she lifted his sleeping body on to her back in a fireman's carry. She jostled him to make sure the dead weight was firmly in place.

She stepped carefully down the stairs with her heavy load and proceeded steadily to the back of the house. She paused at the sliding glass door to open it, get through, and close it with her free hand. She approached the swimming pool and turned to place him carefully on the ground. Now she raised him to a seated position and wrapped her arms around his chest from behind. She raised him to a standing position. She lowered her arms to his waist, allowing him to bend at the waist. Then with all the strength she could manage, she pushed him forward and toward the ground. His face slammed into the pavement near the edge of the swimming pool. She knelt and lifted him by the back of his swimming trunks and slid him into the water. She stood watching for a moment. In a few minutes, he would be dead, and justice would be done.

Confident that there was no sign of her visit, she crept behind the shrubbery, slipped over the fence, and disappeared into the woods.

CHAPTER 63

BREAKFAST ON THE DOCK

JULY 12, 2011

0520 EDT

Somewhere after 5 a.m. I gave up trying to sleep. Rizzo and I had stayed at Goff's until past midnight. We talked, we ate, and we drank. I had downed three beers and a couple of shots of Jameson. And still, I had not slept. Was I where I was supposed to be? Was I doing what I was supposed to be doing? At some level, I knew I had been hiding in my job my entire life. Why should this be any different? Perhaps if I'd been able to sleep, I might have found answers to the questions I was asking. But I had not slept, and I had no answers.

So I got up, took a hot shower, shaved, and put on clean clothes. As superficial as the ritual was, it made me feel better. By 6 a.m., I went in search of coffee and breakfast.

There was a small buffet in the dining room off the reception area of the little hotel. I made myself a large coffee and a breakfast sandwich. The little room was depressing, so I headed for the dock.

A Jack Carter Novel

The sun was up in the east and the sky was a pure cloudless blue. I seated myself on a bench that looked out onto the mooring field in Bristol Harbor. Bristol was the home to many boat builders including Pearson, which made the first boat I had ever owned, a 27. As I watched the boats bob up and down in the harbor, I wished I were sailing. My 38 would not be in Boston for another few weeks, as it was being trucked cross-country. "Independence" was only two years old, and it would've been smarter to sell her in San Diego and buy a new one back here. But she was my boat, and I spent a lot of time and money fixing her up the way I wanted her. So a cross-country trip seemed like the right move. I wished she were here right now. I could just disappear into the Atlantic.

While Bristol had once been a fishing community, those years were long gone. All the boats in the harbor were pleasure craft. Sailboats, trawlers, and speedboats alike, they were all pleasure. And even at 6 a.m., there was not a single person stirring anywhere on any of the boats or docks. Across the harbor, I looked to see if there was any activity at the Bristol Yacht Club. BYC was home to some of the best sailors in the world. Club members included Olympic champions and America's Cup crew members. And apparently they were all still asleep, too.

My thoughts wandered to Mom and Dad. Had I taken sides because I wanted to, or because I needed to? Was it any wonder that I didn't think I could commit to a relationship with Susan, Jenny, or anyone?

Perhaps my biggest problem was that I was not more upset at the prospect of my mother's death. In truth, I didn't really feel anything about it. The thought of my father dying could bring me to tears. But the truth of the matter was that my mother had been dead to me for a very long time. And yet I was still angry, incredibly angry that Mason or anyone could take her life.

So for now, I would retreat into doing my job. We would gather evidence and let the system do what the system needed to do. And if that didn't work out, I would kill Mason Teller myself.

***

My phone vibrated. It was Sarah Walker.

I answered, "Good morning, Miss Walker. What can I do for you at this early hour?"

"Morning, Jack. I saw the press conference from Wayside, yesterday, and wanted you to know that there is zero fallout here at the agency. I did clue in my superior about the use of our video assets, and she seems quite pleased about the outcome. In fact, she wanted to know if you might consider a second career with us." I was sure I could hear Sarah chuckling.

"Please give her my thanks, and tell her I'll think about it. It's always good to have options," I said lightheartedly.

"Seriously, Jack, if you ever want to make a change, I'm pretty sure there would always be a door open here."

"Thanks, Sarah, I'll keep it in mind. And thanks again. We couldn't have got him without you."

"My pleasure. Now just try to stay out of trouble, would you?" And the call ended.

I found myself nodding to no one in particular.

***

For a long while I just sat and watched the boats.

I was shaken from my thoughts by a figure sitting down beside me. It was Rizzo, and he was holding two large cups of coffee.

"I seem to recall you take it with milk?" said Rizzo, offering me the cup in his left hand.

I accepted, saying nothing, and took a sip. It was hot and much better than the coffee I had earlier.

"This is not the coffee from the hotel?" I noted.

"Nothing gets by you," said Rizzo with a chuckle. "There's a little coffee shop and bakery down the street from the hotel that serves a pretty decent brew. I know we cops are supposed to be able to drink anything, but what I can drink, and what I like to drink, are two different things."

"Well, it's certainly the high point of my day so far," I said, and then reflected briefly on my call with Sarah and my other less pleasant thoughts.

"Would I be correct that you didn't sleep much last night?" Rizzo inquired.

"You would be correct."

"Anything you want to talk about?" Rizzo offered.

"Lots of things I probably should talk about, but I'm the strong, silent type, if you hadn't noticed."

"We see a lot of crappy things in our line of work," said Rizzo. "But I get the feeling that there's a lot more going on here than meets the eye. Far be it from me to be nosy, but I'm guessing you and your mother had issues that are unresolved, and unfortunately look like they're going to stay unresolved."

I couldn't decide if I wanted to open up and share my deepest thoughts with this guy, or slug him. For the moment, I decided I would count both as a bad idea.

"I appreciate your shot at grief counseling, Commander," I said without much humor. "And you're right that I probably need to do something about it. But at the moment I'd like to just do my job."

"Enough said, Jack," said Rizzo. "If you need help, I'm here."

CHAPTER 64

JUDD BREAKER

JULY 12, 2011

0730 EDT

The hours posted on the door at the Bristol Autobody Shop said they would be open at 0800. When we arrive at around 0730, the door was already open. We went inside to find a balding 50-something guy sitting behind a computer. The desk and surrounding countertops were piled high with papers. Various auto body parts were used as paperweights. I surmise that there was some kind of filing system at work, but suspected that only the owner would understand it. The auto body repair business was heavy on paperwork due to the nature of the insurance claims process. After more than 30 years in the Navy, I still hated paperwork.

We stood patiently waiting for the man to stop and notice our arrival. After a couple of minutes, he did so.

"What can I do for you fellas?" he asked with a friendly tone.

Rizzo flashed his badge and said, "This is Chief Carter, and I'm Detective Commander Rizzo. We're investigating a hit-and-run and are hoping you might be able to help. The vehicle in question is a 2007 Ford Explorer."

"Why is a Mass State police commander investigating a hit-and-run in Rhode Island?" inquired the man with a puzzled look.

Rizzo had pulled a notepad and pen out of his coat pocket.

"The hit and run happened in Massachusetts. What's your name?"

"Judd Breaker," replied the man, somewhat warily.

"So, Judd, what can you tell me about anyone looking for repairs on a 2007 Ford Explorer?" Rizzo inquired again evenly.

Breaker was now looking at me.

"You're the new police chief in Wayside, aren't you?" Breaker ask.

"I am," I said.

Breaker pushed his chair back, stood, and extended his hand, saying, "It's a pleasure to meet you, sir. I served 20 years as a damage control specialist. You and I have never met, but I'm proud to have served in the same Navy with you. The day we got bin Laden, I cried. It is a pleasure to meet you face-to-face."

Breaker was near tears as he continued shaking my hand. Finally, he released it and looked back to Rizzo.

"I'm guessing I know about the car you're looking for. Fella showed up here first thing Friday morning with damage to the right front grillwork. Asked if we could have it fixed in 24 hours. I told him we could do it in 48, but there'd be a $500 rush charge. He didn't seem to care and happily paid the full $3,200 in cash. Told me he'd take care of the insurance reimbursement on his own. I told him I didn't think that was going to work out for him, but again, he didn't seem to care."

Rizzo turned to me and nodded. Then he looked back to Breaker and asked, "Any paperwork on the job?"

"You bet. Got paperwork on every job," said Breaker.

Breaker went to a pile of papers on the left corner of his desk. He was scanning the paperwork as he picked it up, freeing it from the blinker assembly that was acting as a paperweight. He handed the documents to Rizzo, and I read them over the commander's shoulder.

The customer's name was Mason Teller.

Breaker made us a full copy of the job order and gave us a plastic bag with all the parts that had been replaced on Mason's SUV. We thanked him and departed.

Once we were outside, Rizzo looked at me and said, "I'm sorry, Jack, I'm really sorry."

CHAPTER 65

SEARCHING FOR MOM

JULY 12, 2011

0930 EDT

Farm Pond was only about 100 yards up the road from the Wayside Public Safety Building. We parked in the Public Safety Building lot and walked up Farm Pond Road to the crime scene. One lane was blocked, and there were officers at both ends of the site directing traffic thru the single remaining lane, and preventing vehicles from stopping and blocking traffic. The URT van was parked inside the crime scene with doors open and equipment everywhere.

As we walked into the crime scene, Rose and Detective Britta came toward us.

"We've had two teams in the water since daylight," said Britta.

From where we were standing, I could see two inflatables on the pond, each with one diver onboard.

"How many men in the water?" I asked.

"Four total, two with each boat," said Britta. "They started there," he said, pointing, "and have been working their way in opposite directions since about 0600. They've probably covered a little more than 20 percent of the search grid. The bottom of the pond is heavily overgrown and it's slow going."

We all stood staring at the pond, watching the divers.

Rose looked at me compassionately. I thought of her comforting the Whites, just a few days earlier. My insides were twisting and turning. I wanted to ask her what it was I should be feeling, but could not. I wanted to scream out in confusion, but did not. I wanted desperately to be somewhere else, but could not.

There was simply nothing else I could do.

***

At around 10:30 a.m., the first news van rolled in and set up shop in the Public Safety Building parking lot. Within 30 minutes, there were four more. This was quickly turning into a media circus.

I could not decide what to do about my family. I was still not positive about the fate of my mother. But I certainly didn't want them to hear it on television, before I had a chance to tell them what was going on.

With that in mind, I took out my iPhone and called Ellie.

"What's up, little brother?" Ellie chirped.

"I have bad news, and I need your help," I said somberly.

"Whatever you need, just ask. What do you mean 'bad news'?"

"We believe Mom may have been killed in a hit-and-run," I began, and proceeded to tell her everything I knew about the case.

"I'm already out the door and on my way to Dad. You do your job, and let me know what's happening," said Ellie, a little breathlessly. It sounded as if she were running.

I ended the call and continued to stare at the pond.

***

Rizzo walked down to the parking lot to find out what the newsies actually knew and was now returning. As he approached, he motioned that I follow him into the URT van.

Once inside, he began, quietly, "At the moment, they don't know anything. They're all working their sources trying to get someone on the inside to talk. There are a lot of people on your team and mine who know what's going on, in general terms. So, it's just a matter of time before they put the pieces together. Where's your sister?"

"I got a text from her about 10 minutes ago. She's with Dad."

"Well, with that handled, would you like to go with me to arrest Mason?"

"I would like that very much," I replied with as much control as I could muster.

"If I take you with me," said Rizzo, "do I have your word that you won't shoot him?"

"I promise I won't shoot him. How about you?" I inquired, looking at him somewhat sarcastically.

"I'm the commander, and I'll shoot him if I want to," said Rizzo, without any humor.

CHAPTER 66

DEAD MAN FLOATING

JULY 12, 2011

1200 EDT

There were more than a dozen state and Wayside police officers milling around Mason's driveway. There were another four staties on the rear perimeter of his lot. Rizzo had pounded on Mason's front door for more than five minutes to no response. Now he had called for a battering ram to break in the front door.

While waiting for the guys with the battering ram, the front door of the house opened, and an MSP officer in camouflage fatigues walked out toward us.

"We've got a floater in the pool," he said without emotion. "My team is still clearing the house, but it appears to be empty. The rear sliding door was unlocked, and the alarm system was off. The guy in the pool is wearing trunks. It looks like he was taking a little midnight swim and something went wrong."

***

A Jack Carter Novel

The group now moved into the backyard and gathered around the swimming pool. One of the camouflaged MSP officers was in the pool, standing in shoulder-deep water next to the body.

The officer in the pool addressed Rizzo. "I assume you want me to leave him floating until the ME arrives? He's been dead for hours."

"Son of a bitch," said Rizzo to everyone, and no one.

"Listen up, everyone," said Rizzo."Britta, get the CSI team in here ASAP. Franklin, I want four teams of uniformed officers banging on every door on this block to find out if anybody saw or heard anything. I want a Wayside officer on each team, so we'll get the most from these folks. And I want everyone out of here right now until the CSI team arrives."

Nobody said a word, and the yard was vacant in under three minutes.

When we were alone, Rizzo turned to me and quietly said, "Jack, did you have anything to do with this? Please, think carefully before you answer me. I'm asking you an official question, in my capacity as the state police homicide commander."

I stared back at Rizzo in total amazement and replied, "Commander, I've been with you for almost the last 24 hours. There is no way I could have done this without your knowledge or assistance. And, for the record, I had nothing to do with Mason's death," I said quietly and evenly.

"Okay, now I'm going to give you my own official response. First, everyone in Wayside is going to want to believe you did this. They like your mother, they like you, and most people hate Mason."

I stood quietly, processing what Rizzo was telling me. He was right. Everyone, or almost everyone, in Wayside was going to believe, or at least want to believe, that I had killed Mason, or had him killed.

Rizzo continued, "Next, it's a damn good thing you've got me as a personal alibi. But some folks are going to assume that you did that on purpose and arranged through your many connections for Mason's demise."

Once again, Rizzo was dead right.

"I want you to think about my next question carefully before telling me anything. Have you contacted anyone, other than family members, since last night?"

My call with Sarah Walker flashed to the front of my mind. There would be people who would assume that Sarah was calling to report back to me on Mason's death. And with no record of any outgoing calls to Sarah on my iPhone, it would be assumed that I had used a payphone in Bristol to order the hit. Of course, neither would be true, but that might not matter. So how much should I tell Rizzo?

Without much hesitation, I decided to go for it. I told him about my call from Sarah and that others could easily imagine that my call from Sarah or some other operative could have occurred anytime last night or in the early morning. Hell, I could have done it. I had motive, means, and opportunity to have him killed, while in the company of the Massachusetts State Police Homicide Commander. It was the perfect crime, with the perfect alibi. But I had not done it.

Too bad, I thought.

Rizzo was talking, snapping me out of my reverie. "I assume Sarah Walker will be willing to chat with me and confirm the nature of your conversation with her?"

"I believe she would be happy to do so."

"Then I believe that makes the call from Sarah a dead end. Would it be a good idea for you to show me your phone records right now?"

I understood the question and handed my phone over to Rizzo after unlocking it. He went through my call log, my text log and my emails, and handed the phone back to me.

"I think that ends that line of inquiry," said the Commander, officially.

As if on cue, three CSI officers emerged from the sliding door.

Rizzo's phone rang, he picked it up, listened, and said, "We'll be there in five minutes."

Rizzo look at me, reached out placing his left hand on my right shoulder, and said, "The divers have her. We need to get back to the pond. I'm sorry Jack, I'm so very sorry."

And once again, I felt empty and cold in the pit of my stomach.

A Jack Carter Novel

CHAPTER 67

MOM, DAD, ELLIE AND ME

JULY 12, 2011

1255 EDT

Rizzo stopped his cruiser at the east end of the crime scene. It seemed the place had become much more crowded. We left the car and made our way under the tape and around the URT van.

As we cleared our way through the crowd, I saw Dad first and then Ellie. They were standing next to a gurney, with a thick white cloth draped over a body. Ellie had her face buried in my dad's chest and was sobbing. Dad was stoic. As I approached him, he put his left arm around me and hugged me tight. I felt Ellie reach out and hug me, too. Ellie continued to sob, and we all held each other tightly. The four of us had not been together for decades. Were we together now? One more question that I did not have an answer for.

***

After what seemed like a very long time, we made our way to Rizzo's cruiser, and he drove the three of us home.

As we pulled into the driveway, I noted that there was a Wayside cruiser already in place. The media would be wild over this story. And I was happy to see that we would not be forced to deal with them immediately.

Ellie was quiet now. We made our way inside to find Sally waiting with coffee, cookies, and lemonade.

As the afternoon progressed, close friends and family gathered on the back porch. Everyone had a kind word to share about my mother. I couldn't help but wonder how my father was feeling about her at this moment. Was all forgiven? I got my answer late in the afternoon when the director of the Weston Funeral Home arrived. Dad was clearly taking charge of my mother's burial arrangements. I gathered from the conversation that my mother would be buried in the family plot next to the spot reserved for my dad. Apparently, there were places reserved for all of us, and future generations that were yet unborn. It all seemed very orderly and somehow calming.

**

The visits continued into the early evening.

By the time everyone had come and gone, there must have been more than 100 visitors. Most were familiar to me, although they often looked much older than my memories of them might have allowed.

Among the last to leave was Patrick Kennedy. I walked him out to the circular driveway and stood by his car saying our final goodbyes for the evening.

With no trace of his Irish accent, Patrick said, "Your mother was a wonderful woman, Jack. I know the two of you had issues, but I'm here to tell you that at the end of the day, she did the right thing. Standing up for me costs her her life. And that's not a thing I will forget easily. If you need anything, Jack, anything at all, you ask me."

Patrick reached out and gave me one of his famous bear hugs. I hugged him back as if he were my brother and was somehow comforted. We released each other and sighed heavily.

"Remember, Jack, I owe you and your family," said Patrick, as he opened the door of his SUV and closed it, rolling down the window. He started the engine and drove out.

***

I turned back toward the house to see Chris standing and watching. He moved to meet me.

We embraced, then stepped back to look at each other.

"Did Patrick have anything to say about Mason's death?" Chris inquired.

"No," I said, somewhat puzzled.

"My sources indicate that Patrick's security people took care of the Mason problem," said Chris carefully.

"Why would Patrick take Mason out at this point in time?" I asked.

"Personally, I think there are a number of factors. For starters, Mason has been a pain in Patrick's side for almost a decade now. I also believe that Patrick feels genuinely responsible for your mother's death at Mason's hands. And finally, Mason seems to have been trying to frame either Patrick, or his son Bobby, in his inept way."

I stood there considering the possibility. Patrick did hate Mason and had for years. And recent events could certainly have been enough to push Patrick to action.

"But why wouldn't he just let the system do its job and put Mason away for life?" I asked, knowing the answer to the question as I stated it.

"There's no death penalty in Massachusetts," said Chris. "That would not meet with Patrick Kennedy's sense of justice."

"Is Patrick at risk here?" I asked.

"I doubt it for several reasons," said Chris. "Because of your involvement, nobody's going to investigate this one hard. And my bet is that it was done carefully enough so that it will be booked as an accidental drowning."

"Do you plan to share your theories with Rizzo?" I inquired.

"Nope, and neither should you," said Chris.

Wow, is the only thought that came to me.

Chris put his arm around my shoulder, and we went back into the house.

CHAPTER 68

TALKING WITH SUSAN

JULY 12, 2011

2350 EDT

Everyone was gone. The visitors had all departed by 2300. The family stood talking in the kitchen for a while. Ellie gave Dad and me one final hug then Tom took her home. She was exhausted. Dad walked Sally home and told me not to wait up. Buster went with them, and Bandit was with me.

The two of us were now sitting in the basement, listening to Herbie Hancock's rendition of "I Do It for Your Love" from the *Possibilities* album. The melancholy nature of the music seemed appropriate. While it was late for Bandit, he seemed unusually alert. I've always believed that dogs can sense emotions. I think Bandit was worried about me ... perhaps he was worried about everyone, without really understanding what was going on. He snuggled down next to me and rested his head and paws on my left leg.

Susan and I had spoken briefly earlier, and I had promised to call her after everything settled down. I put on my headset and dialed.

She picked up on the first ring. "How are you?" Susan said softly.

Without thinking much about the answer, I said, "I really have no idea."

"Do you feel like talking about anything?" she said carefully.

"Not really," I said, feeling bad that I didn't want to talk to anyone, even her.

"That's not a problem, Jack. You're in shock. When you're ready to talk about it, I'm here for you. In the meantime, your doctor recommends that you have a double Jameson on the rocks, get some sleep, and call her in the morning."

"Aye-aye, Doctor," I said, and laughed just a little. "I think I can handle that prescription."

"Jack, if you wake up in the middle of the night and need to talk, call me. If you ever need to talk, call me. I'm clearing my schedule for the rest of the week and will be there on Thursday morning."

"That would be nice," I said, realizing it was an understatement as I said it.

"Good night, Jack. I hope you can sleep," said Susan.

"After the last 24 hours, I think I can."

"I love you," Susan said.

"I love you too," I said reflexively.

"Good night, Jack," she said.

"Night, babe," I said slowly, and ended the call.

I already had a Jameson on the table in front of me. I picked it up, and swallowed a long pull. I was conscious of the cold liquid as it flowed down my throat and into my stomach. It was sweet and smooth. I thought momentarily about having a few more to make sure I slept. Then I began to think about the kind of day that tomorrow would be and thought better of it.

CHAPTER 69

RUNNING

JULY 13, 2011

0427 EDT

I was reaching on a southwest wind of about 20 knots. Independence heeled over to the port side with the wind almost directly on my starboard beam. I could see Deer Island Light coming up on the port side, which marked the end of the Boston Outer Harbor.

The sky was a clear blue, with no clouds in sight. It was late afternoon, and the sun was warm on my back. The seas were empty with no boats behind me and no boats ahead. I was alone on the water.

I passed Deer Island Light on the south side. Although the lighthouse appears to be standing several hundred yards offshore, I knew there was a jetty just beneath the waves from the shore to the light. Every Boston sailor knew that passing on the north side of Deer Island Light was a quick ticket to the bottom.

As I cleared the light I prepared to tack and run the boat. My plan was to bring the wind to my stern and bring the main to the starboard side while keeping the jib on the port. As I slowly turned to port, I hauled the boom to center, just as the wind centered behind me. I locked the wheel and reached up, pushing the boom to the starboard side. The main luffed loudly, then snapped to starboard, and the boom swung out over the starboard side, filling the main.

Independence became still and quiet. With her sails split wing on wing and the wind on her stern, the only noise was that gentle lapping of the water in her wake.

We, she and I, were running straight and level at about 11 knots.

We headed northeast into the open Atlantic.

CHAPTER 70

BREAKFAST WITH DAD

JULY 13, 2011

0710 EDT

The shower was hot and steamy by the time I finished. I had not set my alarm and had still woken a little after 6 a.m. I made coffee and wandered around the backyard with Bandit while he did his morning business. Then I sat in the kitchen while he ate his breakfast and had a second cup of coffee.

I was toweling myself dry while Bandit helped by licking the water off my legs. This had become an after-shower ritual that seemed to amuse both Bandit and me.

I shaved, brushed my hair and teeth, and then put on a clean uniform. I pondered what the day might have in store.

Dad was in the kitchen making breakfast for both of us. Plates, napkins, silver, and glassware were on the little peninsula, and coffee and orange juice were already poured. It always amazed me how Dad timed breakfast to be ready within moments of my arrival each morning. It had been this way for as long as I could remember. This brought me around to all the mornings when I was little. Mom would be sound asleep for hours past when Dad and I had breakfast. It was our time then and now.

"How did you sleep?" Dad asked as he put eggs and bacon on my plate.

"I slept pretty well," I replied. "How about you?"

"I slept fine," Dad replied.

I ate my breakfast and thought about the question I wanted to ask.

After much consideration, I asked, "Will you miss her?"

He seemed to be thinking about my question.

He finished his breakfast, wiped his mouth slowly, and then put his napkin down beside his plate.

"Yes and no," he began. "Your mother and I have not been part of each other's lives for a long time. And yet there was some comfort in knowing that she was there. We raised you and Ellie together, and that bound us for life."

We both sat in silence for a while. Then he said, "It's very hard for me to grasp that she's not here, that she is really gone."

He looked at me squarely now and asked, "How are you doing with all of this?"

I paused for a moment trying to find a real answer.

"I really don't know how I feel," I said shaking my head slowly. "She hasn't been part of my life for almost 40 years. After I left for Annapolis, she and I never had another real conversation about anything. To be honest, I don't know if we ever had a connection. She had no idea who I was, even when I was little. But she was still my mom."

Dad reached out and patted my forearm and said, "Have I mentioned lately how good it is to have you home?"

"You have, Dad," I said very quietly. "And it's good to be here."

Dad and I both stood, moved to the end of the counter, and hugged each other for a long time.

I loved him so, and I was glad to be home.

CHAPTER 71

STATE RULING

JULY 13, 2011

1000 EDT

At 10 a.m. sharp, there was a knock on my office door, followed by Rizzo. While he looked rested and alert, his pants and shirt looked as if he had slept in them. He wore boat shoes with no socks and carried two large coffee cups.

I decided these were likely the same khaki pants he had been wearing when I had first met him, six days earlier.

He placed one of the cups in front of me and sat down in one of my guest chairs. As he leaned back and stretched his legs out in front of his body, he said, "I seem to recall you take it with milk?"

"Correct ... did you bring doughnuts?" I asked with a deadpan grin.

"I did not, as I might have been tempted to buy one for myself," Rizzo replied.

"You staties have no discipline," I quipped.

"I beg to differ. If I had no discipline, we'd both be eating a freshly made jelly doughnut right now."

"I see," I said, letting him win the round.

"ME has ruled Mason's death an accidental drowning," said Rizzo, watching me carefully for a reaction.

"I see," I repeated, giving him none.

Rizzo continued watching me for a few moments and then said, "There are rumors about that Patrick Kennedy and Wayside Holdings had something to do with Mason's demise."

"There are also rumors around that I had something to do with Mason's demise," I offered. "Anything from the autopsy that might make you want to investigate those rumors?"

"There were some anomalies worth noting," said Rizzo, rocking his chair on its rear legs. "While Mason's face was badly bruised and his nose was broken, there were only minor scrapes and contusions on his hands."

I waited and said nothing.

Rizzo continued. "ME thinks he was running toward the pool, tripped, and hit the cement face-first ... ME says the .09 BAC was probably a factor in why he barely used his hands to stop himself from hitting face-first and sliding into the pool."

"So Mason was drunk as a skunk, decides to take a midnight swim, runs, trips, knocks himself unconscious, slides into the pool, and drowns?"

"That's the working theory from the ME," Rizzo confirmed, nodding slowly.

"Tox screen turn up anything else?" I inquired.

"ME only pulled a standard screen, and his blood alcohol content was the only red flag," answered Rizzo. "Why do you ask?"

"If I were going to kill him, I would have used a hard-to-trace toxin to knock him out before dropping his sorry ass into the pool to drown," I said calmly.

"Good thing you're not in charge of the investigation," said Rizzo, grinning at me. "Looking for exotic, hard-to-trace toxins would be expensive and likely yield nothing."

"Why do you say that?"

"Anybody with access to toxins that are hard to trace would likely choose one that dissipates quickly. After 12 hours or so, it would break down so there would be nothing to find," said Rizzo confidently.

We sat silently for a couple of minutes. The ME ruling was sound and the toxin I would have used would have been totally gone after six hours or less. While the ME's explanation was solid, it was just a bit too convenient for the circumstances. That said, Rizzo wanted it closed and was here to make sure I would cooperate. Could Rizzo be in Patrick's pocket? I wondered for the briefest moment. A homicide commander would be a very good thing for Patrick to have influence over, if he was making a habit of offing his enemies. I decided not to go there with Rizzo.

"Too bad the ME has ruled the death accidental. I'm a little bored just now and could use another case to work," said Rizzo.

"Personally, I really enjoy working cases that I have little chance of closing," I added.

"Me, too," said Rizzo.

CHAPTER 72

LUNCH WITH CHRIS

JULY 13, 2011

1230 EDT

Chris was already seated in his favorite booth at The Haven when I arrived for our lunch meeting. As I approached, he put his iPhone down and stood to greet me. Our handshake turned into a brief hug.

"How you doing, bud?" asked Chris as we both sat down. Once again, Chris had given me the side of the booth with the calming view of the pond. The water was still, but there was one small boat with two people fishing. Wayside was an interesting place. I was in the middle of the woods and just 30 minutes from Boston. Perhaps my ancestors knew what they were doing when they settled here almost 400 years ago.

"I seem to be doing fine," I answered honestly.

Chris nodded and waited.

"The ME has ruled Mason's death accidental, and Rizzo seems ready to leave well enough alone."

A Jack Carter Novel

"How about you?" asked Chris without emotion.

"Officially, I'm good. Unofficially, I want to know what happened."

"Not going to leave this alone, are you?" asked Chris.

"No, I guess I'm not."

Chris nodded.

Charlie wandered around from behind the bar and approached our table.

"What can I get you boys today?"

"Haven burger, medium with bacon, provolone, and all the veggies except onions," said Chris as if he had placed this order a hundred times before.

"Fries or onion rings, boss?" asked Charlie.

"Both," replied Chris, "and a Yuengling light draft."

Charlie turned his attention to me.

I pondered my options for a moment and simply told him, "Me, too."

I smiled at Chris as Charlie departed with our order.

***

Charlie had taken away our very empty plates.

Chris was finishing a second beer. I was working on an iced tea wishing it were a second Yuengling. I was on duty, after all, although I had no solid plan for the afternoon.

"A unit at Wayside Commons is going back on the market later this week, so I thought we might go take a look-see," said Chris.

"Sure," I said, then adding, "How do you know it's coming back on the market?"

Chris looked at me, grinned, chuckled, and said, "The broker is a friend, and I asked him to give me a heads-up if anything popped loose. They've been pre-selling them out before they build them, but once in a while, a deal falls through. A deal is falling through as we speak, and the unit will be back on the market by Friday."

"Let's take a look," I said.

And off we went.

CHAPTER 73

WAYSIDE COMMONS

JULY 13, 2011

1420 EDT

Chris and I took separate cars, with him leading the way. His pearl black Audi S6 was easy to follow as it gleamed in the bright sunlight.

On the drive over, I checked in with Julie to discover that no one was looking for me. It occurred to me that my staff was conspiring to clear my schedule. I decided that was a good thing, if it was happening.

We passed Route 20 and continued on 126 as it headed toward my dad's house and the club. We took a left onto the no-name street that led to the town center project. About 100 yards short of the fence and guard shack, we made a left onto a private drive called Leeds Way. There was a sign on the right that read "Wayside Commons."

Chris went to the end of the block and pulled into a driveway, and I followed suit, parking next to his Audi.

I emerged and followed him to the front door, checking out the surroundings as I went. 17 Leeds Way was on the right side of the only duplex I could see. The other buildings all contained either three or four units. While other units down the street were landscaped, 17 and 19 Leeds Way were still surrounded by nothing but dirt.

"They're just finishing the building. It will be ready for occupancy in early August," offered Chris as an explanation for the dirt.

Chris unlocked the door, and we entered.

The place was large, new, and felt private for a condo. The back slider opened onto a deck with a view of a large hill. Chris and I walked up the hill and stared out at the town center project, which was mostly open dirt with the outline of a few streets that were being built.

I looked at Chris and commented, "You just want me to be near the town center in case there's any trouble."

"Never occurred to me," said Chris with a smile.

CHAPTER 74

AN UNEXPECTED VISITOR

JULY 13, 2011

1530 EDT

Chris had gone, leaving me with the key and instructions to drop it off at the sales office when I was done.

Chris and I had gone through the place from top to bottom, and I had repeated the process a second time after he was gone.

There was no furniture, so I was sitting at the bottom of the center staircase that led to a loft, guest suite, and a sitting room that could also be closed off as a second upstairs bedroom.

The master suite was on the first floor and included a bath with a steam shower and Jacuzzi tub. The living room had high, vaulted ceilings that made the place feel even bigger. There was a nice little dining room and a gourmet kitchen that was expansive.

The basement was finished including a bedroom, bathroom, and a large living area with a wet bar, home theater, and a billiard table, the only piece of furniture in the entire house. I wondered how that had happened.

I had never owned a home of any kind. I liked the idea that all the outside maintenance was done by the management company, which would allow me to come and go as I pleased. I hoped to spend weekends on Independence once she arrived.

The doorbell rang bringing me back to the present. Surprised, I went to open what I was clearly thinking of as "my" front door.

As I neared, I could see the top of Wendy's face in the door window. Her large brown eyes seemed to sparkle.

I opened the door, and she said, "I hope you don't mind me just dropping by?"

As she entered and I closed the door, I said, "How did you know where to find me?"

"Julie," she said, and continued, "I was checking in to see how you were doing, and she mentioned you were here."

I was confused for a moment as to why Julie would tell Wendy where I was spending the afternoon and then remembered putting Wendy on my "special people" list with Julie.

Not wanting to let on about my "special people" list, I asked, "Do you know Julie well?"

Without hesitation, Wendy replied, "Very well. Julie and I were roommates in college for three years. She's my son's godmother."

I was now pretty sure Wendy knew about my "special people" list and knew she was on it.

Did everyone know everyone in Wayside and Weston?

"I heard about your mom, and all I could think about was how much it hurt when I lost my mom ... how are you doing?"

How was I doing and how much could I tell Wendy?

"I think I'm okay, and I'm distracting myself by buying a place to live."

She considered my answer and said, "Distraction is a great coping mechanism. Are you thinking about buying this house?"

I heard myself saying, "I am."

"Would you like to give me the tour?" she asked, rocking up and down on the balls of her feet ever so slightly.

"Sure," I said, happy to avoid talking about my mother and happy to get some feedback on the house.

***

Thirty minutes later I was sitting in the sales office buying the house, with Wendy along for moral support.

I wrote out a $40,000 deposit check to take the house off the market and start the paperwork. I still hated paperwork, but this paperwork seemed more necessary than most.

Apparently I could change my mind within five days and get my deposit back. And as I sat there with Wendy buying the house, I was reminded that I both needed and wanted Susan's input on the place. My relationship with Susan was yet one more topic that I would need to deal with in the near future.

But right now, I was buying a house.

David, the broker, wrapped up his explanation of the process and handed me a folder of paperwork.

As we stood to depart, it occurred to me to ask, "Does the billiard table come with the place?"

David looked a bit puzzled but then answered, "Of course. It's a gift from your friend, Mr. Bridger."

CHAPTER 75

QUESTIONS WITHOUT ANSWERS

JULY 13, 2011

1725 EDT

After leaving Wayside Commons, I returned to my office at the Public Safety Building and pretended to work. I answered a few emails that were unimportant. I stared at my phone and office door waiting for one or the other to supply a distraction. Nothing happened, which served to confirm my suspicion that my staff had cleared my calendar and was giving me some space. I decided this was okay.

By half-past five, I was standing at the window, watching the traffic on Farm Pond Road pass the Public Safety Building. I noted what I thought was Patrick Kennedy's black Ford Explorer pass, headed east. Given the popularity of black Ford Explorers in Wayside, I could not be sure it was Pat, but I wanted it to be him, and decided to drop by his home for a chat.

***

Ten minutes later, I was ringing the bell on the side door by the garage and driveway. The top half of the door consisted of clear glass panes, and I could see Pat coming to open the door with a big smile on his ruddy face.

"Jack," he exclaimed, as he opened the door wide. "To what do I owe the pleasure?"

I returned the smile, shook his outstretched hand, and said, "I was hoping you could fill in some gaps for me about the last few day's events."

The smile on Pat's face faded for just a moment and then went back to full intensity as he said, "Sure, happy to help in any way I can. Let's go up to my office where we can talk privately."

***

I followed Pat up a steep staircase to a large room over his four-car garage. There was a large cherry desk and leatherbound chairs on one end of the room, which was meticulously well ordered. There were three large computer screens and a single wireless keyboard. The south-facing wall, which looked out toward my mom's house, was all windows for the length of the office. There was a stone fireplace and bookshelves loaded with books and artwork on the north side of the room, which abutted the rest of the house.

Pat motioned me to the east side of the room that had a leather sofa and five leather wingback chairs that would have been at home in any men's club in London. While I sat in one of the well-worn chairs, Pat went to his wet bar and poured Jameson into two short, fat tumblers, and then added two ice cubes to each of the half-full glasses.

He sat in the chair that faced mine at a 45-degree angle, handed me a tumbler, raised his glass, and said, "To your mother."

I nodded, we clicked, and drank.

It felt good, and I relaxed just a bit.

We made small talk for about five minutes, as I considered how to ask Patrick if he had murdered Mason Teller.

"So, Jack, my boy, how can I help you?" said Patrick with his Irish accent firmly in place.

"The ME has ruled Mason's death an accident," I began.

Pat nodded, smiled, and said nothing.

"Some people think you or I may have helped him on his way," I continued.

Pat continued to smile and nod.

"I am personally looking for a little closure, here," I half-pleaded.

Pat's face became serious as he considered my request.

"Mason Teller has cost this community millions over the past decade and made himself a lot of enemies in the process," said Pat evenly.

Now I nodded and said nothing.

"Some people might say that his relationship with your dear, departed mother was the only thing keeping him alive."

I continued to nod.

"Then the dumb bastard runs her down and tries to frame me for the murder. Some people might say he got exactly what he deserved."

"And that is all you're going to say about it," I said, thinking I already knew the answer.

Pat thought about it for just a moment and said, "I have three things to add and then the subject is closed between us."

I nodded.

"First, if someone had killed him years ago, your dear mother would be alive today. Second, I will forever regret that his death did not come sooner. And finally, you need to let this go and move on ... and so do I."

We sat there for a few minutes in silence.

I finished my drink and stood to go.

Patrick stood. He was as somber as I had ever seen him.

"Thanks," I said, "for everything." And I meant it, although I knew I would never be able to fully "let this go" as Pat had directed.

We embraced, and I let myself out.

As I went down the stairs, I could hear Pat pouring himself another drink.

CHAPTER 76

HOME

JULY 13, 2011

1810 EDT

As I stood in Pat's driveway, looking at my mother's house, my iPhone chirped its alert for a new text message.

"Meet me at your new house when you can," said the text from Chris.

"OMW," I thumbed and sent.

I drove slowly past her house, then headed for mine.

***

I found Chris sitting on the back deck of my new house, with a cooler full of Honey Browns, one of which was mostly gone.

"How long have you been here?" I asked as he handed me a cold beer.

"Just a few minutes," he said as he leaned back against the railing and finished his beer.

I nodded and then told him about my conversation with Patrick.

"Letting it go is good advice," said Chris.

I nodded, not really sure if I agreed.

"You are having dinner with me, Mandy, and the kids at 7:30. Your dad and Sally are joining us, too. Mandy insisted," he said as if to close the matter.

"Okay," I said, and thought how much I liked Mandy and Chris.

"Which means we have time to play a little eight-ball, and break in your new table."

"Cool," I said feeling some calm, "and thanks for the table."

"My pleasure," said Chris, as we headed inside.

"Any more surprises for me?" I asked, half kidding.

"You bet," said Chris without missing a beat. "But they won't be surprises if I tell you about them now."

"Right," I said, chuckling to myself as I followed Chris down the basement stairs.

A Jack Carter Novel